In the city of Sylvow, brother and s
made a childhood promise to each other. he would look after
the plants and she would look after the animals.

*Unlike most promises, both of these were kept – each in their
own way. Claudia is now a vet – looking after pampered
pets or putting down strays and leading a mundane life in
the city. Leo, on the other hand, disenchanted with modern
urban life, has abruptly abandoned his wife and disappeared
into the surrounding forest, his only contact with the outside
world being a sequence of dramatic and prophetic letters –
increasingly convinced that a semi-sentient natural world is
preparing to rebel against its human irritants.*

*Nature is a strange thing – although we have done an amazing
job of cataloguing and observing it, we still know very little
about it. Nature always surprises – and always changes,
especially under an external influence such as humanity's
devastating effect on the environment. This book follows
its cast of characters through a spectacular clash between
everyday life and life on the evolutionary scale – as society
dissolves and is stripped away under the onslaught of surreal
environmental disaster. Douglas Thompson has dug deep into
the inevitable guilt that we all feel, as a culture/species, for the
disastrous state of civilization and its effect on both ourselves
and the world around us – in the process touching on elements
as diverse as literary surrealism, philosophical tract, horror,
disaster novel and visionary science fiction.*

DOUGLAS THOMPSON

DOUGLAS THOMPSON
SYLVOW

"His eyes flashing with rage, the pied piper pointed a threatening finger at the Mayor. "You'll bitterly regret ever breaking your promise," he said, and vanished. A shiver of fear ran through the councillors, but the Mayor shrugged and said excitedly: "We've saved fifty thousand florins!" That night, freed from the nightmare of the rats, the citizens of Hamelin slept more soundly than ever. And when the strange sound of piping wafted through the streets at dawn, only the children heard it. Drawn as by magic, they hurried out of their homes..."

- Jacob and Wilhelm Grimm.

SYLVOW
by Douglas Thompson

Publication Date: August 2010

ISBN: 978-0-9562147-7-5
NOTE: **Sylvow** is a work of fiction, and therefore all characters within the text have invented names and are not intended to resemble real people.

Quotes in the foreword by Martin Bax are from the *Meditations of Marcus Aurelius* translated by George Long, 1862.

Thanks are hereby extended as appropriate to the editors of the following magazines: Andrew Hook at New Horizons, Stephen Theaker at Dark Horizons, Paul Sutherland at Dream Catcher, and above all Martin Bax at Ambit for being the first to see the light of Leo ...

Chapter 1_Sylvow, appeared in Ambit Magazine, Issue No. 192, April 2008.

Chapter 4_The Equation, appeared in Ambit Magazine, Issue No. 195, January 2009.

Chapter 5_Veronika, appeared in New Horizons Magazine, Issue No.3, June 2009.

Chapter 6_Beautiful Dreamer, appeared in Dream Catcher, summer 2010.

Chapter 7_The Forest Of Veils, appeared in Ambit Magazine, Issue No.200, Spring 2010.

Chapter 8_The Doctrine Of Signatures, appeared in New Horizons Magazine, Issue No.5, June 2010.

Chapter 9_A Game Of Chess, appeared in Ambit Magazine, Issue No.197, Summer 2009.

Chapter 14_Vivienne's Garden, appeared in Dark Horizons Magazine, Issue No.55, Autumn 2009.

ACKNOWLEDGEMENTS

───────────

Rona MacDonald, for cover photography and love. David Rix, for the vision, hard work and genius to bring this book to life. Matt Benians, for the promise he made his sister.

In memory of Allan Berwick: architect, photographer, and friend.

CONTENTS

Maybe - an introduction by Martin Bax   p 11

1 . . . . Sylvow   p 15

2 . . . . Conversation Piece   p 29

3 . . . . Furniture   p 35

4 . . . . The Equation   p 47

5 . . . . Veronika   p 67

6 . . . . Beautiful Dreamer   p 85

7 . . . . The Forest of Veils   p 103

8 . . . . The Doctrine of Signatures   p 139

9 . . . . A Game of Chess   p 159

10 . . . . The Pollination Crisis   p 179

11 . . . . The Warlike Music of Rain   p 197

12 . . . . . . First Days of the Dog Rebellion   p 219

13 . . . . Leo's Last Testament   p 237

14 . . . . Vivienne's Garden   p 249

15 . . . . The Red Queen   p 265

16 . . . . Flood Tide   p 281

17 . . . . Critical Shift   p 289

Afterword by David Rix   p 301

MAYBE

An introduction by Martin Bax

Sylvow . . . Well *maybe* it all began with the Roman Emperor Marcus Aurelius Antoninus. In his *Meditations*, he wondered *"Either it is a well-arranged universe or a chaos huddled together, but still a universe. But can a certain order subsist in thee, and disorder in the all?"* And in that universe, note the recorded vegetation: *"A cucumber is bitter – throw it away. There are briars in the road – Turn away from them. –This is enough. Do not add, and why were such things made in the world?"*

The Romans suffered one of their worst defeats in the Teutoborg forest, now modern-day Osnabruck. But by AD 179 the Emperor had again subdued the Germanic Tribes, and then that became as far as the Roman Empire ever reached. Marcus Aurelius died at Vindobonna (Vienna), and remember it was just after this that Gibbon felt Rome began to decline but the forest – and then Thompson's mythical city of Sylvow – grew and developed. During the Hitler Wars, the forests of Sylvow protected patriots from the Nazis. But now the city – a late XXth Century City – exists surrounded by the Forest where this furthest battle of the Romans was fought.

Now it's a standard 21st century city. A government somewhat fascist but *seemingly* ordinary – a city with banks, businesses, schools and tree-lined streets. And here the first event, when Anton turns a corner and meets not trees but forestation, which

11

causes him to crash, in body and mind. And other ordinary people – a psychiatrist, a vet – but her brother Leo has already left for the surrounding forest and his first letter records his meeting with a Roman centurion. So what sort of world has Thompson produced?

A classic science fiction world? Not really. Not a Drowned World or a Burning World but more like J G Ballard's High Rise, where you'll remember we start with a man eating his dog and perhaps here too is something of Crystal World – Ballard's crystalline forest. Anyway – starting from some sort of 'genre' but moving somewhere else. Anton, accompanying the two girls, Claudia and Vivienne (for sex, *maybe?*), is vainly searching the forest for Leo while the Sylvow government tries to establish some control over the forces they do not understand. Children are 'lost' from the city, adopted by animals (wolves, very Roman). The city is overrun by deer, which humans start to eat though the horned beasts defend themselves. Strange ships float up in the now half-ruined city. Don't get involved or you may wake up wondering if you are a Roman after all…

But all is well. I have the great Emperor's meditation beside me still: *"Either there is a fatal necessity and invincible order or a kind of providence, or a confusion without a purpose and without a director. If then there is an invisible necessity, why dost thou resist?"*

Thompson likes his *maybes*, his doubts and ambiguities, the darkness of the forests of our minds. Come in and enjoy this wild walk in the woods, and step out again unscathed – *maybe.*

-Martin Bax.

1.

SYLVOW

A bearded dishevelled figure, old beyond his years, shuffles into a forest clearing. Above him the tall oak and beech sigh in the wind, an enormous breathing sound like a land-locked ocean of the mind. He kneels down and sits cross-legged, surrounded by tiny flowers that thrive in the hallowed semi-darkness: yellow Violets, purple Phlox, white Dogwood: *Viola rotundifolia, Polonium reptans, Cornaceae...*

From his tattered haversack, he produces a Polaroid camera and carefully takes a snap in every direction at thirty degree intervals. Then as they develop he lays the photographs out over the moss and ivy in front of him, noting over them in pen the angles and attitudes of the flowers, their Latin names.

He closes his eyes and meditates. The forest's breathing moves into him, the wind-sound rushing, slowly fusing with his lungs and heart. His mind settles as if falling through countless layers of fallen leaves, fermenting, re-metabolising. A half hour passes.

He opens his eyes, and takes the same photographs again, and lays the Polaroid images out in a row, held down with pebbles, each below its neighbour taken earlier. The scene is like a fortune-teller interrogating Tarot cards. He looks on in awe, his fingers tracing angles over each image in turn, noting that every flower and leaf has turned itself towards him.

*

Sylvow is where the Roman Empire finally faltered. I have always considered it somehow significant to have been born just a mile north of where their northern boundary still lies in ruins. The mystery of why Roman civilisation first began to fail and go into its long decline, starting perhaps from this point, has long intrigued me.

Scholars put it down to the miles of impenetrable forest that encircle Sylvow in every direction, in which any alien army is likely to become ensnared and disorientated. This was certainly the case with Hitler's Nazis, millennia later, who were quite unable to dislodge the partisans who lived rough in the forest, even throughout the long cold winters. Then the darkened forest, long a source of folktales and childhood fears, became a mother again in the eyes of its people, and an implacable foe to the invaders.

But since then we have forgotten that relationship somewhat. The Industrial Revolution started here also. We are curiously apt to forget this too, but in the history books you will find that Sylvow's great minds were among those who first devised steam engines and mills and foundries, and began to fell some of the trees to fuel their great world conquest, the expanding empire that still rules this world, now with computers and cars and aeroplanes.

We have felled many trees, we have eaten into Sylvow's encircling boundary of forest. She suffers a little every day for us, but our wounded mother remains intact, and still dwarfs us in terms of scale, longevity and patience.

Though the natives of Sylvow today are scattered across the globe like castor sugar, in the mind of anyone born here there is always a forest, real or imagined, just out of sight or buried in memory. It is a dark and unreasonable place, where human laws do not hold sway, where a man could survive indefinitely with the right knowledge of roots and leaves, but where if he once becomes lost without path or compass: then he might wander aimlessly for a lifetime and never return to the world.

*

Claudia held the little insect in her hand, and cursed herself that she no longer remembered its Latin name. *Tanyderus Pictus.... Protoplasa Fitchii... no... none of those.* She wept when she remembered the childhood vow she had made with her brother: that he would look after the trees and plants, and she would look after the animals.

Now that she had children of her own, it moved her all the more acutely to remember this: the strangely endearing arrogance of two children imagining that a world so old and vast as this one; could possibly require their puny assistance in being catalogued and cared for.

And yet, perhaps they had been right, and the world of adulthood was where the real foolishness lay. They had remained true to their promises. Leo had become a landscape architect and she a vet. But now, outside beyond her little balcony stuffed with plants, on the twentieth floor of an apartment block: she could see the neon city flickering in the dismal rain, its signs shouting

17

about sex and money like a toothless old harlot, a starlet whose fleeting beauty only lives on in faded films. Every day the leaves seemed more caked in dust, her throat more torn by the brown sandstorms that blew inwards from the ravaged fields of the deserted villages. The city was like a line of concrete cliffs on which wave after wave of people broke, daily migrants from the countryside, refugees from the Oil Wars. Most seemed to be dashed on this edifice sooner or later, and were washed up like flotsam to beg on its meagre shores, the narrow pavements.

*

Anton turned the car into the Avenue of Martyrs, a habitual turn of the arm designed to take him into a habitual street: the last one on his drive home from another twelve-hour day. But this time something went wildly wrong. Although darkness had fallen, what he saw could only be a hallucination, no optical distortion could account for it. Instead of the usual scene of sapling cherries, planted only a year beforehand, now he suddenly saw a forest of hundred-foot trees, some whose roots were buckling the tarmac of the ruined roads either side. Huge leaves blew and flickered overhead like sails in the night wind. He swerved and lost control of the car.

Later in hospital, as the morphine kicked in, he saw climbing roses emerge from the Ward Sister's pockets and move their way over her arms and chest. He tried to cry out as they bared their thorns and twisted into her ears and throat, piercing her soft white flesh. But then as she was standing over him, talking, saying something inaudible to the doctor, red roses emerged from her eyes and mouth and flickered there, attended by occasional bees that then flew off across the ward like words too fast for his brain to capture. Now her chest was transparent as glass and he could see the stems of the roses twisting there, sustained by discoloured water that rippled with her every movement.

*

Claudia kissed her son and daughter's foreheads and stopped at the door, to look back at their sleeping forms. An ancient scene which always reminded her of a litter of kittens or puppies and made her puzzle over what technological inoculation had driven her species to swarm like bees for the last several millennia, to hang its children up in baskets floating in the night sky. *Rooms Only 60 Dollars A Night* ... said her hall floor in red letters, a flickering intermittent projection from the building opposite. It was like an invitation to wander forever, such a reasonable rate, to forget all friends and family and everything more burdensome than an unhappy news bulletin.

She looked in on her husband who was working late again, looking over his case notes in the eerie light from a computer and an antique desk lamp. She said goodnight, knowing better than to urge him to stop soon, knowing this would anger him. But this time his attention seemed already broken, and he turned his screen to show her its contents. *Did you know that C G Jung began noticing changes in his patients' dreams as World War Two approached? Before anyone knew consciously, before even the politically astute were forecasting it, it was there in ordinary people's dreams...*

But how is this relevant to a patient you have? -she asked.

He seemed to ignore her and clicked to the next page he had up: *...and decades before the first railways were built or even forecast, illiterate Gaelic Highlanders began having* *dreams and visions of fiery black horses that would belch steam and draw carriages across their fields. There are several cases here...*

*

When the hospital staff took Anton in a wheelchair to the waiting taxi, he swore from that moment forward to use his crutches only sparingly and to stay out of sight until his recovery was complete. He had no desire to be seen as a cripple, even temporarily.

But back at his home, things seemed imperceptibly different. The milk had gone off in the fridge and a few apples had begun rotting. Some potatoes were putting out roots, a yoghurt had turned into a teaming colony of bacteria. At first he thought the odour of all this unwanted growth was what was unsettling him. But even after the Cleaner had finished and left, the flat did not feel his own. He had rarely found the opportunity to watch the light change throughout the day and now, as it played through the blinds, he found himself strangely transfixed by it.

This was unlike him. He had plenty of work to continue at home on his laptop, his boss was just a phonecall away, but gradually he lost interest in any of it. His thoughts began to drain away, his mind emptied, he ate less. At first he had tried to think constructively about his life and how to get it in order, do something about finding a wife, a better job, the old circuit of hopes and fears. He was still young. But in the bright light from the white metal blades of the blinds, he felt his mind flare up and burn out like a filament. But it was the only one he had.

He watched night fall, the moon rise up like a threatening sickle, ready to harvest the dreams of men. He found inexplicable tears streaming down his face as the city lights came on and pulsated like semaphore, words of a language he had lost the will to hear. Forgetting his own body completely, he rose from the chair and his weakened legs collapsed under him. In total darkness he dragged himself along the polished timber floor of the living room, and pulled open the door of the fridge. The yellow light spewed out: a dreamlike door to a lunar world of memory and desire. Water poured in slow motion from its shelves. Water lilies and pondweed and toads and fish flapped onto the floor.

He rolled around to face the living room wall, and moonlight and fridge-light met there and mingled in an eerie tryst. He saw now that there was ivy growing over the television set, the sideboard, his favourite paintings. In the hallway he could see a long plantation of olives and grapevines, roots erupting through broken floorboards. They suddenly struck him as resembling a cohort of Roman infantry, awaiting the order to march into his defenceless lounge and impose order.

*

At the veterinary practice, Claudia found herself unusually moved by the animals' complaints. After years of this kind of work, you began to regard each pampered pooch as a physical extension of the vanity and hypochondria of its owner, you began to withdraw the moral dispensation given to smaller creatures swept up in humanity's grand plan.

But this morning it was there again, the reason she had taken up the job: that look of nobility and innocence in an animal's eyes, that fragment of God's will looking back at you, unadulterated by guilt and self-consciousness. All of humanity were culpable, it seemed to Claudia, for what humanity had done. From Hiroshima and Auschwitz right down to the abandoned or abused child or the dog starved to death in the birdcage of a lunatic. But animals didn't build bombs or cages, so a crime against them was somehow worse, an affront to nature itself; surely not a force to be trifled with.

She held the Alsatian's paw in her hand and puzzled over its inflammation, while the nurse and the owner babbled inanely about burns and broken glass. Being cryptic, she retreated for a minute to her library and then returned via the pharmacy with some lotion and swabs.

The skin isn't broken at all, she said. *This animal has multiple nettle stings or perhaps poison ivy inflammation, I'll need to do a few more tests to be certain...*

But he never leaves the house! -the owner squawked indignantly, -*we're on the twelfth floor, he's locked in all day and night, we have no garden, he exercises on a roller...*

The phone rang, and her secretary said it was a national newspaper asking for a quote about the current wave of violent dog attacks. Claudia grimaced and sighed and declined the opportunity and put the phone down, but before she could continue it rang again. She nodded, and said *Yes, straightaway.* She hung up and reached for her coat, a pack of syringes and bottles of sodium pentothal, chloral hydrate and potassium chloride, -*I'm sorry, you must excuse me now, I have to go, that was the Police, they say there has been another dog attack on a child and they need me to play Death The Destroyer for them again. It's been like some sort of epidemic this week...*

*

In the evening, as Claudia sat back after dinner, the distant traffic noise was joined by the sleepy music of the machines: machines beginning washing the plates and knives soiled by the sauces from the vacuum-packed meals that the other machines had cooked; machines washing clothes that other machines had cut and sewn. Her two children sat in front of their little screens, their blonde locks bobbing attentively to the cues and signals of their digital dreamworlds. Ignored over their shoulders: the television raged with the sound turned down, displaying constant news images of war and torture.

Now Claudia and Franco finally managed a conversation: *I was strangely emotional at work today, I had to put down another two Rottweilers for the Police, but I should be used to that by now, I'm overwrought maybe, but I'm not sure why.*

Your brother, Franco said. *It's been a while since he sent you a letter, you're probably worried about him...*

Not consciously, -she said, -*it's been six years after all. This is how I live, how we live. Nobody can find him, he doesn't want to be found, and yet he lives. He seems happy in a way, or absorbed at least.*

Bit tough on his wife though. Shouldn't you visit Vivienne again sometime soon?

Claudia sighed. *Perhaps... but she seems so inured to it now, so distant. She does not want to be comforted. I even sometimes wonder if she wants Leo back. I mean would she recognise him? Would we? Anyway, I have another letter from him, didn't I tell you? It arrived only yesterday, let me go get it for you.*

While Claudia opened drawers in the hallway, Franco talked absentmindedly: *...of course he could be quite mad by now, like one of my patients. There's one of mine has been really perplexing me this week.*

Oh yes...? -she said, handing him the letter, brightening up to hear him talking freely about his work for a change.

He says the streets are full of trees everywhere he goes, his cupboards full of lilies and daffodils. He said my waiting room was filled with alpine succulents and hardy annuals.

Delusional?

Of course, but we had to have his stomach pumped the other day, it was choked with ivy, as if he had been eating the stuff.

That's odd, Claudia said. *That's like my dogs and cats who had been stung by nettles and thorns, one of them even had hedgehog spines in its snout.*

Nothing unusual surely?

In highrise apartments? And lots have been going missing apparently, pet birds escaping too.

Yes, Franco nodded, *and I saw whole squadrons of geese and lapwings flying over today, but it's May, not autumn.*

Isn't that what they're supposed to do when there's an earthquake coming? A disturbance in the Earth's electromagnetic field? You know, like rats off a sinking ship..?

But she saw that Franco's attention was now locked into Leo's latest letter:

Dear Claudia, Try to make Vivienne understand why I had to leave. We had everything, all the standard accoutrements of normal urban life except children, thank God. How can anyone raise them into this nightmare, where you need to travel in a metal shell like a hermit crab every morning, scuttling in phalanx through the warzones where the restless barbarians are held in camps, subdued on drugs and lottery tickets?

One night I sat on the doorstep looking up into the midsummer night sky after Viv had gone to bed, and I listened to the leaves whispering on the night wind, reminding me of all the unreconciled fragments of what might have been, of what could still be. I was suddenly filled with an unanswerable question, as if a space had opened up inside me that could not be defined or satisfied, and that nothing human could fill.

I caught a train to the edge of the city, and set off into The Forest, walking, and I'm walking still. I sleep under fallen trunks or in temporary dens of mosses and leaves. I make notes each day and occasionally venture out onto a tarmac street by cover of darkness to find a post box. But for whole months and seasons now I am on the move without any contact. The trees move past me endlessly, towards me, through me, the sun sways and pulsates across the leaves making music like prayers. The morning mist drifts through the trunks, grey veils of sleep as time itself freezes. I am closer every day now to the centre of everything. The less I hear of human voices, the more I begin to hear the voice of The Forest. It reverberates through me, assimilating me. Maybe one day I will become a tree and then nobody will ever find me again. Every memory of my past life comes closer here and plays through me as I walk, gradually forming into a pattern as beautiful and inevitable as tree bark or fallen leaves.

The Forest says it is closing ranks again, tightening its grip around Sylvow. Yesterday I met a Roman Centurion and he walked with me for a while: we conversed using the Latin names of trees and flowers, which he was delighted to hear me recount, reminding him of home. He showed me where Hermann Goering had buried some gold bullion and some French Impressionist masterpieces.

But these are all human things. The trees live so much longer than us, and move and think more slowly and deeply. Our empires rise and fall while they breathe and sigh. You think I have left you, but it is you who have each left yourselves and wander lost as strangers now. But don't be afraid. The many paths are one path, and wherever you start you too will end in the heart of this forest, embraced by the cycle of youth and decay, immersed in silence....

*

In contrast to the early days after Leo's disappearance, now Vivienne had no difficulty sleeping, quite the reverse. She would snooze for whole weekends, half waking intermittently, the sound of the wind or rain outside mixing with her increasingly outlandish dreams. It was as if her head had become a haunted movie theatre, a room of the sky where vast messages were encoded in patterns of cumulus and birdsong. She had begun writing the dreams down, in the hope of eventually piecing together the pieces of a huge puzzle, her own life, the world's fate.

Waking finally, her long lithe figure wove down the hallway, topped by a flattened flame of blonde hair obscuring her face like a curtain. She staggered into the living room. The patio doors looked out onto an absurdly overgrown back lot, a tangled jungle of ivy and wildflowers. Now something impossible happened; but living in a world increasingly encroached upon by dreams, nothing surprised her. She stared out at a particular branch on a bush for no reason, for a minute on end. Then like a film playing backwards a magpie flew down and landed on exactly this spot and stared straight in at her, looked directly at her in a way no bird ever does. Then as she walked towards it, the thing flew down onto the threshold of the patio doors and left something from its beak there, then fluttered away. Opening the doors, Vivienne bent down to lift up the tiny winged glider of a sycamore seed.

A moment later the doorbell rang, and still clutching the seed Vivienne went to the front door to find Claudia standing outside, hair dripping from the recent rain, holding a gift of a bag of fruit in her hand.

It's started, hasn't it? -she asked, without even saying hello.

What? -asked Claudia. *What's started?*

Without answering, Vivienne took the bag of fruit from Claudia and retreated to the kitchen. Used to this eccentric behaviour from previous occasions, Claudia simply closed the door herself, hung her own jacket up and followed her. Along the way, she was disturbed to step over her discarded T-shirt and pants.

She found Vivienne naked in the kitchen, cutting the fruit on a glass chopping board. First she sliced one of the apples in half and, instead of seeds the core released an army of black ants onto the worktop. Next she split a peach in half and, instead of a shrivelled stone, revealed a tiny beating heart the size of a small dog's.

At this, Claudia stepped backwards in shock, her hand to her throat. Vivienne took the last item; a blood orange, and peeled its skin and outer segments away to reveal a glowing blue orb: a tiny turning world caressed by clouds, beneath which a pupil and iris now rotated and set its gaze upon them both with a hypnotic power.

Vivienne spun around, and the revelatory force of her beauty hit Claudia like a mirror refracting and focussing the sun's rays. The two women embraced and kissed, one naked, the other in a black suit, outstretched arms touching, both holding the same kitchen knife, fusing, twin-backed, like a faceless angel of retribution, conflation of ego and id, animal and human, as the room filled with heartbeats and the eye of the world sliced the air to ribbons with its tireless gaze of light.

The sycamore seed, grown to the size of a bat, flapped around the room on its leathery wings, snapping at flies and dust mites before settling on the cold light bulb for sustenance; content to wait there until nightfall and the release of all the doomed human energy it craved.

~

2. CONVERSATION PIECE

I have something to confess, Vivienne said, pouring Green Tea into Claudia's cup as they sat down together at an old cracked marble table in her back garden.

Claudia raised an eyebrow, saying: *So have I, actually...* And then nervous laughter broke out, quickly blossoming into a memory of the warmth of the previous years of their friendship. This thought was like the climbing plants, the honeysuckle, ivy and roses, particularly the roses with thorns – mingled with an odd feeling of regret as to how they had inexplicably drifted apart recently.

Yes, Vivienne sighed, rubbing her fingers along the marble patterns as if trying to feel them, as if they might be human veins or the grain of wood, *-Just like old times, eh?* Her eyes lifted and she blushed and Claudia remembered how she often felt as if Vivienne could read thoughts, or hers at least. *Friendships have to be maintained like gardens, don't they?* -and she waved her hand around her to indicate the burgeoning jungle that her garden had become in the absence of Leo's labour and expertise, the festoons of creepers and draping leaves, the carpets of damp moss.

But this is beautiful, -Claudia corrected her, anxious to head off any suggestion of depression or self-pity or reproach. Vivienne's eyes widened while Claudia blinked in the sunlight filtering through the whispering leaves overhead. *I mean the overgrown garden, meeting after a long time... it's all good. Perhaps it all has its place within the picture of our lives.*

Even Leo leaving me? Is that what you mean, that perhaps even that can have some meaning, some place in the scheme of the way things are and have to be?

Claudia nodded carefully... *yes, perhaps... and my brother* **left us***, Viv, he left all of us, not just you.*

Oh yes... Vivienne said, lighting a long white cigarette and exhaling. *Now I remember... he abandoned all of humanity but I just happened to be his wife...*

Claudia made to correct this note of sarcasm but before she could, Vivienne placed her hand on hers to stop her: *Listen, before you go on, my dream, my confession is that I had an odd dream about you just before you arrived... how funny is that when you hadn't phoned or left a message, how could I have known?*

Claudia shrugged her shoulders, sensing that she should just play audience for a few minutes.

In my dream, Vivienne began, her fingers and eyes exploring the table again, -*a bird arrived outside the window and gave me a sycamore seed that grew into a sort-of vampire bat-thing that flapped around the room. Oh yes, and you had arrived and gave me a big bag of fruit and we cut it up in the kitchen and I was totally naked while you stood there watching me.*

Claudia smiled and nodded her head, amused by her friend's imagination.

But the fruit... -Vivienne continued, -*was all weird. One piece was full of ants and another contained a beating heart and another a little blue planet that was also an eye.*

Very peculiar, Claudia nodded, becoming slightly uncomfortable, her hand in her left pocket brushing the edges of the letter from Leo that she had brought to show Vivienne.

More than peculiar, Vivienne exclaimed, *...it went queer after that, I mean gay. Sorry, but you and I embraced over the rotting fruit and I kissed you... then I woke up, and I'm sorry but I have to confess this: feeling slightly aroused by the whole thing.*

Claudia laughed out loud, genuinely surprised by this revelation and by Vivienne's candidness in revealing it. *Is this where I analyse you like my husband would do? Tell me about your childhood and all that? Or where the porno soundtrack kicks in and I tear your clothes off?! They say we're all a bit of each, straight and the other thing I mean, it's no big deal. You're not saying you've been a secret lesbian all these years are you?*

No Claudia, Vivienne smiled sweetly, -*although if I was of course, I'd like to think I wouldn't be afraid to tell you. No seriously, I think it was just a kind of sensual thing, an awakening of some side of me that has gone to sleep.*

An animal side? You always did think too much. You and Leo were made for each other in that respect, sorry ARE made for each other, because I believe he will come back one day.

Ha..., -Vivienne laughed half-heartedly, with quiet resignation, -*Well that's just it though Claudia, Leo wasn't in this dream, not even his presence unless he was the bird or the sycamore seed. Often in my dreams he has been like a backdrop, a stage curtain, or just an atmosphere that hangs over everything.*

Have you been having a lot of dreams?

Oh yes, and I've taken to writing them down.

Oh Franco would love that, you should let him read them through some time.

You're kidding, Claudia? He would have me sectioned inside a fortnight. But anyway what I was trying to say is this: Leo wasn't in this dream, and I felt empowered as if a time had come for me stop waiting and grieving and to take charge of my life instead, to become a woman again.

Hence my presence.

Yes, exactly. We were silly teenage girls together once, chasing men, remember?

She knows I have this letter somehow, -Claudia thought to herself, does she even know what's in it? Does she want me to give it to her, or will she be upset?

What? -Vivienne asked, reading the doubt on Claudia's face, as if she had heard her thoughts. *So is it time I found somebody else, Claudia?*

Take a lover as they say?

But Christ, is that all we are then, us women, biological timeclocks, genetic gateways, flowers in Springtime?

As if on cue, a bee flew between them and Claudia waved her hand at it and they both watched as it divebombed a hydrangea bush and lodged itself into a flower, its furry little black posterior wagging contentedly.

There! -They laughed. *Is it time I was re-pollinated, Claudia?*

I think, Claudia laughed, putting her hand on the table this time, *...that it's dangerous to see a partner, old or new partner, as the centre of your life. That's always a burden for them and for you. Maybe you need to get a job again, anything really, some new friends too, just begin another chapter of life... see what happens.*

And if I get a stamen thrust into my stigma, so much the better eh?

Ohhhh... O grade Botany, very good girl, gold star there alright. But the bee's only looking for honey remember, he doesn't know he is propagating and procreating on behalf of all those other species. He doesn't understand the higher purpose that he serves.

And neither do we, Claudia, let's face it. But if he stays home the world dies.

Yes, pretty much so. No less an authority than Einstein observed that if the bees disappeared, Mankind would have only four years of life left, although what a physicist was doing speculating on botany I'm not sure. The point is that if we are good instruments then Nature will use us and reward us with a little pleasure.

Or if we won't play ball? Discard us? Crush us underfoot?

Oh, recycle us at least, surely? Which is our eventual fate anyway.

Then the only question is pleasure. Take it or leave it. These might be dangerous thoughts Claudia, you should write this stuff down. It reminds me of the old days, you always did bring out the best in me, my little philosophical playmate.

The moment has arrived, Claudia thought, and realising it would deflect or perhaps stave off altogether the bleak prospect of a dissection of her own troubled relationship with Franco, she pushed across the table towards Vivienne the letter she had just received from Leo.

Just as Vivienne reached out her hand to receive it, her lovely brow furrowing in curiosity, some kind of aerial commotion occurred, whether bird or branch or wind it was difficult to say, and a single sycamore seed landed and bounced on the surface of the letter. Claudia gasped as Vivienne retracted her hand in horror. Both women's eyes widened and rolled up to meet the other's: one amused, the other suddenly chilled with fear.

~

3. FURNITURE

In the years since Leo had left, one of Vivienne's Sunday afternoon rituals had become to walk through the antique furniture stalls in an old market half a mile from her home. She wasn't sure what she was looking for there or why she found the place so calming to her spirit. Although some of the furniture was brought out onto the street, most of it remained inside the cold dark warehouses that smelt of wood polish and dust.

Perhaps this smell and sight of gleaming dark-stained wood reminded her of her grandmother's house, of an imagined former era of romance and Victorian opulence. Everything was there: silver tea trays with elaborated edges delicate as lace, old mezzotints or oil portraits of nobody anyone knew anymore. Grandfather and mantelpiece clocks that didn't work, wardrobes with surreal elaborate handles and feet: as if they were turning into the skin of blackened crocodiles. Cupboards which seemed like old Victorian or Edwardian ladies that you could just open up with a swift flick of the hand on a cold silver flourish to reveal the sweet musty emptiness inside. Drawers and shelves as bare as the deserted rooms they had come from: where she imagined the shafts of sunlight had rotated like clock-hands as the monotonous music of passing trams and buses filled the streets outside.

Vivienne sometimes imagined fondly that pre-feminist world of long afternoons of idleness while your servants did the housework and your husband earned the money. In fact, the furniture reminded her of a world which she had never known and could surely never miss. But somehow she did. A world of Empire and Colonies, now condemned to history books and cold warehouses.

She had bought one piece maybe six years ago and she and Leo had re-varnished it themselves. But now perhaps she just came to look, with some vague notion that somewhere hidden in an obscure nook or cranny she might chance upon a wardrobe or table which expressed the essence of her soul more perfectly than a painting or a poem and would feel compelled therefore to purchase it in order to make sense of her life.

Perhaps she had found just such a piece and was running her hands over it in awe when she met Joe for the first time. He was wearing dark brown overalls stained with dust and wax, camouflaged as if he were part of the very fabric of the place itself: so much so that Vivienne didn't even notice his presence until he spoke gently, close to her left ear. *It's a lovely piece isn't it?*

Of course it should have been an appalling question, the sort of sales pitch that Vivienne usually regarded as an intolerable intrusion, a *faux pas*, a crudity designed to rob the customer of their personal space and their licence to daydream without commitment. But somehow the sonority of his voice, its softness and genuineness made her turn and look into his face. His eyes were blue, resembling turning globes she thought – where she might expect to see cloud cover flicker and the weather change at any moment. His mouth moved into a smile and all the little hairs of his close-clipped beard lifted and rotated like the fur of some graceful animal.

I love it too, -he said at last, not waiting for her answer, exhaling and running his hand over the other side of it: the long curvaceous doors, the beautiful inlaid glass panels crazed with age, *-but I can't afford to buy it... I only work here.*

I could buy it -she said, surprised to hear her tone of voice so relaxed as if she were addressing someone she had known all her life. *You could help me carry it home.*

She smiled, and after a moment's surprise in his eyes he looked down and blushed. With the spell of that first moment's innocence broken, now Joe noticed her black fur collar, her immaculate dark skirt and stockings, how expensive a woman he was in the presence of.

Will you deliver it? -she said, and he wiped his eyes, glad to have a practical distraction to his awkwardness. *Of course,* -he said, *-but you realise it needs varnish, several coats, can you do that yourself?*

Yes, she said as he was writing down her address, *-But you could bring a can and show me how...*

*

When Joe arrived at her house, Vivienne made him coffee and then watched as he lightly sanded the surface of the wardrobe, his hand moving in circular motions, the sound he made strangely soothing like waves breaking on a shingle beach. Then he applied Teak Oil and she noticed how his movements followed the grain and brought it out into the light: the fantastic fingerprint of a once-living tree. Then his hands were flip-flopping over the ornate skirt and legs and feet of the thing: the bobbles and volutes, all of that Victorian flourish.

*They made their table legs look more and more like
human legs...* he explained after she remarked upon it, *-so much
so that then they felt the need to cover them up with tablecloths
and counterpanes and doyleys...*

She sat down next to him on the edge of a chair and he
paused for a second to look up from his place on the floor. She
wore a long floral dress and, with a movement that was somehow
at that moment completely natural to both of them, he put some
Teak Oil onto his hands and rubbed it onto her bare ankle and
foreleg and caressed it. She closed her eyes in an expression Joe
recognised from the face of every woman he had ever made love
to.

Suddenly they were giving in to something unexpected
breaking into their lives: an invisible wave rolling across the grid
and weave of the streets of this and every other city in summer.
Soon they were chess pieces fallen over on a chequerboard,
routines thrown into disarray. She was in his arms and her hair
in his eyes, losing her breath and her past, as their futures shrunk
from bleak years down to minutes and seconds of anticipation.

*

They began to see each other regularly, and every antique
clock Joe saw while he worked seemed to mark the time until
they could meet again, visit some restaurant or cook at home
together. For Vivienne, a life somehow suspended since Leo's
disappearance was now in motion again. Her weekends moved
from grey abstractions into missions to buy clothes, get her hair
trimmed, tidy her apartment before their next date. Her time was
short again and she wondered how she had ever filled the vastness

of it with just thoughts and daydreams alone. Her friends asked about her new acquaintance and, out of a desire to fend off their prying rather than any kind of snobbery, she would let them run with the label of *Her Furniture Man* until they lost interest. She would keep him under wraps.

*

When Joe stayed over, Vivienne would sometimes wake up to find he was running his hand gently over her whole body in slow caressing movements as if she were the most magnificent piece of furniture he had ever found.

Joe was a straightforward and moral man, and although exhilarated by their affair he didn't mention it to even his closest friends and family, conscious that she was technically still married. Making love to her he almost felt for a second as if he could become her, become part of her perfection by completing it, like a long lost handle or a missing drawer for a damaged wardrobe. It was an abstract fantasy but he could not see it in reality: his own body in the mirror was to him just a mass of angular lines and sags, all hair and sweat. If she was a work of art then he must be the waste material, he thought – the off-cuts destined for the bin.

Yet for all her beauty she had one imperfection that Joe spotted and never dared to mention. But it began to disturb and obsess him nonetheless. She had a faint long white scar across her stomach. Instinctively, when half-asleep, he would think of sanding it down and polishing it out like a piece of fine birch veneer. He knew she had no children by this man Leo whom she still spoke of reverently even though he had abandoned her, so the scar could not be from a Caesarean. He knew what appendix scars looked like. The explanation of an abortion appalled him somehow and all the more so when he realised he was sexually intimate now with a woman he did not know well enough to ask this simplest of questions: *what caused the scar?*

Sometimes they would lie awake late at night at weekends, smoking in bed, discussing their lives. It troubled him that she still had photographs of Leo on her dressing table and mantelpiece. He had handled second-hand furniture all his life, indeed he obviously preferred it to new: its smells, its age, its exquisite grain. Why should it worry him that bodies were second-hand too? Just as a beautiful table he polished might have come from an Edwardian salon he had never seen, its owners dead, so then might any woman have been made love to by other men, been soaked in their sweat and flattered with their gifts, immortalised in a thousand photographs now framed or hidden away. He tried to accept the thought, but it irked him like the itch of a blemish on his own skin.

He admired the old piano she had in the hallway and asked if she played. She said only Leo had played it but he could do so now if he liked. He sat down and admired the fine walnut carcass, the ebony keys, the complicated sheet music he couldn't read. Joe had no formal training but had learned to play by ear on the hundred antique pianos he had refurbished over the years. He would just play in any key and let a long meandering melody evolve, something different each time that expressed his mood of the moment but which he never repeated nor felt the need to record or write down. Now he wove a sad cascade of notes on the air, lazy like the shafts of late sunlight landing on her dark polished floor. As he played, he thought about Vivienne and Leo and the unreachable life they had shared together, of which this house was still the museum.

When he finished he found Vivienne in another room with her face turned to the wall and lined with tears. *What was that music?* -she whispered hoarsely, almost angrily, and it occurred to him for the first time that she hadn't shown this much weakness in front of him before. *It was nothing...* -he said truthfully, *-I just made it up as I went along.*

Mysteriously, this seemed to make her angry again: *It must be something... you can't just make that up... if you have that kind of talent you would have to use it for something wouldn't you?*

I just did. -he said and saw that they stood on the edge of some strange gulf between them. He was a tradesman, content to live and die in humility and obscurity, while she and her beloved Leo were *professionals*: those who feel they must achieve something special in the world's eyes or die trying.

*

One night as they finished making love and he withdrew: they found that they had had an accident. Vivienne went pale and rigid in fear and seemed ready for a moment to blame him for something that was probably both their faults or maybe nobody's. Vivienne was disturbed by the ease with which Joe seemed to contemplate the possible consequences, which to her were terrifying. *I can't afford to have a child right now! I might be too old anyhow.* She expressed every form of indignation in fact, other than to voice the idea that troubled her most: that the two of them were not a compatible couple, were not people she could ever imagine as parents of the same child.

Worst of all was when Joe verged onto the subject of abortion and how he would always rather bring a child up than contemplate terminating a pregnancy. Vivienne stopped him talking, almost to the point of putting her hands over his face. *You don't know what you're talking about,* -she started to say,

-you know nothing about what it means... to be a woman, she meant, and that he could have no jurisdiction in the terrifying domain of her body.

After the fight, as if in the wake of a storm, they had a curious conversation on this premise: *-What is the most sacred place that you know or possess?*

Next morning she showed him: lowering a hatch in the hallway, they both ascended into the large attic where Vivienne kept her paintings. The eaves were packed with a hundred canvases, most turned to the wall. But there on the easel was a portrait of Joe himself: alone, asleep on the bed half naked, the covers strewn around him in chaotic folds and brush strokes. *But when, how?* -he gasped.

I sketched you one morning while you slept, -she said.

Is it dry, is it finished? -he asked.

It is finished. -she told him and he smiled, not realising that she was also answering another question: one he had not yet asked.

*

He thought it cowardly that she should phone him to break off their relationship. But with an enormous effort of will he managed to talk as if this outcome did not disappoint him but then he asked one last thing of her, in fact he begged her: that she should meet him in the evening so that he could show her the place most sacred to him.

It was a pleasant summer evening when they both stepped out of her car at an old barn building beyond the city outskirts. This was his family's original workshop, Joe explained, where his grandfather had first founded a carpenter's business almost a hundred years before, made his fortune then lost it in *The Great*

Depression. He pulled back the rusting door and the wheels and track howled like a dinosaur. It disturbed him to notice that already their body language had become formal, how this woman whose skin had been so intimate to him was now to be out of bounds and that even to touch her incorrectly might be deemed a violation.

Tired and disheartened, he nonetheless felt the need to carry out this one last rite, as if he wanted to prove something to himself and her. Like the music he had played on her piano he wanted her to acknowledge that he, and indeed any man, could have greatness and yet choose to squander it on a whim. He wanted to show her how the wind does not listen or, if it does, it doesn't care for one word of human babble.

Here was the first chair he had made as a child, now discoloured by rot and mould. Here were some of his Father's and Grandfather's work: humble workbenches, kitchen tables, rocking chairs, nothing of great value. He had left them here purely as sentimental symbols. Then he opened the back doors of the shed and led her out into the woods behind. She became slowly enchanted as he led her into a landscape of chairs and wardrobes and tables vanishing into nettle and tall grasses, ivy, hawthorn and birch. Was it possible that he had damaged some of the furniture on purpose and trained creepers and roots to work their way up like this – clutching and strangling and seeking out every opening they could thread themselves through? No, incredibly this was Nature's work alone.

Her breath was taken away when she reached the edge of the forest and saw reaching into the distance in the gathering twilight beneath the leaves: the ghostly forms of chairs and tables that had been seemingly eaten by trees. Progressively decayed, now root and trunk and branch were interwoven with the decaying wood, as if their slow blind gestures had found then caressed and embraced what they recognised as their own.

My God... -she said, turning to him wild-eyed; *-it's beautiful... and horrible...*

I wanted you to see it, -he said, running his hand through his hair, his eyes smarting in the angled evening light. *This is how it ends you see... everything...*

For a moment she almost recoiled at the coldness of his words before he went on: *Every chair or table or bedstead is just a tree that somebody killed then turned into the strange spectacle we call furniture. But trees die anyway. Decay is part of life, everything is fleeting. It's only the desire to preserve, to suffocate under varnish or oil that's vain and human. It's all a beautiful lie, but Nature isn't fooled and Nature isn't listening...*

She stared into space for a long time as he left her alone at the edge of the woods. Finally she stretched her hand out to touch the arm of an ancient chair half woven into the branches of a silver birch and it crumbled into dust in front of her: only brown mulch and crawling insects were left writhing in her palm.

Back at the barn she heard a noise of tapping from inside then saw a rivulet of some bright liquid pouring out from the barn door into the concrete drain outside. For a crazy moment she thought he might have hanged himself as some melodramatic gesture or that this was his fresh red blood, his wrist cut through with a band saw.

Relieved, she found he was just mixing an old pot of varnish and starting to apply it to a chair. *It's ok,* he said, *you can leave me here now. I made this a long time ago and I always meant to seal it. I'll walk back, I know the way like the back of my hand.*

She saw then that it was a primitive chair, perhaps the first one he had ever made, not a patch on all those beautiful antiques he had sanded and polished every day: heirlooms too elaborate for his simple tastes.

She stood there for a moment and looked at him, trying to preserve the scene in her eye like a photograph before the light faded. He looked up and smiled widely: *It's ok now...* -he said, as if comforted by the feel of work in his hands then laughed: *Really... it's ok.*

Getting into the car she realised that he hadn't even asked her why she was ending it. How could he be so accepting? Her period had been frighteningly late and the fear that she had fallen pregnant had kept her awake all night, filled with a strange hatred towards this harmless man. Even driving home now, as the sunset turned red in her wing mirror and the blighted fields gave way to suburbia, she could not lose that taste of irrational fear that had soured and severed forever the bond between them.

~

4. THE EQUATION

Doctor Franco Reinwald had finally consented that his most enigmatic patient Anton Perlato should receive electro-convulsive therapy. All else had failed and, during an hour of unusual lucidity, Anton had even seemed keen to submit himself to this somewhat controversial and old-fashioned treatment.

Now it was evening and while Anton lay back in a hospital bed to have the electrodes applied to either side of his head, Franco sat down in his living room, ten miles away, preparing to be confronted by his wife Claudia over his failure to spend enough quality time with their son Vittorrio.

At the same moment, little Vittorrio himself sat up in bed in the next room and ran his hands over a huge fallen leaf he had hidden under his pillow. The texture of the leaf delighted him: particularly the underside with its complex network of ribs, its spreading delta of veins.

Thirty miles away at this same moment, Claudia's brother Leo had ceased walking for a moment and was running his hands in awe over the deeply fissured bark of a cedar tree. His eye followed the bark up the immense height of the tree to its distant tip: it was a giant.

Suddenly, from the midst of the brooding evening clouds overhead, a fork of lightning snaked down and struck the cedar, propelling Leo backwards for ten feet until he hit a neighbouring tree and collapsed, winded. The tip of the tree turned instantly to black charcoal and fell off, leaving the remainder in flames.

The switch was flicked at the sanatorium and Anton's body arched upwards briefly then relaxed as 800 milliamps passed through him, his brain circuitry degaussed, re-booted, rerouted, scrambled.

Vittorrio watched the leaf in his hand in wonder under the covers as he thought he saw the fantastical network of veins momentarily light up. It was like a family tree or a river distribution pattern seen from space. Delighted, he lifted the soft fragrant leaf to his face and pressed its texture against his forehead and breathed its aroma in.

In the gathering twilight, Claudia stood at the living room window and saw the distant lightning fork beneath the rainclouds building up to the east. She thought briefly of her missing brother, then turned to continue her line of argument with her husband.

But you're a psychiatrist, ok? So what I simply don't get is how you can be disinterested when your four-year-old son says he has an imaginary friend who is the spirit of a man who died in a car crash two years ago?

I didn't say I wasn't interested, Claudia, you're putting words into my mouth as usual.

Maybe that's because you don't use enough words, Franco. After listening to everyone else unwind all day, you'd think you'd want to follow suit back here, but you're like a closed book half the time.

I think, if I might return us to the point rather than the personal attacks, I think I said that Vittorrio's words didn't overly concern me. He's just a little boy. Children have imaginary friends and gothic imaginations, it's normal.

Today he told me the name of the friend, the registration of his wrecked car and the names of the two streets at the road junction where he says the accident took place... And all of this delivered in a cheery little voice by the way, as if it's just his mother who's weird for getting unnerved by this kind of thing...

Well you said it, right there. Maybe Vittorrio's correct in this instance. It's just a game and you need to take it as such... I don't mean enter into the spirit of the thing and stage a séance, I mean just ignore it or pacify him like you would any of his other games.

Mmmm... Claudia sighed. *But you haven't heard his voice when he talks about his friend... it's weird, like an adult's... and this is what I mean... You haven't heard him because you hardly spend any time with him these days.*

Franco was cornered, and took off his glasses and polished them. This always made him look more vulnerable to Claudia, the soft cheeks and sensitive brow, and she felt for a moment two contradictory emotions simultaneously: the frisson of the memory of her first inklings of love for him, and the more recent terror that she was the only adult in a house, indeed a world, filled with needy children.

Vittorrio had lost consciousness in the next room, face wrapped in his beloved leaf. Leo had picked his aching limbs up from the forest floor after a moment's disorientation and was laughing to himself now, wilder than ever and invigorated at nature's latest show of force, seemingly just for his benefit. Anton, memory and awareness temporarily wiped, was being returned carefully to his ward by the sanatorium sisters. The thunder was fading and soon everyone would be fast asleep for the night, the storm gone over the horizon.

Meanwhile, the million trees of the encircling forest, tired of breathing the discarded carbon of the puny city in their midst, sighed and took their first breaths of oxygen like a rare cigar, and wondered whether to leave any for the humans in the morning.

*

Anton's recovery was so unexpected and sudden that he discharged himself from the sanatorium before Doctor Reinwald had even had the opportunity to re-assess him. He walked the streets towards his home, and felt as if he had just awoken from a three-month long nightmare. He talked to a few people in the shops and found that the old terrors and tensions had magically evaporated from him. Better still, he felt a connection with strangers, as if rather than be gripped by his own insecurities he could sense theirs and move to assuage them. He made strangers laugh, and looked forward to doing even better with his friends and family. He had drowned, short-circuited perhaps in the sea of human terror and now he saw that everyone swam in this sea everyday. Now he knew he could help them, and that help was what everyone needed, whether they realised it or not. Now all their television and gossip and chit-chat made more sense to him. They were each alone and frightened and their words to each other were like a million caresses, administered invisibly like a healing balm. They were sending and receiving signals of mutual respect and reassurance. He had simply misunderstood the social currency of the human race and, convinced it could harm him, turned his brain into a bastion against it, an upside-down place.

One of the strangest symptoms of his illness had been a total lack of dreaming. Now as he returned to his first night in his own bed for many months, he would find this normal facility for nocturnal fantasy returned. It was as if all his brain's powers of invention had been temporarily employed in fictionalising the real world into a nightmare while he was awake and, now that this was over, these powers were free again to roam harmlessly by night.

*

At work, Franco heard a disturbance from outside his counselling room and, excusing himself from his patient for a moment, paced out into the waiting room to discover that people were panicking and running for the stairs on account of a bee the size of a fist that was battering itself against the window. Franco was bemused at first until he moved closer and began to appreciate its true scale. A wave of primordial fear swept over him, he even shivered. He shouted to everyone not to be afraid and to stay still, then as if in answer the bee shifted to the left and entered the room through the one window that no one had yet had the presence of mind to shut.

Franco told himself the kind of advice he gave his children at times like this: that bees were harmless, that like every animal they had a simple objective which almost certainly was something other than attacking a life form a hundred times their size. Food or shelter or mating, he told himself, as he held back visions of the huge bee latching onto his face and stinging and probing his nasal cavities like succulent flowers. He placed a plastic lunch box with a fragment of jam sandwich in its path, and choosing his moment suddenly rammed the lid back over the box, trapping the creature within. The wave of applause from his patients and staff began to briefly exhilarate him until he felt the sickening urgency and strength of the angry monster in his charge. Fighting back an urge to drop the thing and run, he shouted instead to his nurses to bring him packaging tape and further containers to secure the prisoner.

There had been a plague of unusually large insects recently, some photographed in the local newspaper, but this specimen struck Franco as truly exceptional. He told everyone he would take it to his wife to examine, a trained veterinarian. But deprived of air and kept in the boot of his car, he secretly hoped it would safely expire before nightfall. A cowardly act of murder no doubt, not good science, but he had a vision of his wife's misplaced respect for all living things leading to the thing running rampage in their apartment and maiming their children.

Driving home, he had to stop three times to open the boot and check that the creature had not been playing possum to trick him, imagining the rumbling of the car's motor noise as he drove to resemble the sound of an uncanny resurrection.

*

The next day, Claudia received a letter from her brother Leo:

Sometimes I see the trees as diagrams, proxies for the human networks of births and deaths. I mean I stumble upon a tree and I suddenly know that it is the mother of my wife's family, or the daughter of an ex-neighbour or my first teacher. Then I sit and gaze up into its canopy of branches and leaves and there I see reaching into the past and future the various unions and issues, intertwinings and divergences that create the human race. Brothers, sisters, sons, cousins, the trees like humans: are joined together under the earth by roots, united after death and before birth, when seen sideways out of time. The forest is a collectively conscious organism, as are we, and its roots reach up into our very bodies like arteries and veins. Destroy the forest and we destroy ourselves. But is the converse true I wonder? If the earth-brain root system were to decide to strangle us tomorrow, to euthanise us like the misbegotten chimeras we have become, what then, would be the net loss to the planet? The withered and desiccated carcass of our civilisation would doubtless make useful compost for the next unwritten chapter of evolution. The persistence of life as a whole, we may be sure, would be undeterred, perhaps redoubled. Dust to dust, as the priests say. Therefore by the very measure by which we deplete the soil that nourishes us and our crops, so we bring upon ourselves by slow degrees our own inevitable famine and extinction. It is biblical, but it is also scientific, mathematically true, an equation.

How are we to know when any species, in this case ourselves, is reaching this tipping-point in its betrayal of its own supporting eco-system? -The point at which it is about to be trashed by nature? -When its scrap-value, so to speak, exceeds the daily cost for its survival?

1. Elements within the species will mysteriously lose the will to live, and begin to die prematurely. This is Gaia's drawing-away of vitality from the doomed branches.

2. The species will swim in its own excrement. Thus physically, artistically and spiritually it will begin to die of poverty and infection.

3. The species will begin to eat itself. This is Gaia's preparation for the great repast, a fusion of the ingredients.

4. The species will be attacked parasitically by other lifeforms. The process might be thought of as an act of love.

5. Its own end will be intimated to it by tremors, dreams and portents. Prophets will be chosen from within its own number.

Claudia, her blood beginning to chill, closed the letter in horror, unable to read on any further, dismayed by the progressive insanity of her errant brother. Short of breath, she opened the patio doors and leaned, weeping to herself, over the handrail of her balcony, gazing blindly at the traffic down below. From the many potted plants swinging overhead, a beetle fell and moved into her curls of black hair. She felt it and reached up, half crying out loud, ridding herself of the creature and retreating in doors in panic.

*

Something was driving Anton irrevocably onwards, a feeling of pre-destination seemed to be residing in his feet. He was walking through a deep pine forest without any memory of how he had got there. Suddenly he reached an opening in the trees: a long steep fire-break criss-crossed by muddy fissures, leading down to a green valley far below. Then to his left he heard a low voice, saying something in a language he didn't understand, maybe it was Latin. He spun around and perhaps fifty yards up slope he saw an old man had also just emerged from the trees on a parallel path and was staring down at him. Instantly, strong winds picked up and all the canopies of trees overhead started making a deafening sound together like waves of the sea. The stranger seemed unperturbed, almost as if he was orchestrating the weather.

Who are you? Anton shouted against the wind, spellbound by the strange aura of this man, as if he had just stumbled on a rare antelope or an apparition of Bigfoot. The look in the man's eyes was tired and yet extremely calm and focussed. As he looked closer he wondered if perhaps he was not so old as he looked, just unkempt. Then the stranger simply lifted his arm and pointed down the hillside over Anton's shoulder. Anton turned, following his finger and saw to his right, perhaps half a mile down the slope: a small boy dressed in white had just emerged from the trees and now turned and looked up towards them. Their three figures seemed somehow aligned in an obscure equation in space and time.

Instinctively, Anton waved and shouted to the boy and began to move down the slope towards him. When he looked back a moment later, he saw that the old man had disappeared.

*

Driving back from a veterinary emergency at a farm in the country, Claudia was passing through an obscure northern village when something odd caught her eye. Slowing down she noticed a street sign with the name *Charlemagne Boulevard*, one of those that Vittorrio had said to her in connection with his imaginary friend. With a drowning feeling beginning to build inside her, she turned off at the end of the town and slowly drove back along the main street, reading the name of every avenue leading off. She couldn't remember the other name, but she knew, like a premonition, that she would know it when she heard it again. *Versaille Row*. Her stomach lurched and she pulled over and switched the engine off, wound down the window and breathed deeply.

Trying to act naturally, she got out and walked back for a hundred yards until she stood at the junction of the two streets. She put her hand to her throat and shivered as she saw that the garden wall of the house on the corner had been rebuilt, probably after an impact. A woman in a neighbouring garden was mowing her lawn, and had begun to notice Claudia's interest. She switched the machine off as if to come towards her and Claudia was suddenly filled with confusion. She turned to walk away but seeing the woman was not discouraged, felt unable to ignore her as she spoke: *can I help you?*

I'm sorry... Claudia blurted out, stumbling as she reached for, of all things, her dark glasses from her bag. *It was my son... I was just being silly...*

Oh, I'm so sorry... Please forgive me... -the woman gasped, her reaction seemingly inappropriately effusive, confusing Claudia further as she touched her arm. *It was a terrible thing... it's been a while now since anyone left flowers, I didn't realise...*

Oh no, no, please...! -disgusted by the misunderstanding she had inadvertently generated, the stranger's kindness somehow threatening, Claudia panicked and hurried back to her car, hands in her hair, unwittingly enhancing further the tragic image of a distraught mother. Her hands were shaking when she placed them back on the steering wheel.

*

When she returned home that night, expecting to be greeted as usual by Vittorrio in his school uniform, Claudia was perplexed to meet Franco waiting in the hall of their apartment with a dead insect in a lunch box.

Later, when Franco brought the children back from swimming lessons, he in turn was surprised to find Claudia in full veterinary surgical gear in the study with a large poster of an anatomical diagram of a honey bee pinned to the wall above her. Only when the children were safely off to bed did Franco dare to re-enter the room and survey the bizarre scene again.

This is fascinating... Claudia said, *... the thorax and scopa... everything is outsized by a factor of about thirteen. This is the biggest yet, I better take it to the Institute in the morning.*

What's causing these freaks? -Franco asked. *Radiation from Sizewell B or something?*

Claudia laughed. *You should know better, Franco, as a medical man. Radiation causing gigantism is the stuff of Marvel comics, it really has no such redeeming features, it only kills cells, causes Cancer and...*

I was probably joking. What then?

Well, I can only guess it's some kind of change in the food chain, arrival or removal of a predator, some new threat or advantage has made it useful for them to increase in size.

But flowers aren't getting any bigger are they? I thought they were sized so as to fit into flowers?

Quite so, then we must ask what this monster is adapted to pollinate. I've analysed the pollen traces on its legs but I'll need the results of full lab tests to be sure. It looks like Japanese Knotweed, Giant Hogweed and maybe Rhododendrons. Invasive, fast-growing, non-indigenous species in other words.

So it's following changes in the habitat?

Yes, but rapid changes, damaging changes perhaps, where we have cleared large tracts of forest and disrupted their familiar eco-system. This is panic-adaptation, emergency pollination.

So will these bees increase the spread of these species?

Undoubtedly.

Then that's bad news for the forests surrounding us?

Not necessarily, Franco. The reports of these creatures have all been in urban areas.

Franco furrowed his brow, adjusted his spectacles and examined the hideous beast upturned: its many black hairy legs in the air, twitching spasmodically every time Claudia applied pressure with tweezers and scalpel. *Don't you remember the story a few years back that their numbers were dropping, and they thought our mobile phone networks were interfering with their navigation systems?* Franco also found himself remembering as he said this, about the interference on the television in his waiting room as the bee had attacked, but dismissed the notion.

Don't you see? -Claudia sighed, taking her surgical mask off from around her neck. *They're spreading these plants into the city for some reason, presumably unintentionally, since we don't yet credit them with a centralised intelligence. They are Nature's ultimate guardians and gardeners, the pollinators. They are seeding our city for us.* She turned to look at Franco and it occurred to him that she seemed almost exultant at her own alarming conclusions. *We're being fertilised, Franco. Ploughed and sown for an alien crop...*

*

Vittorrio Reinwald, aged four and a half, in his white nightshirt and bare feet, walked through the streets of the city at night. He crossed boulevards roaring with traffic, moved down streets pulsing with thieves and pimps and prostitutes and yet remained unscathed, moving in a trance as if protected by an invisible aura.

He would remember almost nothing of this evening later, perhaps he was sleepwalking. The bored commuters passing by saw him like an apparition, a *Christ Child* walking blindly between cars that swerved and sounded their horns. Stray dogs barked, then cowered away from Vittorrio, as if subdued by some inner light.

Some citizens who glimpsed him momentarily, those seated in passing trams, believed they had been dreaming or had misunderstood their own eyes, but were left feeling strangely comforted afterwards. Others, mothers, crossed themselves in doorways, then phoned the police or ran after him. But all were strangely repelled at the second before they could move to touch Vittorrio. Perhaps they were scared to wake the child, or scared to wake themselves from the beautiful dream he seemed to be enacting for them.

At the end of one street, he finally found the forest and his little feet left the tarmac at last and padded along the carpet of pine needles. Down an impossibly long vista between tall trees, his tiny figure sauntered, dwarfed by the dark green overarching pines and the full moon above: sailing serenely amid brown clouds ruffling in the night wind. The forest sighed and whispered, surrounding him, an ancient mother singing him to sleep, enclosing him in its cool green shawl.

*

When Claudia found Vittorrio's bed empty in the morning, and the curtains blowing, her howl and ensuing hurlings of herself against every available wall reminded Franco of nothing so much as the giant insect he had so recently intercepted. Even after the police had been called, the street searched, and he held her, pinned like a butterfly against his chest: her violent jerking and guttural vocalisations reverberated through him and threatened to overwhelm him at any moment. Perhaps this urgent need to restrain his wife from self-harm helped him to forestall his own emotions and concentrate merely on survival from one moment to the next.

It was nearly twenty-four hours before Vittorrio was found by a police search party with sniffer dogs led there by Anton Perlato. They came upon him in a forest clearing at sunset, wide awake, cold but contented, with two curious fox cubs and a vixen for company; who upon seeing the torches, turned towards the rescuers and hissed briefly in hostility then vanished into the undergrowth leaving the child alone.

*

When Vittorrio was returned by Anton and the Police, Claudia held him and sobbed uncontrollably against his little body. She brushed his blonde hair from his eyes, asking if he was alright, searching to see that her son's personality was intact, that he was not *a changeling*, as the old women of a previous generation would have called it.

Hè seemed relaxed and happy but glad to have his mother run a hot bath for him. Touchingly, his sister Lucia came and hugged him, then presented him with a little crown of daisies she had made for him. Claudia wept to see how the children interacted with the lightness of a dream, Vittorrio stroking Lucia's hair in a simple gesture of gratitude. She wished she knew how to live as children live, she thought, as if death is an illusion and all of life is a blessing and a game to be laughed off, as harmless as summer rain.

When Franco came home from work and entered the apartment, Claudia saw a rare side to him. With all his many layers of formality and control suddenly stripped away by joy, he almost collapsed as he embraced Vittorrio, and Claudia was fascinated, almost jealous somehow, of those fat tears that spilled onto his cheek. His son was still covered in bubbles from his bath, his towel like a little Roman toga and water and soap spilling over Franco's immaculate black suit like spume and spray from some tidal wave of the heart, ash and lava from an emotional volcano.

Later in a quiet moment as she dressed him for bed, Claudia asked Vittorio how he could have travelled alone for so long a time without being afraid. What had made him do it? There had been a voice, he said, or several voices talking at once, in his head and all around him, and they had reassured him and guided him away from harm. They had wanted him to reach the forest. They were the voices of the trees themselves, they were old and kind, they had showed him nuts and berries to eat. *But surely they weren't as comforting as Mamma's voice were they?* She asked. *Surely you won't listen to them again? Now that you understand how leaving your mother and father and sister will kill us with worry?*

Vittorrio smiled and whispered in his Mother's ear that he knew the trees would not call him again because of what they had told him. *Next time... They will come to us, Mamma... soon, very soon... they will come here.*

Claudia backed away, hoping to conceal a moment's fear in her eyes but soon saw that her son's eyes were already closed in sleep. The streetlight shadows of leaves and branches played over his face, feather-light but inquisitive, as if pawing him like a fox cub. Leaving the room in the twilight, she was struck for a moment by the disquieting and irrational thought that everything wooden in the room, floorboards, doors, tables, wardrobes, represented some kind of latent threat and might all be waiting to be reclaimed by their rightful owner: the forest from which they had been made.

*

It's an amazing coincidence… -Franco began. *I asked you to drop by so I could thank you in person for finding my son and returning him to my wife. What can I ever do to thank you?*

Nothing, please Doctor, -Anton said. *You treated me and cured me after all, I have my life back now, or maybe it's a new life altogether, a better one. But at any rate I feel cured and I'm sure I will get a job soon and resume normality. So maybe I have repaid my debt to you, it is fate… or perhaps…*

Yes? -Franco was intrigued by the sudden doubt in Anton's voice and Anton had to pinch himself for a moment to remember that he was no longer being analysed.

-It was as if I was being guided to him. I can't explain it. I wasn't looking to find your son or any lost child for that matter. There was this old man in the woods, or what I thought at first was an old man…

Yes, my wife said you had mentioned something like that.

Well, there was something uncanny about him.

Franco paused and frowned with a sudden impulsive curiosity, and against his better judgement ventured into uncharacteristically irrational territory: *Anton, can I show you something? A photograph of somebody?*

By all means. Anton leaned close over the Doctor's desk and peered at a photograph of Leo Vestra as a young man with his arm around his wife to be, the beautiful blonde Vivienne.

Could this be the man you saw, aged and worn after several years of living outdoors, living rough I mean, like a tramp?

Anton peered for a long time, particularly at the eyes, comparing them to his memory of the strange dishevelled wanderer he had seen. *Yes....* He affirmed finally, *it's certainly possible, that could well have been him, aged as you say.*

Doctor Reinwald sighed and returned the photo to his drawer. *I knew it... Leo... he is, was, my wife's brother... now he is some kind of forest mystic, a rural vagabond.*

Why? -Anton was the intrigued one now, *...does he choose such a life?*

Well now... how long have you got? Traffic jams, pollution, overcrowding, poverty, social division, crime, the ongoing rape of our natural surroundings on an industrial scale. The reasons are legion, Mr Perlato, just take your pick.

He didn't seem unhappy... Anton said quietly.

Ahh... if only the same could be said for my wife, his sister... but that's another story. Thank you again, Anton, for all that you have done. You will have my enduring gratitude I can assure you. I hope we meet again... and here Franco finally smiled and laughed as they shook hands... *-but not here of course, not like this again. You will stay well, I trust.*

But Doctor Reinwald... -Anton said, thinking and pausing at the door, *-I think maybe you've misunderstood me. I led the police to your son, but when I said I saw him and this man you call Leo in the forest, I didn't mean that I was there or saw them in reality. I meant I saw them in a dream, Doctor. I dreamed about where they were, and then the next day I led the police to that spot.*

*

That night, unusually, Franco had a nightmare about Leo. He saw him as he imagined him from Anton's description. Long matted hair and beard, bloodshot eyes, skin pocked and grey. He saw Leo sit down somewhere in the forest close to a beehive and rub a trail of honey on his cheek, leading up to his left ear. In time a bee landed on the trail and crawled into Leo's brain. Somehow, as Leo meditated, various bees entered his head and began to colonise the mysterious disused third of the cerebrum. Then the days seemed to pass as Leo marched through woodlands with a colony of bees growing inside him. He eventually reached a break in the woods and spun around and opened his mouth and roared like a lion. From his open mouth, a swarm of bees flooded out and swept down the hillside along a gully between two flanks of tall pine trees. Franco saw their progress as if he were a bee himself: the cliffs of green branches spinning giddily past him.

At the bottom of the hillside, the bees descended upon a burned out car and coalesced into a cloud in the shape of a man hunched in the driver's seat. For a moment there was the hideous illusion of a corpse being swarmed over, devoured by bees. Then there was a sudden flashover and the car appeared intact again and moved off backwards towards the road.

Franco woke up with a shout, sweating, as he realised the man in the car driving backwards was himself.

Sitting up in bed, he looked to his left and saw to his surprise that Claudia was not beside him. Getting up he followed the light in the apartment until he found her in Vittorrio's room, kneeling over their son's bed, just watching him sleep. Franco entered the room and stood over her, placing his hand on her shoulder. Then in turn, after a while, she placed her own hand over his.

Standing looking at the moon on their balcony before returning to bed, Franco sensed that they were both thinking about Leo. *Will he ever return?* -he whispered, almost to himself.

Claudia sighed and gazed down to the quiet streets below, where only a few late cars rumbled and hissed in the first drops of midnight rain. *Will we?* -she murmured, then turned to him, wild-eyed and half-asleep, scarcely understanding her own words: *Will we?*

~

5.

VERONIKA

"What has all your study of the wonder of Creation taught you about the mind of the Creator? An inordinate love of beetles..."

-JBS Haldane.

"Alas for us, I want to cry, our bones are secret..."

-William Gass, *Order of Insects.*

Doctor Franco Reinwald was surprised and a little intimidated to find that his next patient was, in the current language of youth culture: a *Goth*. He had been spotting gangs of these obscure creatures on street corners in the city centre for years, mostly outside bookshops and art galleries on Saturdays. He had little idea what they thought they stood for, but suspected that they had even less idea themselves. Was it possible they were expressing some societal angst by proxy, or just their own personal pain? The pallid make-up, the obsession with death and violence, it all slotted in neatly with the standard teenage difficulties. To tell them what straightforward anthropology they were therefore enacting might shock them into giving it up and growing up on the spot, Franco mused to himself. Dressing up as if it was Halloween or a funeral every day could in fact be viewed as a logical strategy for counteracting the pressures of the lifeforce pushing the young towards sexual interaction and meeting parental expectations.

Old Freud would have loved this... Franco found himself saying out loud as he rubbed his goatee beard, before his patient had even opened her mouth. *Death and sex fused in a youth cult that steals its name from the great Germanic barbarian race that finally wrecked the Roman Empire. Classic... even classical stuff. Warlike uniforms. A dress-code infinitely more onerous and arduous than the suits and jeans and T-shirts of the oppressed parents. So much for rebellion...*

Sorry? -the creature in front of him asked, wide-eyed, all black eye-shadow and multiple piercings. Leather armour, knee-high shining boots, fishnet tights (artfully torn), superfluous bike chains. A spraypainted skull across her chest with some obscene caption beneath it. He knew not to try to analyse the words. They would not be original but borrowed from the lyrics of a Thrash Metal album of electric growls indistinguishable from the noise of a broken washing-machine. All the black leather reminded him of insect armour, like some of the freakish specimens that had been showing up on his surgery carpet all summer. But then there was the face. Blood red ruby-rouged lips, wild green eyes with the cruelty of a tigress.

Veronika... Miss Steiner... he began again, *I see from your notes that you've had problems with depression and you've been referred here by your GP.*

I'm sorry... she said, *but what you said back there was insulting...*

Yes... you're right. It just slipped out I suppose.

Like Hell it did. You're just a close-minded old bore. A square. How the hell are you going to understand my life with that attitude?

Veronika... Franco sighed. *History repeats itself. My father fought in a war so terrible that nobody thought anyone would want to have a war again in the future...*

Your point is?

Well, you do watch the evening news? Then you get my point. I was a punk rocker you know, dressed more outrageously than you. We had a reputation for spitting on old ladies and the like, which was nonsense of course, but our parents were terrified of us. But at a punk concert surrounded by thousands of other kids like myself, it wasn't threatening at all. It was great, a feeling of real belonging...

C'mon Doc... Get up on your desk and pogo then, I'll photograph you on my mobile phone... Sorry, but that is quite funny... -She was laughing now, wiping a tear from her eye.

That's OK Veronika, you're quite right. I insulted you first. But it's a form of communication after all.

Do you insult all your patients?

Some of them, yes. It's one way to assess their level of self-esteem.

And how was mine? -she smiled precociously.

Franco, to his surprise found himself grinning in return. He felt a twinge of vanity, but resolved to repress it. *Good! Recovery from anything only comes with wanting to recover. Recovery must become what your self-esteem desires.*

You mean you think I want to be depressed? -she asked, incredulously, unimpressed again for a moment.

At a subconscious level at least, possibly. We're not all masters of all the compartments of our consciousness, you know. That takes self-discipline, hard to achieve when you are young, but it comes with maturity.

Really? -she said, as her sly smile slowly spread like a Cheshire cat's and she eyed him ruefully.

So the tiger is tamed, Franco thought.

*

Franco and Claudia had not had sex for 3 months. Supposedly this was because Claudia had contracted some fungal infection, which she seemed to vaguely blame on him despite all the evidence to the contrary.

She had even cheerily offered to show him the micro-organisms responsible under her microscope, but Franco had politely declined as if dodging an introduction to a trailer-trash cousin-in-law.

Now instead of sex they would lie in bed on Sunday mornings and look up at the ceiling where a mysterious patch of black mould had been gradually spreading for the best part of half a year.

Are we going to paint it then?

As I keep saying, we painted it last year and it came back. I think we have to go up into the attic and investigate it from above in case it's a patch of dry rot or something.

Yes... she drawled, leafing through a magazine, -*when are we going to paint it then?*

Franco covered his eyes, but she didn't notice and went on:

I got another letter from my brother by the way...

Franco opened one eye, then the other, put the hands back down again. *Really? How is he?*

Oh, still mad as a hatter... -Claudia laughed manically, then burst into tears a moment later. Franco rubbed her back as she handed him the letter and began reading:

I'm not coming home anytime soon, Claudia. The forest is my home now. It is everybody's home really, if only they could see that. It was once, in the distant past, and will be again in the not so distant future. Ask your dogs and cats. They'll be glad when the crunch comes and urban refugees come here building campfires and roasting squirrels. This is how they first befriended us and came along for the ride, so many millennia ago. Listen to your animals, look deep into their eyes. Gaia resides in them more deeply than in us now. We have wandered too far from hearth and home and now our bodies wither and die in the smog and congestion, our souls weep at the boredom and incarceration of everyday life. We caged the animals in return for their loyalty, but we caged ourselves more subtly, more damagingly.

You are what you eat and drink and breathe, so what are we now, most of us? Carbon Monoxide, Lead, Fluoride, Monosodium Glutamate. Metal and ash and oil. If we are not what we were, then what is it we have become? Android Clowns? Surrealist Machines for endlessly wasting energy and resources in absurd ways? New models of cars every year. Every desirable home in the country extended a thousand times until it looks like a nursing home. Perpetual makeover, the cult of the new. Consumerism and Economic Growth, our holy cow and holy grail, are in fact synonymous with Environmental Destruction, maybe they always were, right from the first. Only their exact opposite: Stasis and Equilibrium are the key to Eternity, the mislaid key to our physical and spiritual survival.

Gaia is everything. If we oppose Gaia then we must be eliminated. The process has already begun. Mankind is rotting from within as Gaia withdraws the

Human Spirit from its bodies, like the drawback before a tidal wave.

Pay careful attention to the armour of the Barbarians. A sign of the coming end will be that the children will adopt the religion of death. It is the fate of the minds of the children to feel the first waves of the future. Thus to them will be given the intimations of destruction. Skulls and blood will be their emblems. They and their children will be the army of scavengers among the bones of their parents, in the time to come, dressed in black armour to shield themselves in night.

Wow... Franco could only mumble hoarsely, as he took off his specs and rubbed them. He didn't dare reveal his real thoughts, even to himself: that it had been a long time since he had got the chance to analyse a patient this mad, and felt strangely jealous.

*

Shopping with Claudia the following week, Franco unexpectedly caught site of Veronika and a boyfriend hanging around on a street corner looking gothic and deathly. It occurred to him that there was something vampiric in their demeanour, a professed inclination to drink blood.

Vampires were an entirely fictitious creation, currently seized upon by popular horror fantasy films out of, one presumed, sheer boredom. Being Franco, part of him wanted to ponder what deeper societal angst the archetype of the vampire might be a latent signifier of. Was there a connection with menstruation?

He wanted to continue this pressing internal dialogue, but was diverted temporarily into a department store for a pointless debate about duvet covers with his wife.

*

While Claudia went to the hairdressers, Franco chanced upon Veronika again, a few blocks away. She was alone this time, sitting on the pavement and looking so dejected that Franco felt compelled to risk his medical detachment and professionalism by going over to speak to her.

Veronika... -Her eyes rolled up vacantly and he saw that she was drugged up on something. He tried using her nickname: *Roni... are you OK... are you feeling alright?*

Her eyes finally widened in recognition: *Doctor Reinwald... Hey... how are you? I'm just won...der...ful...*

Roni, have you taken something? It's OK, I'm not the Police or anything. I'm just concerned. If you're depressed then drink and drugs are the last thing you should be taking...

Herr Doctor... She said at last, fixing her spinning stare upon him with Herculean effort... -*You're a big handsome hunk... did anyone ever tell you that before?*

You're out of it, Veronika, you need to go home, you don't know what you're saying...

Doctor, Doctor... she sang, and leaned up and whispered in his ear as he tried to pick her up off the pavement: *...Don't you think my mouth is like a ripe apple? Wouldn't you like to push your little maggot into it and corrupt me...? Ooze your white slime down my virginal throat?*

Franco back away from her, disgusted, angered, embarrassed, conflicted between helping her and discouraging her. *Veronika, where do you stay? You need to go home and sleep this off, can I get you a taxi?*

Suddenly her boyfriend had reappeared and was standing over them. His outfit was even more outlandish than Veronika's. Angular sections of silver metal seemed to be emerging from his chest at a multitude of angles as if he were the genetic fulfilment of a collision between a human being and a Ford Focus. He was obviously styled as a forager from a post-apocalyptic waste dump, but the apocalypse was running disappointingly late.

Hey Benny… Veronika drawled, *Doctor Dreamboat here was just telling me how he's going to take me home so I can SUCK HIS COCK in the back of a taxi…*

The magnetic millipede instantly flexed and lifted and pinned Franco against a shop window. *Fuckin' old pervert… ah'll make ya suck mine,* -he intoned through his metallic teeth, face leaning close to his.

Two policemen had appeared behind him now, and laying hands on leather shoulders, disentangled the scene. *Old pervert… trying to shag my girlfriend…*

Everyone including Franco (now mopping his brow with a handkerchief) turned to look at Veronika for a moment who laughed and sighed: *No… not true, Officers… don't be fooled by the suit, this old guy is my drug dealer…*

Psychiatrist… -Franco interrupted, grabbing her shoulder, -*I think she means psychiatrist.*

Same difference… Veronika snorted.

I've been treating her for depression… and I saw her here sitting on the pavement and I became concerned…

Aroused, more like… -Veronika whispered. The boyfriend lunged over and slapped her, and they were both led away.

*

A few nights later, Franco had a curious and disturbing dream in which he saw Veronika being made love to by a giant beetle. It alarmed him that a patient he hardly knew could so quickly have entered his subconscious. Perhaps he was not the sober master of his own mind that he imagined himself to be?

He could see in the dream that the giant beetle had represented Claudia's boyfriend but he had also partially identified with the monster himself. Its many legs and antennae playing and probing and piercing her pale flesh had provoked from its victim a kind of combined moaning and screaming that he found both distasteful and arousing. Was the beetle really himself? The ambiguous mixture of revulsion and attraction on the part of Veronika, a representation of her own feelings towards him, as an older man? Why, as a dispassionate professional, was he interested in such feelings towards him anyway?

He also remembered that as he had moved inside the body of the beetle, the walls had seemed to shake in a way that frightened him. Out of a corner of his eye he had seen that the room was filled with hundreds of little pots of diluted paint or coloured water. Or were they glasses filled with blood?

*

Sorry about the other day, Doctor... -Veronika smiled sheepishly from behind the half-open door of Franco's surgery. *-I was out my face basically, guttered, loaded, wasted. I slept for 2 days afterwards.*

Come in and sit down, Veronika. You missed your last appointment I see. But we're here to talk about your behaviour together, not to make excuses. Just relax and trust me... do you do this a lot?

What, make excuses?

No, I mean sleep for days.

Yes, were you never hungover Doctor Reinwald?

Not for entire days.

It's my beauty sleep, not bad for me surely? Don't doctors always prescribe lots of rest?

Routine is best for all of us. Regular sleep, therefore no bouts of insomnia and nocturnal introspections.

How boring...

Health is boring until you lose it then ill-health is Hell on earth. Always carry a map of the route back to the world with you, that map is Routine.

Route, Routine... that's very neat, Doctor. I'll bet you never explore a foreign city without a map... Do you know what the name Veronika actually means, Doctor Reinwald? Veronika had an irritating habit of changing the subject whenever Franco seemed to making progress with her analysis. *It means "True Image" in Latin. Veronica wiped the face of Jesus on the way to the cross and found the imprint of his face was miraculously left on the cloth afterwards.*

Very impressive, Veronika, he sighed, *-Except that I don't think you'll find that in the gospels if you care to dip into them. It's actually a mistranslation from Etruscan, it really means Bearer Of Victory.*

Really?! -She was suddenly both humbled and jubilant. *But that's even better? Wow, how come you know that?*

It was my Mother's name, so I'd appreciate if you treated it with respect while you borrow it for your time here on earth.

*

Franco awoke with a shout to find that the blackened patch on the ceiling overhead had finally burst open and was showering Claudia and he with thousands of black beetles. His shout woke Claudia, whose hysteria instantly overtook and surpassed his own until they were both running around the room yelping like asylum patients.

Only when their two children appeared at the bedroom door did they stop jumping around, look at each other comically, then resume the process with renewed purpose.

Ten minutes later, with their bedclothes binned and burned, Franco was able to return to the scene and start taking the ceiling down and vacuum it out while Claudia calmed down the children.

Have you killed all the bad beetles, Daddy? -his daughter Lucia asked him when he came to tuck her in at bedtime, -*They're everywhere...* -she whispered, wide-eyed in her perpetual fantasy world, as her brother Vittorrio giggled and ran to hide under the bedclothes. -*Not just here, Daddy, Vittorrio says they're in every house, every street and park, just waiting to take over...*

Back in the study, he found Claudia had set up her beloved microscope again. *Come and see, Franco.* Now that she was calm and back in her professional mode, she could examine the dead specimens with an entomologist's detachment.

It reminds me of a patient of mine, Franco said, as he marvelled at the complexity of the little creature. *She's one of those Goths, you know, dressed in black leather and chains. Some of them are supposed to be into sadomasochism and all that sort of stuff. It's like they're wearing shiny armour, all that metal...*

Inside out, -Claudia muttered.

What was that?

Exoskeletons. They're the opposite of us, you know. Their bones are on the outside, fused into flat plates. That's why they're articulated into sections, cut into bits, hence their Greek name, Entomo, insects, it means cut into segments.

Cutting... Franco mused. *They're into self-harm, some of them you know, I was reading about it on the web...*

What, beetles?

No... he laughed, *beetles probably have more sense. Cutting themselves with knives and bleeding a bit. Maybe it releases endorphins in the brain, an addictive high, but I'd say a jog in the park was easier.*

I understand that Franco, don't be so judgemental. Young people have always been unhappy and self-loathing at times, it's part of coming of age.

Since when? Not in any other species, I'll bet.

Not so, and I should know, speaking as a veterinarian. Parrots pluck their own feathers out when they're unhappy and bored. Chained dogs will pull until their necks bleed, chew their own tails.

Caged and chained, and by us, -Franco sighed, *-you just said it exactly there, without realising what you said.*

There's more of them than us you know, beetles I mean. Seventy percent of all life on Earth is insect, and forty percent of that are beetles. And they have some interesting abilities, like Holometabolism, the ability to change from eggs to maggots then gestate in cocoons before emerging as beetles or butterflies or whatever. In the cocoon, they completely dissolve themselves you know, break down until only a few cells of their original selves remain, then regenerate from those as a new life form.

That's quite something, eh?

But their armour has a critical drawback, Claudia said, lifting the specimen up to her face, impaled on a pin, *-and this is where we have one advantage over them. In order to grow they* have to moult, completely shed their body to reveal a new one underneath. That's a pretty costly exercise in biological terms, wouldn't you say?

*

So why do you think you are depressed, Veronika? –Franco sighed.

Dunno. Isn't everyone?

Let me re-phrase that. Why do you think you attempted suicide?

Because life is bloody dull, Doctor, and hopeless, isn't it?

I don't see it that way. If you are fulfilled, you shouldn't feel like that, Veronika, you should enjoy every day.

Do you?

This isn't about me of course, but yes, I think so, most of the time.

Why? How are you fulfilled?

This isn't…

About you, yes, you said that…

But, my work interests me, especially when I am able to help people, and my children are a joy to watch growing.

Your wife, you haven't mentioned your wife yet.

I was coming to that.

And do you? Do you come to the thought of that? Of her? Your wife, Doctor Reinwald? I don't think so, judging by the way you eye my legs and breasts every chance you get…

I beg your pardon, my sex life is relatively ordinary and normal, I love my wife. And you shouldn't put your anatomy on *display if you don't want it viewed, it's a normal male reaction, the eyes move before the brain can...*

Bollocks.

Sorry?

Bollocks. Your bollocks. I'll bet your bollocks are full of snot every day. I'll bet they're full of snot right now and you'd like to lose it all over me...

Veronika, this isn't constructive. Is this some kind of a defence mechanism? We're trying to cure your depression...

Not empty your sack, I know, I'm sorry. I'll bet you think all I need is to get married and have children and have a nice little day job and I'd be happy, now isn't that so?

Well, what's wrong with any of these things? Biologically speaking, you must see they are what you are evolved to require. Get them, and Nature will reward you with a little happiness.

How quaint. How dictatorial. You make it sound like Nature, whatever that means, is the biggest most tyrannical headmaster, or headmistress, in the whole wide world. The biggest mafia boss with the toughest henchmen, and the only way to survive in this one-horse town is to do right by her and she'll reward you with a line of cocaine. Or endorphin, dopamine, adrenalin, oxytocin or whatever.

Where are you going with this, Veronika?

*Where are you going, Doctor Reinwald? Where is our entire society going? Wake up. Don't you see the score here? It's not just me that's unhappy and dysfunctional, it's all of western capitalism, the **Duff-Hell-Opt** world, shopping and selling and socially climbing, swarming over each other like rats, competing not co-operating, everyone looking for some materialist Shangri-la of consumer happiness, when all the time happiness lies somewhere else entirely...*

Franco was becoming astonished by this diatribe, his mouth fallen involuntarily open, his spectacles ready to fall off his nose.

Where? -she finally asked then answered the question for him. *…In a glass of clear water from a mountain stream, in a white puff of cloud on a summer's day above an uncultivated meadow, in a kiss that doesn't taste of dust.*

She had got up out of her seat now and moved towards him. His hand tensed on the desktop. *Paypackets!* -she exclaimed as if to distract him, -*Our whole lives are about pay packets. Some predetermined scale of inequality and the joy of rubbing other people's faces in how much more than them you earn. Is that a worthy or noble goal for an entire society? Or an undeclared war?*

She had suddenly kissed him before he even knew it was happening, then withdrawn, rubbed his face in it, as it were. A rapid, invasive gesture lasting only a second, then clutching at his groin as she turned away. *There now… You're awake again, alive. I have your attention at last. When does all the merry-go-round stop, Doctor Reinwald? When does the machine stop and the monkey step out?*

Veronika… he shouted as she walked to the door, -*this is just your highs talking, you know you're going to come down again, this is what you need the medication for…*

But she was gone and the door closed after her.

*

When Franco arrived at the door of Veronika's flat, he should have immediately realised something was amiss. Unlike the helpless washout she had seemed on the phone, she was greeting him at the door in a black leather dressing gown which parted like subtle wings to reveal a silver needle that she thrust into his side. He fell to his knees in pain as the door was slammed and locked behind him, and stepping over him in red glossy heels she withdrew the syringe and drawled *that should do you...*

Within minutes it was as if some furious prehistoric animal was thrashing about inside his body. He staggered across the hallway, starting to foam at the mouth, and she intercepted him, dragging him then tripping him up and over onto her bed.

He wanted to resist her, to escape, but found that he had an erection so angry that his whole life essence seemed anchored there, his very blood flooded with a gathering poison that could only be vented from this throbbing centre. The beckoning release for all this pain could only be that soft white triangle of legs and arms that seemed to be forming on the bed in front of him in his blurring vision. For the first time in his life, he experienced copulation not as an act of entry but as a repeated series of attempts to withdraw, but it was these very movements that seemed to delight his voracious host.

He screamed as something moved inside her. Blood emerged as he withdrew and, deranged now, he plunged his hand back inside her and pulled out by its clutching mandibles: a beetle the size of his hand, all black wriggling legs and antennae. She was laughing hysterically as he backed away and the creature fell writhing onto the mattress.

Running to find the back door, stumbling, trying to pull on his clothes as he went, he wiped blood on the walls and moved down the stair and through her disused basement, past a gallery of unborn children, swaying from the ceiling in the half-light like Chinese lanterns, wrapped as silk worms in the pupa of gestation, the shrouds of unfulfilled desire.

The door burst open and released him into her garden. He gulped down air like cold water and brushed past ferns and thorns and cacti, Nature potent and chaotic and harsh, clawing at his brow and hands, drawing more blood.

He fell on his back on her lawn and found the sky above again: clear blue and racing clouds, wavering beyond the clothes line and the geraniums. His vision was clearing slowly, telescope-like, from the centre outwards. The jagged leaves and branches around him whispered and laughed in conspiratorial tones. Had he really ever thought that all of Nature was his benefactor, that he was master over this world? Now he was damned. Now he was young again. Now he was an insect. Now he was inside out.

~

6.

BEAUTIFUL DREAMER

"*Beautiful dreamer, wake unto me, Starlight and dewdrops are waiting for thee; Sounds of the rude world heard in the day, Lull'd by the moonlight have all pass'd away...*"

-Stephen Collins Foster.

Anton gazed out from the ninth floor cardiology ward to where a seagull swung by at a comparable height to the hospital window. It seemed like an image of freedom, a flag of white hope, as if thrown out like a fishing line from the ailing heart of his father behind him, the voluptuous movement of its wings conjured from his laboured breathing.

On the hills he could see the distant lines of enormous wind turbines turning slowly, and beyond them the army of trees encircling the city, like the first Roman legions that must have paused there two thousand years beforehand, poised to attack and conquer.

He turned around and was surprised to see that for the first time his father had sat up in bed and turned himself to try and see the view also, as if following his son's example. Anton rushed back to his bedside and helped him lie back down, knowing what effort even this movement must be costing him, the strain on his wasted arms.

He would remember this moment for many years afterwards and ponder over its symbolism. Did his father wish to pass into the body of his son, to travel with him to horizons as yet unglimpsed, days out of reach beyond his own span of time on earth? Was such a shared journey possible?

*

Anton's father disliked the framed photograph on the wall in front of him in this private room they had moved him into: a picture of an enormous beach on the Isle of Harris, one they had visited together many years ago on holiday, when Anton had just left school. He said he hated it now because of its uncertain sky, a kind of grey burgeoning of cloud that looked on balance more likely to result in rain than sunshine.

Anton's father described how it made him recall a particular afternoon during the war. When sailing towards Naples they had seen a sky like this one and, finding themselves off-course, had been dismayed by the lack of clues the weather allowed them to confirm their position. Spotting land was easy on a sunny day, because cumulus would build up by the hour like shaving foam over any land mass due to warm air convection, announcing its presence to a distant observer, even when it still lay below the horizon.

But this grey bleak day, this endless sky, had gone on forever that afternoon, deceiving them, deluding them, refusing them the slightest clue of redemption or failure to find land, until they were almost upon it.

*

On his second night in hospital, Anton's father told him a strange and garbled story. Only some time later did he wish he had listened a little closer and tried to get to the bottom of it. Then some aspects of it made him shiver.

He had said that four people had come in and stood around his bed and looked at him, but that they had not been doctors. *Were you dreaming? Were they somebody else's visitors?* -Anton had asked him.

No, the lights had been up and they had been as clear as Anton was, apparently. *A big Swedish chap and a woman with a hat and a shawl, and another chap..... one who looked oddly familiar, I had the feeling I had seen him before...* Dad had muttered.

Anton had checked discreetly with the nurses afterwards, and there had been no such visitors.

Later a doubt crept in. His father had not implied there was anything supernatural about the encounter, so was it just the delusion of a confused and ailing man? But he had not been on morphine at that point.

At home, Anton checked the family tree that his cousin had recently researched and found his eyes drawn to previous generations from Gothenberg. He looked out photographs that had mouldered in the family albums for decades: faces familiar but of people that had died long before even his father was born. An absurd thought struck him. Had his father seen some kind of spectral welcoming party, a delegation sent from the ranks of his ancestors?

*

Perhaps in retrospect, Anton's father's fate had been sealed before he even entered hospital. The heart attack at 5am on the Friday morning had done damage to the heart and, through circulation loss, also to the lungs and kidneys, all of which would be hard to repair.

At that exact moment, Anton, seven miles away, had woken from a nightmare in which he saw his father sleeping on top of a wardrobe while his mother watched anxiously from down below, scared he would fall off.

When his mother left a message on his mobile later that day, Anton listened to it with a strange air of *déjà vu.*

That evening, after the doctors gave their opinions, Anton's father had said: *I think I've had it this time, son.* And Anton had replied: *well, you've said that before, Dad. There's no reason why you shouldn't be able to make a recovery...* -but sensed that neither of them probably believed it. He sensed also however, that the pretence of believing it was something they both needed now as a means to get through the coming days with dignity and decorum.

Incredibly, his father wanted Anton to leave and not "waste time" with him when he could be getting on with his own life. *This is boring for you, son,* -he had said.

Nonsense Dad, Anton said, *I'm just designing a building inside my head right now, don't worry about me...*Anton had trained as an architect, something his father had dreamed of doing himself.

A building with no way out? -his father asked and, wrongfooted by this verbal spar, Anton answered and found the last syllable choking him with the emotion of its religious meaning:

My father's house has many mansions...

*

For years, Anton had dreaded the eventuality of his parents becoming old and infirm. He had dreaded his own imaginings of incontinence and derangement, of unmentionable smells and sights. The bad news was that those we love must age and die, the good news was that the love made it easier, not harder. There was nothing disgusting in Anton's father's demise. In these last days he resembled nothing so much as a wizened little owl, perched on his hospital bed, his eyes glittering and sharp and alert, his jowls and beak honed and dignified by age into an exquisite sculpture. He was beautiful. He complained, not of being mistreated, but that his son should not waste time tending to his dying like this, but go out and get on with his normal sunlit life instead, leaving the dead to it.

Sorry about all this inconvenience... he said, and Anton answered: *Don't be silly Dad, you're no inconvenience at all.*

Well, it's a bit inconvenient for me! -He replied grimly, and then they both laughed heartily, before tears formed in Anton's eyes.

Anton pointed out to his father that this was just how he had tended to Anton when he was helpless and incontinent, that is to say: a babe in arms. He thought, then laughed a little at this, but without emotion. Perhaps it had really not occurred to him that Anton was simply re-paying the debt of his existence, ferrying someone out of life who had ferried him into it. There was a symmetry to life that was poetic, not sordid. Had he read *Little Bo Peep* to his father to send him off to sleep each night on the ward, it really wouldn't have been inappropriate.

*

As he left the ward, Anton felt an unexpected and vaguely comical need to salute his father, and to his surprise the old man's face immediately broke into a glittering smile as he returned the military gesture.

So long, Admiral... He would always remember his father for this moment and this gesture. They were soldiers of life, parting of necessity to take up their respective duties with resolution, resignation and dignity: one to go on living, and the other to die.

*

Walking away from the hospital in the afternoon, returning to his office, it occurred to Anton for the first time how little everyone really knows about their parents. More to the point, how little they *want* to know, in a queasy sort of way. His father's own parents had died before Anton was even born.

Although he had heard plenty of anecdotes about them, they were all his father's versions of them, filtered by God knows what kind of unconscious prejudices and censorships, and imperfect knowledge eroded over time by re-telling. The truly reliable and indisputable facts of anybody's life were pitifully negligible if you stopped to think about it. Who had his father really been? As children, we want our parents to be Gods, immoveable, immutable, eternal. But to ever truly get to know them, we would each have to re-imagine them as people: and therefore imperfect, lustful, dangerous, unpredictable, flawed, foolish. Who dares, what son or daughter on Earth, really wants to entirely bridge that gap?

*

The next afternoon, the doctor told him he thought his father was "on the way out", and looking at his sleeping form, his head thrown back, Anton had already judged for himself that he would not be waking.

What was the thought, the memory or revelation that finally drove Anton to break down in tears in the office toilet that evening once all his colleagues had gone home? A lightning bolt broke through his weeks of numb denial of emotion, and removed the impasse to his pent-up grief.

It was a dim memory of a summer's morning, lying in bed and hearing his father singing in the kitchen downstairs in his beautiful baritone voice: *Beautiful Dreamer… Awake unto me…*

It was a moment of sunlit happiness, of a young father who loved Anton's mother, before all the uncertainty and disturbance had set in like rot. Anton wanted that young man back. He wanted all the previous versions of his father that the final withered dying father had obscured in his mind. It occurred to him that we are each such a continuum, a string of subsequent and previous selves on a precarious journey out of beauty towards decay, out of folly into bitter wisdom, out of love towards love, through all the shades of light and darkness in between.

Beautiful Dreamer... It was a memory of when Anton's father had loved his wife, Anton's mother. Or had he?

*

By the evening, Anton's sister Petra and her husband and three children were all gathered around their father's hospital bed as he slept noisily. Head thrown back and breathing laboured, his throat gurgled slightly with the fluid in his lungs. The drip feed attempting to re-hydrate his kidneys was, as predicted, putting strain on his heart and as a consequence everyone now knew he probably had only hours or days left, during which time he was unlikely to wake again.

The children were crying at the sight of their grandfather but incredibly, Anton was trying to make them laugh philosophically about it, as his father had done, before losing consciousness. *Why do we keep crying about death as if one of these times it won't happen? Isn't it a necessary part of life without which the old couldn't make way for young whippersnappers like you?*

He felt his father's fingers twitch in his grip, in approval he felt sure, rather than protest. The crying was stopping. Anton had almost been unable to face coming to the hospital again tonight, after his breaking down with emotion. But he had forced himself on leaden feet to take the now habitual route from his office across the park, under the University spire and into the hospital grounds. It had been hard to keep going until he saw the children and took the hand of his sleeping father. Then a mysterious strength, even an unexpected joy or exaltation had passed into him as he spoke to comfort them.

Now he crossed to the window and looked out again at the horizon and the encircling forest, the distant windfarms, the road junction down below where passing pedestrians flickered to and fro as the ambulances and taxis filtered across them. *You know, twice a day I've been coming here for the last two weeks and each time I've got up and looked out this window at various times of day, there's always been people down there crossing that road. Young people, old people, students, businessmen, pensioners, but always people, late at night, early in the morning, people, and you know what occurs to me?*

The tearful eyes all turned towards him. -*That maybe the only real truth of the matter is that people are flowing across that street like blood. They all think, and we all think, that they are individuals, and for all we know maybe molecules of blood think the same. But maybe they're only blood, a collective entity. And no matter when you choose to look at that junction you'll see in effect the same thing: not a person, but people, blood, flowing.*

Anton felt his father's hand twitch when he took it again. Could he hear their words? Comprehend their discussion? Or was it all mixed up with some morphine-induced dream he was now having? Maybe it was hard to answer that question with your head, but it was easy with the heart.

*

The next morning Anton woke early, with a feeling of terrible tiredness and sadness, and something entirely new: a dull pain in his left-to-middle chest, below his heart. On his way to work, all these feelings were intensifying by the minute, on the walk to the station, sitting on the railway carriage into the city, as his eyes scraped at the morning light breaking the overcast sky, no longer asking for hope. He felt as if all his energy were being invisibly drained from a remote location, and of course he knew where.

Every night before Anton had left the ward, he had held his father's wrist for a moment, half in jest, telling him he was giving him an injection of energy to see him through until morning. They had laughed about it, but had Anton and he actually formed some kind of temporary link? He felt as if his father was pushing into his outline, as if Anton had been keeping him alive and now both their bodies, invisibly joined, were dipping down, swooping like seagulls over a lonely ocean into which they knew only one of them would fall.

Walking through the pedestrian precinct at the exact instant of his father's death, Anton found himself glancing sideways, his eyes alighting on a shop window display on the other side of the street. Then something extraordinary happened.

The grey sadness and tiredness that had been building inside him suddenly broke through for a second and took over his vision, soaked right through it like flames consuming an ancient strip of film. He saw something, fleetingly, subliminally, and only a week later when he passed the same way would he fully realise and come to terms with what he had seen.

The fashions of all the clothes were late 1940's, the colours drab, the windows grimey with all the smoke of a post-war city. He was looking back in time to when his father had been the same age. But more than this, the slightly exposed curves of the manikins, one of them half-dressed: were momentarily shorn of all sexual charge. Anton was seeing the world, for just a moment, as the dead must see it, coldly, supremely truthfully, stripped of all the prejudices of the flesh.

Then the dull pain beneath his heart suddenly disappeared.

Five minutes later and a block further on, the ward nurse phoned to say his father had just died. *I know,* he replied.

He caught a taxi to the hospital and was led into the now-darkened room. He looked at his body, saw that it was peaceful, and went to part the curtains and gaze out again at the ever-present view. The horizon, the distant windmills, the perpetual flow of people at the traffic junction below, only slightly lessened at this early hour. At the exact moment he chose to look, there was a woman with a child in a pram crossing the road and Anton smiled and laughed to himself as if Fate or his father could communicate through the language of events. *Yes, I get the message,* he whispered in the darkened room. ...*Life goes on.*

He turned around and leant over the bed and kissed his father on the forehead, kissing him goodnight as he had been unable to do while he was living, scared even then that such words or gestures would seem like a betrayal, an execution. They had both been content to persist with the tacit fantasy of his recovery and survival.

I love you, Dad. -he said, using only the present tense, feeling his presence within him and in the air around him. No tears came, no vast outpouring of emotion. He was just glad his father was at peace now, and felt he knew with physical certainty that death was not the bleak negation that devotees of Science believed in, but a redistribution, an assimilation, a release. He had never seen or touched a dead body before, but now it was not so bad. Still warm, the only difference was the peace, the absence of suffering. Only a vessel was being dispensed with, and a hopelessly broken one at that. He couldn't cry because he couldn't see the loss. That would come later.

*

Anton immediately recognised his mother's shuffling footsteps as she turned the corridor corner to enter the ward. They embraced and he diverted her into a waiting room, while the nurses "prepared" the body. *It's ok mum, he's at peace now, he didn't suffer.* She was tearful but he could see she was in shock, and nothing was seeming real to her. After a while Anton realised she had walked from the car park on her own and he felt appalled. *Where on earth is Claude, why didn't he come in with you?*

Well, he and your father didn't always have the best of relationships as you know...

I never understood why, Mum, and he never even came to visit him... now how is he going to cope, when it's too late for a reconciliation?

Death in the modern world is a surreal and shocking event, not because of its rarity but perhaps the opposite: the way everyday life rages on all around afterwards as if nothing has happened. While his mother went into the darkened room to bid her husband farewell, Anton found himself asking the nurses what to do with his father's body next as if he had been landed with an awkward logistical problem like a minor traffic collision with a damaged car requiring recovery.

*

As Petra drove them out to the suburbs afterwards, the sun was flooding down and the first Spring flowers opening, birds flickering between hedgerows excitedly. The normality of the world was momentarily absurd. They crossed a few hills and the beautiful suburban village of their childhood appeared before them again: all dipping fields and winding roads.

Their mother talked wistful platitudes of how their father could only have made it home with a dripfeed and catheter, a district nurse, a night watcher, maybe even a kidney dialysis machine. He had been suffering and could only have suffered more, but now it was over.

Her voice coasted up and down as the car traversed the hills and Anton wondered at the reserves of mysterious strength she held, and grasped the hope that they could all feel grateful for their father's long life rather than sorry for themselves or each other.

When the car turned into the drive, he remembered the reason why this hope might yet be dashed. Their elder brother Claude stood on the threshold of the back door of their mother's house looking like the only worse news they could hear that day, a fountain of resentment and black depression.

His clouded face and knotted brow were like the unexpected thunder and lightning that would surprise everyone on the afternoon of the funeral.

*

Only hours after Anton's father's death, while his mother and Petra were away at the undertakers, Claude broke down in tears and spoke of how their father had been a philanderer. How he had planned to leave them when Claude was only thirteen, Petra ten, and Anton seven; how he had sounded Claude out to judge whether the children would forgive him or be able to cope with such a trauma.

Anton was more sceptical than stunned over this revelation. How could Claude have kept it secret all these years? Was this just the twist in his own grief talking? His bitterness over the lack of love his father had shown him in deference to Anton, the unreconciled friction between their two egotistical characters, domineering father and wayward eldest son? He scarcely believed a word of it. Indeed it was laughable, but nonetheless he begged Claude never to breathe a word of it to their mother. If there was even the slightest grain of truth in it then who was to say what their mother might think, without her husband there to defend himself and his own memory?

A lifelong bachelor, Anton suspected that Claude didn't have the psychological insight to know a womaniser when he saw one. Anton didn't think his father fitted the type, there was too much honesty and open-heartedness there. Like Anton and Claude themselves, their father had been more the type to imagine a dalliance with another woman, to have committed a kind of adultery of the heart and mind and blamed himself for that, than to have actually carried the deed through in the real world. Surely it would have jarred with the devout Christian principles of his own Victorian mother.

*

The day of the funeral it was another bright Spring morning as birds sang outside, and Anton, Claude and Petra lined up to thank all the mourners as they filed out of the chapel. They were surprised when one young man none of them recognised seemed to skip and dash past them rapidly, as if reluctant to talk.

Driving away to follow the coffin, Anton caught sight of the young man a block away and wound the window down to talk to him. He seemed alarmed to find himself cornered and almost backed away like a fugitive before Anton tried to disarm him with a casual remark: *Would you like a lift up to the cemetery, we have a spare seat in the back?*

Oh no thanks, he blushed, his eyes flashing from sky to pavement, looking around for an excuse, *-I have to meet someone shortly...*

On a curious and sudden hunch, Anton gave him his card and asked him to call him later before he left town so he could buy him a drink and talk. The other passengers in the car immediately assumed the two of them knew each other, and the stranger looked up and nodded and grunted non-committally before slouching off towards the village centre as Anton drove on.

*

The priest had spoken of Anton's father's life, how he had studied at the University after the war. And now as they turned away from the graveside, Anton and his mother and brother and sister looked down onto the distant city whose wide sunny panorama seemed dominated from this location by the soaring University spire.

This was the same building Anton had walked under every evening as he went from his office to the hospital ward to visit his father.

Only a few hours later, when they were all returned to their mother's house drinking tea, Petra's face was suddenly crossed by fear, and the conversation died as they all sauntered to the patio doors to look out: the sky was darkening rapidly and violent thunderclaps shook the sky. In the city centre, passers-by were amazed as the University spire was struck by a fork of lightning. The event was caught on amateur camera and broadcast on the evening news. The heavens opened and rain and hail blasted down like knives. Nearby, another lightning fork came down and struck a woman in her car in a traffic jam, making more headlines on the newsstands the following day.

These were all exceptional events, August weather in April, like the freakish culmination to an air of unreality that had been permeating Anton's mood for weeks since his father's illness began.

*

Just before Anton had finished packing up and was about to say goodbye to his tearful mother and leave town again, his mobile phone rang unexpectedly and the nervous voice of the mysterious young man from earlier in the day came on the line, speaking almost reluctantly, monotone, unsure of its own motivation.

Darkness was falling and the rain still plummeting when Anton entered the unprepossessing local tavern and found the young man waiting at the bar, still dressed in his black suit and tie. His name was David, he said, he was Anton's half-brother, *a love child* (the term made him wince) his father had conceived by an old flame. David brought out a photograph of a beautiful woman, his beloved mother, who had died some ten years previously. Next to it in his wallet, was a photograph of Anton's father, *their* father, as a dapper young man in post-war hat and coat, bearing a cheeky resemblance to a youthful Frank Sinatra.

They drank some strong spirits and exchanged melancholy stories of parallel lives, of shared absences, of the haunting imprint of a father who neither ever really understood or saw enough of. Anton's head began spinning, he saw the years telescope out beneath his feet, as if the foundation stones of his life were laid over a trapdoor. *But what about you?* -Anton finally asked, *Do you have a wife of your own now, any children?*

David snorted and smiled, laughing sadly and mumbled cryptically: *I'm still very young... And I have you now.*

Moved and confused, filled with a wave of unreality, Anton followed David out into the car park at closing time. Ahead in the darkness, the rain on his shoulder and back seemed to be almost deconstructing him as he walked, his hair and skin grown translucent with moisture, his footsteps suddenly softer than falling leaves.

How shall we stay in touch then? -Anton called after him, -*Should I ever tell my mother or Claude? What if you're mentioned in his Will?*

What good would any of that do? -David spun round, smiling, light-hearted, almost cavalier. -*And who would ever believe you? ...Why do you believe me?*

You... You... bear such a resemblance to him... as a young man! -Anton stammered, tears in his eyes at last, arm outstretched in a gesture of embrace.

But his hand passed straight through him.

~

*"I think we are in rats' alley where the dead men lost their bones.
'What is that noise?' The wind under the door."*

-T.S.Eliot, *The Waste Land.*

Vittorrio and Lucia cowered beneath the blankets as the night wind raged outside, the noise merging threateningly with the raised voices of their parents arguing in the next room.

The wind seemed to be harrying fences, billowing trees, bending creaking branches to breaking point. In Vittorrio's mind, the wind and the night were like one entity now, fused as waves of some nocturnal ocean that was sweeping and engulfing the whole city, testing everything in its path.

The argument in the next room made no more sense to him than the angry sounds outside, blind rage, pleading indignation, sighing despair. What would be left standing in the morning? Who would make sense of the debris, pick out what fragments were salvageable and make repairs?

With one eye open beneath the covers, Vittorrio caught sight of his posters in the moonlight on the opposite wall: Aztec and Inca cities, *Pompeii, Angkor Wat...* obviously sometimes things were not always well again in the morning. Logically such a time had to come for some people, when on an arbitrary whim their lives were just totally wrecked by the untrammelled forces of nature. Then they just packed up and walked away from it all to become nomadic hunter gatherers again. History was littered with the ruins they had left behind each time it happened, all those archaeological digs. Was it lack of resources or lack of heart that turned them away in the end, unable to face the rebuilding? Vittorrio decided to ask his father some of these questions in the morning, if the house was still standing.

*

And I don't want that witch anywhere inside this house while I'm away... -Claudia sighed bitterly, shaking her head from side to side as she spoke, her hands in her hair, eyes downcast to the floor.

Franco stood at the window with his back turned, staring out into the raging night as if it was some inscrutable puzzle he could unlock with a skilful glance.

I understand, he mumbled gruffly.

But do you? -Claudia came back, head forward like a bird of prey. *I don't want her anywhere near the children, **Our** children, you understand?*

Of course, he said, sighing, and returning to sit down facing her, taking his glasses off.

You silly old fool... she muttered harshly as she looked again at his vulnerability, the half-blind eyes, his baby-soft cheeks.

I'm the same age as you... he replied rather lamely.

Yes, Franco, old in today's youth-obsessed culture, passed it. Don't you see that this silly little tart is just playing with you? Wrecking your life, our marriage, for a laugh?

He started to shake his head then put his glasses back on and nodded: *I admit the possibility*...

And you'll expect me to take you back after all that? After you're the laughing stock of the whole town?

I expect nothing, he replied grimly, *not from you, nor from the creator of the universe. This is just what it is, the situation, I make no excuses.*

You realise I will leave you when I return if you haven't sorted yourself out... if you haven't got her out of your life?

He nodded his head silently.

We're not going to be one of those weird couples with an OPEN RELATIONSHIP Franco, you might want to live like a freak but I certainly won't.

I'm not turning into a freak or a hippie, Claudia, let's not be childish. This is a calamity, something that has hit me, hit this marriage out of the blue, and now I am trying to understand it, to come to terms with it, find a solution and find how to move forward.

Ah-huh... and will this search for a solution involve you fucking her again, do you think?

Claudia... Franco sighed in despair, *I hate hearing you use language like that, it's horrible, it's not like you*...

*Oh really? And what **is** like me? What the hell do you really know about me after all these years? What is the correct language for a situation like this? Swahili? Esperanto? I'll bet she uses a lot more colourful language than me. So answer the question, will you be fucking her, Franco?*

*

The older you get, the less coincidences surprise you. Three days before her pre-arranged holiday with Vivienne, Claudia ran into Anton in the street. Or rather, Lucia spotted him among the crowds on Market Street and trotted over to him and said: *Hello, you saved my brother, you brought him back. Are you an angel? Please come and see my mother, please save her next... please come.*

Claudia was hiding her sleepless eyes behind her dark glasses when she realised she had momentarily lost sight of Lucia. She looked around startled and then like the answer to an unasked question: Lucia emerged from the crowd leading Anton by the hand. She recognised his face, failed to remember for a moment who exactly he was, unlike her daughter.

Mrs Reinwald... -Anton began and reached out his hand, squinting to see past her glasses and verify her identity. She put her hand up to her hair self-consciously as she took her glasses off, concerned it would be obvious that she had been crying recently.

It's Anton, he explained, to save her embarrassment, *Anton Perlato, I found your son when he went missing,* -and he smiled, turning to look at Vittorrio who was holding her other hand.

For a moment she was overwhelmed by the strangeness of the scene, like they were a surrogate family together, as if her whole life had taken an instant and oblique shift sideways.

Anton seemed to read this, and carefully returned Lucia to her other hand, all the time watching her eyes, as if he were carefully adjusting the balance in an artistic composition, a still-life with flowers.

How are you? -she asked, then realised the hollowness of the question. In the stress and relief of her reunion with her son a year beforehand, she had failed to ask or learn anything memorable about this man, although in retrospect she felt she should have.

I'm fine, Anton said, then frowned at the thought that he had answered one meaningless platitude with another one. The market crowds flowed by either side of them as if they were ponderous boulders in a river in spate. The effort required to either terminate or perpetuate the conversation suddenly seemed beyond either of them. They floated and then drowned in this uncertainty.

Then Lucia pulled on Claudia's hand and resolved it with a single word: *ice cream.*

*

Over their Latte and Machiatto, Anton unwound and gave an authentic answer to Claudia's earlier question: *Well, I've been O.K, very much back on the straight and narrow since my difficulties, thanks to your husband, and how is he by the way?*

Claudia tilted her head and lifted a single hand in a gesture of open verdict: they would come to that later.

But then my father died...

Oh, I'm sorry, Claudia said, reaching her hand out a little across the table, and she saw from the moisture in his eyes that the matter was still raw.

It's ok, really, Mrs Reinwald. He was 76, a decent enough age for a man who had survived several heart attacks and a by-pass operation. It's just one of those things we all have to go through... one day.

Claudia's eyes flicked involuntarily to the children, and Vittorrio slurping his strawberry slush-puppy through a multi-coloured straw asked: *Will Daddy die one day, Mummy?*

Oh goodness Vittorrio, not until we're all old, you'll be all grown up by then with a wife and children of your own.

Do you have a wife, Anton? -Lucia asked, wide-eyed and Claudia chastised her: *Sweetheart, that's a rude thing to ask.*

Anton suddenly laughed with a light-heartedness that seemed to cheer up everyone around the table. *No, princess. I haven't found the right girl yet, but I will one day, don't worry. It's fun waiting to see who it will be...* He turned around and led her eyes with his hands to consider every face in the crowds streaming past their table. *Look... any one of those girls and ladies strolling by could be Anton's wife one day, isn't that exciting? Look, that one! This one!* The children laughed and became inspired by this game until Claudia had to calm them down.

What about you? Anton asked, *and Franco...?* he said, finding it strange to be using the doctor's first name now.

He could see affection and happiness in her eyes towards him now, but it shifted and receded at her discomfort as the spotlight turned onto herself.

Things have been hard, she began, *we've been working too long hours. Franco...* she began again, then looked meaningfully at the children as if to signal that she couldn't really take the conversation in the direction she wanted it to go. *Well, he could do with more time off. He could do with a friend, like you for instance. He sorts out other people's problems, but I wish he, we, had more time to sort out our own.*

And you? Anton asked, stirring his coffee and fixing her eyes intently.

She raised her eyebrows, as if unclear of the question.

Do you have friends, holidays you can take?

Oh yes, and she snapped out of her reverie as if relieved to have an apparently simple question she could answer. *My friend Vivienne and I... we're taking a walking holiday next week.*

Where? Anton asked.

Into the forest, Claudia replied, *all of it, some of it, an expedition with rucksacks and thermos flasks and tents, just like when we were kids.*

What Anton said next both alarmed and reassured her: *are you going to try to find Leo?*

She had forgotten that Anton had known anything about her brother, and felt suddenly uncomfortable that this deeper motive could be laid bare by a virtual stranger.

Anton saw her disquiet and moved to reassure her. *Your husband told me about him. How he wanders in the forest and writes letters. I'm sorry, I didn't mean to intrude.* He glanced at the children. *It's just...* and he searched Claudia's eyes to see if she had been irrevocably insulted. *Well, this is another of those strange coincidences that keep building up these days.*

Go on... Claudia said, rubbing Lucia's hair with her hands.

Well, you know I was an architect...

No actually, I don't remember if I knew that, or if Franco mentioned it.

Well, I say was, because I resigned my job the day after my father's funeral.

But why? -Claudia asked.

I suddenly realised what was important in life. In order to do that, maybe you've got to see death at close quarters, ponder what a man's whole life amounts to in the end, before you can look at your own with clear vision and think how to shape it and change it. Life shouldn't be about sweating and slaving in front of a computer all day. It's about fresh air and sunlight and exercise, that's what we've evolved to enjoy, not eating dust and synthetic hamburgers. So I packed it in and applied for a job with the Forestry Council.

Forestry? Claudia asked, surprised.

Yes, I've been getting trained up for the last three months. It's meant a cut in pay but I get free food and lodgings half the time when I'm out on placement. And I'm full of fresh air, up to the brim with all the sunlight I can handle! I'm a forester now.

But that's... wild. I mean well done, congratulations, if that's what you really want to do. You're really sure you'll be happy, are there career prospects, I mean promotions over the years?

Anton laughed out loud again, and now the children were giggling with him before they even understood the joke. *You're not getting it are you? -with all due respect.*

Claudia stared blankly.

Once you breathe the fresh air and spend a few days in the woods and sleep like a log, ha ha ha... the children giggled again like little puppets, *then you realise that money, promotion, careers, overtime, overwork, unhappiness... these are just things you are doing to yourself. Torments, self-imposed. Life isn't about these things. You only really need food and shelter and some honest, preferably physical work, Everything else is...*

Vanity? Claudia suggested, *Extraneous? Unnecessary? Counter-productive?*

Anton still seemed lost for the right word and turned to Lucia who said simply: *Ka-ka.*

Everyone laughed apart from Lucia, as Claudia prepared to take her to the toilet. *Now you stay here with Anton and be good, won't you Vittorrio?*

Uncle Anton. Can we call him Uncle Anton?

Anton laughed again. Claudia paused to ask: *but what was the coincidence, Anton, about you becoming a forester?*

Because I can guide you now, of course. I have access to the right maps and kit and survival training. I can guide you though the forest, I can help you to try and find Leo.

Will you really be able to find Uncle Leo? -Vittorrio asked, once his mother and sister had left the table.
Well Vittorrio, I found you didn't I? Anton answered, smiling sweetly.

*

The night before setting off on their expedition, Vivienne had a dream in which she and Claudia were in a forest made of spider's webs. But with the peculiar half-logic of dreams, she was immediately given to understand that all the webs leading off in every direction were somehow the physical legacy of every conversation she had ever had: every one leading out to each person she knew, each of whom was a dim tree trunk wrapped in silk, hidden in the murky distance of sylvan twilight.

As she spoke, she saw that her words were making more spider silk, issuing from her mouth. She flinched and twitched in her growing cocoon, and saw that she was becoming increasingly entwined and encased. Then she realised that her web was connected by a thread to some central monitor, and that up above her, a large and many-eyed spider was shuffling along at treetop level. The dream ended as she caught sight through the branches of the creature's black furry legs and several bulbous eyes that were rotating towards her. She noticed that the creature wore a Roman Breastplate and clutched a bundle of spears.

*

The doorbell rang and Vivienne answered it sleepily to discover to her surprise that Claudia had brought company. Then she remembered what Claudia had said about having found a forest guide to bring along.

Sorry, slept in, running late again, she said, and fled from the door in mock shame for a moment before halting and returning to shake Anton's hand and introduce herself in uncharacteristically timid style, long dishevelled blonde hair covering her face like jungle creepers.

Had she not been so stunningly beautiful, Anton thought to himself, he might have concluded she was an eccentric social misfit or worse.

When she returned to the living room ten minutes later, fully dressed and packed, he revised his opinion. She seemed in fact, terrifyingly perfect in every sense.

Why are you doing this for us, Anton? What's in it for you? Hoping to get gang-raped in the woods by two dirty old women?

Viv! Claudia exclaimed, but Anton was laughing again in that disarming way of his, as if all of life were a comedy film he could bring to a halt in a second with a quick signal to the director.

Strangely enough, Claudia never really asked me that question, but the reason is probably that Leo intrigues me from what I've heard of him. Maybe I'd like to meet him, or to read some of his letters if you would be so good as to share them with me. Also... Claudia's husband treated me, cured me we should say, after I had some kind of breakdown last year, when I was working too hard. Maybe I'd like to help her and him both now ...

And Vittorrio, -Claudia added, *Anton, how can you forget to mention that? Remember Viv, I told you someone had led the police to where Vittorrio was? That was Anton.*

Mmm... Vivienne eyed him suspiciously, -*you're very open about having had psychiatric help.... as indeed I suppose you should be, although this isn't America yet, but there shouldn't be any stigma, should there? In fact, that's commendable, Anton, you seem pretty well adjusted now...*

Well, I realised what actually matters in life recently, and once you get that revelation it's hard to just forget it.

Anton's father died recently... Claudia explained.

In a gesture that amazed everyone, the normally somewhat aloof Vivienne put her hand out and stroked the side of Anton's cheek as if he were a pet dog and whispered: *you poor baby...*

A strange atmosphere filled the room as the two of them held each others gaze for a moment.

Claudia spoke into the silence at last, out of embarrassment, but the spell wasn't broken yet. Vivienne was stepping backwards as if frightened, unnerved by the inappropriate gesture she had just made. But Anton, unperturbed and still holding her gaze calmly, curiously said: *do you believe in fate, Claudia?*

Well, it believes in us I would say, Claudia smiled at the door.

Then I should tell you about the dream I had, about Leo in the forest. But it will keep for the journey. Now we should really get on the road I think, we have a long way to travel before nightfall.

*

Driving north through the poorer districts, Vivienne said to Claudia: *you know what Leo would say, don't you? How strange it is that everyone keeps carrying on as if nothing is happening, as if their world isn't going to end....*

Is that what he writes in his letters? Anton asked.

I thought Claudia had let you read them?

Well, the latest one.

So he could try to pinpoint his whereabouts, -Claudia interjected, *from the post mark.*

Fat chance, we've tried that ruse in years gone by. He's on the move all the time, particularly when he thinks anyone is looking for him.

How will the world end then? Anton asked, oddly fascinated. *What does he mean?*

He says Nature is preparing a cataclysm for us, didn't you know? An extinction level event after which the insects or the Rhododendrons are going to take over. He says the human spirit is already ebbing away like... what does he call it, Claudia?

Drawback, I think.

That's it, you know, like when the tide goes out just before a tsunami comes in.

Stopped at the lights, Anton tried not to stare too openly at the drunks and drug addicts falling about on the pitiful little park with vandalised benches that constituted the only social centre to this neighbourhood.

As if guessing his thoughts, Claudia said: *he wasn't, isn't, a snob my brother, Anton. He meant our lot just as much, maybe more. The rich middle-classes, decadent and bored, wife-swapping, bed hopping, depressed, suicidal, rotting from the inside out.*

So is this mysterious event, the ending of our world, a natural disaster or a man-made one? Does Nature do it to us or do we bring it on ourselves?

There was a long silence as they drove and then Vivienne said **both** quietly, in introspective mood again, *that's his whole point I think, because of Gaia, once you get what he means by that, you realise both can be true at the same time.*

But can't we do anything to stop it? Anton asked, *Presumably Leo wants us to try to stop it?*

Ahh... time and causality, that old chestnut. I'm afraid there's a problem with that too, Anton, according to Leo that is. Correct me if I'm wrong Vivienne, but basically Gaia exists outside of time, which means it has access to the future.

And therefore, Vivienne said into his other ear, taking over: *this catastrophic event in the future whatever it is, has already happened. All we can do is go on driving towards it, like we're on rails.*

To Hell with that, Anton said, and as if to crystallise the metaphor took an unexpected left turn in search of a short cut to the outskirts.

*

I think you might be labouring under a false assumption, Vivienne said later, eyeing Anton sceptically, before helping him load some of the equipment out of the jeep.

Yeah? -he looked up, running his hands through his hair, a slightly vain gesture which irritated Vivienne.

You're assuming the catastrophic event is a bad thing...

Boy, you are two serious ladies... Anton stood up and laughed. *I thought you said you'd known each other since you were little girls. Did you talk about stuff like this when your pals were playing with Barbie?*

Vivienne made Barbie and Ken play together... Claudia laughed, and Vivienne tutted at an old story being trailed out again, -*and made Ken anatomically correct, shall we say, using a bit of black pipe cleaner. She was.... quite advanced for her years I think you could say.*

Yeah, and Claudia was amazed when her first boyfriend turned out to have something pink rather than furry and black between his legs.

They fell over laughing, while Anton looked at them both incredulously with his eyebrows raised. *Seriously again....* He said, *seriously now... presumably the end of the world is by definition a bad thing isn't it?*

Only if you're human, Vivienne said, smiling, but growing quiet again.

But we're all there is aren't we? Are chipmunks going to rule the earth, or woodlice?

Nobody rules the earth, Anton, the earth rules us. Maybe we're just a project, like the dinosaurs were. They died out, but life didn't... Claudia said.

Anyway, they didn't all die out. Crocodiles and coelacanths and ferns and horsetail weeds and gingko trees: some things made it through... -Vivienne corrected.

The gingko trees survived at the centre of Hiroshima you know, Claudia added, *the only living thing that did. You can't blind a thing that's blind already.*

I read once, Anton said, lifting his rucksack, *that when the British set off the H-bombs on Christmas Island, thousands of birds were blinded instantly, left screaming and blind, wondering where they were and what had happened until they slammed into rock or trees.*

A crime against Gaia of the highest order, Leo would say... -Vivienne sighed. *Maybe even enough to merit the penalty of extinction.*

Hey, you're pretty serious yourself, Anton, what's all this metal gear you've got in the back pack?

Global Positioning System, laptop, satellite uplink, distress flares, infra-red camera.

No shit. You're for real aren't you? Why are we going to carry all that stuff?

Anton stopped and put his pack down. *The views, the fresh air and the wildlife will be stunning I promise you, but once we get into the heart of the forest we will be surrounded by dense woodland for up to seventy five miles in every direction, several days walk to get out of. The forest is vast, Vivienne. If we make a mistake, we die. If we travel carefully and patiently with the right equipment then if we still make a mistake we can at least get helicoptered out.*

Wow, boy scout. You sure talk a good adventure for a reformed pen-pusher. Lead the way, Rambo.

*

Franco placed his hands on his desk to stop them shaking as he waited for his next patient to enter the room. Why had he allowed her to take this last minute appointment when it would have been so easy to invent some excuse and have her quietly removed from his client list and passed on to a colleague?

But here she was, and to his amazement she was wearing a suit, and apart from the red lipstick and a nose-stud all of her gothic trappings were temporarily gone.

Surprised, Doctor Reinwald? -She hovered at the door and he had to flicker his hand in irritation to signal to her to close the door over. Embarrassment: perhaps this was his biggest fear, and the accusation of professional misconduct, and of course his marriage.

She looked good in the suit, and her hair was now long and straight and no longer dyed: revealed as the lovely flaming red she must have been born with.

She sat down in front of him and smiled, searching his eyes for emotion, like reading a magazine. He looked back with all the blankness and bewilderment of a newborn child, and with some difficulty: returned her stare.

Job interview? -he asked finally, realising this was not the sort of opening question he would usually start a session with.

Yeah... Veronika sighed, and crossed her legs and took out some cigarettes and matches.

*There's no smoking here...*Franco said, but numbly and without conviction, like a talking computer, then again: *...this is a non smoking surgery.*

She lit up and leaned back in her seat, eyeing the paintings on the walls, sizing up the place like she might be planning to move in on Monday. *Would you like me to suck your cock?* -she finally asked quietly, absent-mindedly, getting bored.

Veronika... did we, did you... use protection... when I was at your house, when I...

When you...? When you what? Oh go on and say it, Doc, when you ejaculated inside my vagina.

He winced, involuntarily.

Oh you were good by the way, vigorous, violent, and let me see, what's the opposite of premature?

That would be the drugs you shot into me, I would imagine, Franco replied, *I suppose there's no point me asking you for the names and molecular compositions of those. Are we playing a word-association game?* **Laborious?**

Oh... tut, tut, tut... you're too hard on yourself, tiger. **Involved** *was the word I was thinking of, long and involved. There, that's much better.*

We're not though are we?

Involved? Well, let me see. It's been several weeks so I guess by definition that's a no, but then again this casual sex thing is a dangerous game you know: messing with primordial forces. I get the psychic smell of you all over me and visa versa, and then hey presto we wake up thinking about each other, all that sort of shit. That's how it usually goes, isn't it?

What was the job interview for?

Is..., Doctor, I'm going there next, and guess...go on...
-she smiled, holding her cigarette up over her head.

Sex therapist.

Very good, Doctor, a sense of humour, self-deprecating even. No. An administrative assistant in a lawyers office. You ready for that blow-job yet?

I hope you don't blow the job, Veronika.

Two jokes in one day, lover. You been popping your own prescriptions?

I hope you get the job and move on. You need to move on. What happened was... I'm sorry, a sordid incident, for which I take some responsibility, despite what was basically an assault on me, I should have known better than to visit you at home. I don't do house calls.

Veronika stood up and wandered around the room then went and lay down on the sofa.

What happened was an aberration... -Franco continued, *and it mustn't happen again. You're clearly more or less cured, unless you're going to tell me otherwise, and we don't need to continue your treatment... Veronika?*

Yes, Doctor? -she drawled sleepily.

What are you doing?

I'm masturbating of course, Doctor. Clitoral stimulation you'd call it, although I doubt if you've ever discussed it much. As the old joke goes, I've decided to start without you...

Jesus Christ... -Franco opened his desk drawer and fumbled frantically for the old key to the door, the one he hadn't had call to use in years. He bounded across the room and managed with some delicacy to lock the door without making enough noise to arouse the suspicions of Rosemary, his middle-aged secretary whose radio was on quietly, tuned to classic FM.

Veronika, please stop this, he said, standing over her, ... *get your hands out of there.*

What? -she said. *What's the big deal, never see a madwoman jerking herself off on your weekend tour of the asylums?* Her left hand clutched his wrist, and this arm of his in turn was clutching her right wrist, trying to slow her movements. *Crazy woman masturbates in psychiatrist's office... not even a great headline I would say...pretty run of the mill really... you must see shit like this every week you poor devil, no?*

Please stop... -he begged. But she pushed his hand lower and he found himself soothing her, curing her, her eyelids fluttering. *Hippocratic Oath...* she muttered, *...you have to alleviate my suffering...*

Running out of breath, she looked more beautiful by the minute, her cheeks slowly taking on the innocent red of ripe apples until the little panicked sounds from her mouth made him lean over and kiss her, still imploring her to stop, swallowing her breaths.

*

The first night in the forest, Anton had a curious dream about Vivienne.

Perhaps it was his instinctive fear of sleeping in the open, but the setting for his dream was an exact mental replica of the clearing where they had gone to sleep, right down to the pine needles and cones, the rolling hillock beneath the deep shade of the trees, the bark on the thick trunks as fissured as the faces of blind old men.

High up, from out of the canopy of pines, he saw a light then a fluttering butterfly descending in spirals, flitting from tree to tree but somehow growing in size all the time. He felt that the butterfly could sense he was watching it and sure enough as it grew it made its final descent towards him until, six feet high, it landed with its wings furled in front of him. He could see it was like a Red Admiral: fabulous patterns of red and black with two emerald eyes that he couldn't discern in the half-light to be either real or decoration. He reached out his hand towards it and the wings of the butterfly slowly and majestically unfurled to reveal the exquisite body of a naked woman underneath. Somehow he sensed this was Vivienne, but her head and neck were buried in some kind of black furry mask, the body of the butterfly itself perhaps. Before he could reach out and touch her flesh, it occurred to him that maybe the naked body was only another disguise, an illusion like eyes on the outside of the wings, and that if he touched the skin it would not respond like flesh but give way softly and sickeningly, revealing itself as some insect contrivance of feathery tissue. Afraid but fascinated, he held his quivering hand out below her vulva, like offering crumbs to a pet bird, and in time its folds opened and a red tubular tongue distended towards him. Telescopic, it finally revealed within its innermost tube a shining silver needle that pricked his finger and he cried out in his sleep, seeing a great ruby-red teardrop of blood there, winking like a wicked eye.

*

Next day, they encountered a hidden glade by a river where numerous outsized insects flew past them that Claudia marvelled at and took notes and photographs of for her dairy: giant dragonflies a foot long, butterflies the side of a fist. Anton trembled at the prescience of his dream but felt unable to share it with his companions.

*

Pitching a tent and sleeping al fresco was a novelty for the first night, but as the days went by and their rations ran out the hard reality began to set in: physical discomfort and exhaustion and an increasing sense of isolation due to the vast green army of trees around them. Anton tried to keep the journey interesting by relating everything he had learned about tree species: Larch, Cedar, Douglas Fir, their ages and projected heights, here was a stump whose rings revealed it had been planted around the time of the American Civil War. Here were two yews: one female the other male, having sex in slow motion over decades with the aid of every passing breeze. Here was an oak colonised and all but killed by ivy which entirely covered it: keeping its host alive just enough to sustain it.

At first, Vivienne and Claudia found his tales of how to catch animals boring and a little childish, until it dawned on them they were going to have to use them soon. *But I'm a vegetarian!* -Vivienne exclaimed indignantly.

Not this week you're not, Anton said abruptly as he marched on, *unless you want to die.*

I can eat fruits and nuts! -she called after him.

Not enough to sustain the kind of strength you need to keep walking like this. Believe me or don't believe me, it doesn't matter, you'll be ripping the squirrel steak out of my hands within forty-eight hours, I guarantee it.

There were rivers of course. He began with fish, easy enough to catch, and baked them in a sand oven made from the embers of their camp fire.

But how on Earth do you think we can find Leo, in a forest this size? -Claudia asked, picking fish bones from her teeth as delicately as she could contrive to.

Anton pointed to the fire. *No matter how tough Leo is, and he's obviously pretty tough, he's going to have to light fires now and again. This sector, the one we think he's in, is pretty flat. At dawn and dusk I climb a tree...*

I thought you were just looking for nuts for me... -Vivienne laughed.

From any treetop I should be able to see a long way, and I have a telescope. If he's around, he must light a fire and we might see him. Then there's tracks. It looks vast and uncharted to the naked eye, but from the maps you can see there are certain logical routes and arteries Leo must take now and again. Fresh water sources for instance. He can't be wandering randomly, despite what he says, or he'd be lost and wouldn't be able to find his way to the various villages where he posts letters. To me, that means he has maps, mental ones at least, and he's following routes on which we might find his tracks or other traces, shelters and dug-outs for instance.

After dinner, Anton would sit alone and write his diary while Claudia and Vivienne had time to themselves, talking quietly.

Anton recorded some his first impressions on entering the woods:

Tree bark: like flakes of skin, deeply fissured, twisting over itself, layer upon layer. Uprooted trees; the clay-red soil exposed underneath, rainwater pools forming there. Incredible height of dead-straight pines. Water plummeting through rock pools, rapids, forming grottoes, criss-crossed by fallen trunks, pines growing at the edge of cliffs: blind, the trees don't know the precariousness of their situation and grow regardless.

The mosses on the grotto walls: a hundred unnamed species, a botanist's wet dream, soft as sponges to the touch, saturated with rainwater. The rocks underfoot glitter with iron pyrites, fool's gold. Metallic sheen to every wet rock. In the shadow-twilight under the big trees: a hallowed carpet of pine needles leads upwards, vanishing into the morning mist, the roar of a waterfall nearby reverberating through our bones.

He looked up and saw that Vivienne was standing over him. *Here, you said you wanted to read more of Leo's letters,* she said. *Here's one I looked out this morning, sort of relevant to our discussion…*

Anton took it and began reading as she walked away:

So through environmental calamity Humanity stands at last on the brink of its own destruction. No. Humanity walks backwards towards the edge of a cliff, while chattering incessantly about the price of oil and other rubbish. No. Humanity, a rather annoying little insect, has finally succeeded in making enough noise by jumping up and down on a hot summer's day to rouse the large slumbering creature upon whom it rests, whose blood it sucks, so that the beast is just about to roll over and crush it into pulp. How did we get to this stage? Every life form, every design has its inherent flaws, potentially fatal. Were it not already too late, our first project might have been to map these flaws and use them as a template with which to correct our vision and see beyond the mirror's edge. Here are the five key blindspots of the human brain:

1.   Didactic Thinking. The unconscious presumption that an answer will be simply one thing or the other, black or white. This simplification is always our first approach to a problem, but carries with it the inherent failure to accept complexity and see where multiple factors are at play to produce shades of grey.

2. Projection. The unconscious presumption that other people think like us. This carries with it the consequent failure to recognise, analyse and predict motivations alien or novel to our own, in other words we fail to empathise effectively, because projection is easier.

3. Timeblanking. The unconscious failure to grasp the linear impact of time. A comfortable present, i.e. the day in front of us if pleasant, will always seem more real than any misfortune which may inevitably arise later out of our actions that day, no matter how dire those consequences, provided they are days, weeks or years hence. Given a combination of danger with time, we tend to ostrich time rather than starting running.

4. Flattery. The social herd instinct of humans pre-programmes us to like those who like us. Thus flattery, entirely regardless of whether it is meant or feigned, will completely shut down the critical analytical function of the recipient's brain for an average of two and a half minutes. The effect can only be overcome by extreme self-discipline and extensive practice.

5. Conflation. It is a common philosophical assumption that the human mind is always looking for absolute truth, when in fact it is only programmed to always make the best-fit sense of a situation no matter how little information is available or how flawed the information is. Not making sense of a situation is apparently not an option. To the human mind, a wrong answer is better than no answer. Hence why every tribe on earth has its own elaborate creation myth and accompanying rituals. The range and complexity of modern science should not blind us to the same persistent underlying truth, which has remained unchanged since the days of the caves: it is ludicrous to think that a talking chimpanzee can fully understand the universe that so dwarfs it, the gaps in our knowledge are vast, the inventions we plug those gaps with are only temporary sticking plaster, thus all our "truths" and assumptions remain wholly unreliable.

*

Franco found himself crying in the car outside Veronika's house. It had been raining for the last hour and the windscreen wipers were responding on auto-pilot, a mournful little movement, intermittent like a housemaid of the world sweeping up after each fresh calamity. The radio had just announced an earthquake on the other side of the planet in which children had been entombed in their own school. Franco remembered a line from Bob Dylan: *just when you think you've lost everything, you find out you can always lose a little more.*

The door opened and Veronika sat down on the passenger seat. *As Bugs Bunny used to say, what's up Doc? What's wrong?*

This is wrong, -he sobbed. *I can't do this.*

Veronika sighed and put her hand on his knee and said gently: *Look at me.* Then for the first time, she used his first name:

Franco.

He looked up and met her eyes and she held his gaze calmly for a minute, then said: *...Tell me about your childhood.*

Then they both started laughing.

*

On the fourth day travelling, Anton, Claudia and Vivienne found a track not marked on any map. The tire marks of some unknown off-road vehicle led to a strange clearing in the woods where they found yellow tape tied between trees, as if indicating a crime-scene or tree-felling in progress. But Anton could tell from the silence, the occasional nesting birds, that they were entirely alone and the scene had been abandoned months beforehand. They made their way tentatively past the yellow tape and spread out to explore the area.

Anton heard a whistle from Claudia and made his way back towards her through the thin saplings that were already re-colonising the blighted arena. She seemed apprehensive, and was gesticulating silently towards a strange hillock a hundred yards to her left. Anton approached carefully and circled it, kneeling at its edges to try to understand its meaning.

He could hear the hum of bees from somewhere within the mound, as if a hive was concealed there. Ants were patrolling the perimeter, biting his feet, knees and hands. At the centre, flies were hovering and feeding over what he thought at first was cow dung, but what as his eyes focused through the miasma of noonday heat, seemed to resemble the browning folds of brain tissue, possibly human. From beneath and within this a complex array of electrical wires could be seen leading away in every direction towards the periphery of the mound, where many arrays of batteries lay partially buried in the earth.

Anton backed away carefully, and gestured to Claudia and Vivienne to stay back.

What is it? -They whispered when he returned, and he looked back over his shoulder, troubled and confused.

I honestly don't know, but I don't think we're supposed to be here. There's something unsavoury about this, let's just quietly get out of here, shall we?

You seem rattled, Vivienne said as they reached the yellow tape boundary again.

Maybe you should be, Claudia said from where she stood up ahead reading some sort of notice nailed to a tree. *This says this is a Defence Ministry Restricted Area, Danger Of Death... they do like their hyperbole and melodrama those military boys, don't they?*

Does it say what kind of danger? Anton asked.

Claudia shook her head, *nothing so helpful I'm afraid, why?*

The one piece of hardware I didn't think to pack was a Geiger counter. Sunburn I can handle, but Leukaemia I could do without contracting on holiday.

Pahhh... Vivienne said, *...Looked like a harmless old pile of electrified dung to me. Could be any number of other silent killers anyway... spores of Small Pox or Anthrax if that's any comfort...*

Just at the moment Claudia yelped and ducked as a particularly large dragonfly buzzed past her head like a model helicopter. *What the...*

Jesus... that one's practically back to Jurassic proportions, Anton gasped, fumbling for his camera.

They all watched as the creature approached the cordoned zone, slowed and hovered uncertainly, then diverted its path in a different direction.

*

The children had been badly behaved in the morning, too much energy and mischief in the air, as if the departure of their mother on holiday was a green light for an adventure of their own.

Now Imelda, the Reinwalds' housekeeper, having carefully tired them out in a lunchtime game in the park, sat Vittorrio and Lucia down in the study with various games and puzzles in the hope that they would play quietly or get bored and take an afternoon nap.

They sat on their little chairs and eyed the marble chessboard on the table between them. The study was the finest room in the house: original oak panelling to dado height and oil paintings on the wall above, polished wooden floorboards on which the children scuffed their shoes now, swinging their feet between the chairs.

Vittorrio took the ivory and ebony chess pieces from the box and began to set them up as his sister watched.

Why do they go that way? -she asked

It's how papa sets them up, he showed me.

Which one's the Queen. Can I go the Queen?

*There's two queens, silly, the black and the white. You don't **go** the Queen, you go black or white.*

Is that her?

No, that's the Knight.

But it's a horse, not a night, is it the Queen's horsey?

Maybe, it's called a Knight, like a knight in armour, you know, jousting and all that stuff, it's a tradition, it's the rules.

Did Papa teach you all the rules, do you remember them?

I think so. But I guess we can make new rules if we get bored. The Knight can do things none of the other pieces can.

Look, he's allowed to jump over other people and move in a funny L-shape like this...
Why?
It's just the rules, since ages ago, since Vikings and stuff, since the Stone Age. All the other pieces have to shuffle around a step here or there, forward or diagonal, but the Knight gets to jump.
What does this one do? -Lucia asked, her hand on a Castle.

That's called the Whistle. You pick it up and blow through the hole on top of it and see how many Pawns you can blow over.

Lucia giggled, *and this one?* -she said, holding up a Bishop.

See that roundy shape? -Vittorrio continued earnestly, *that's called the Stishup. You put him up your nose and hold your head over the chessboard and wait until you sneeze, cos' that's him condemning them to death.*

Lucia was excited now, clapping her hands together: *what happens to the pieces that die?*

They just go back in the box until the next game of course, Vittorrio mused, puzzled by her curiosity.

No blood? No hanging or beheading? -she whispered conspiratorially.

Vittorrio smiled mischievously and leaned down over the board until their two noses pressed together, sharing a secret. *Have you got a hacksaw?*

*

After he had cooked everyone a dinner of roast rabbit, Anton went to sit on his own on a hillock at the edge of a clearing, leaving Vivienne and Claudia to talk quietly together by the fire. The sound of the evening birds and chirping crickets where he sat drowned out whatever they were saying. The lowering sun turned blood red like a throbbing heart, a solitary eye that looked into his soul. In the heart of the wilderness at last, he had nowhere left to hide. His mind emptied, he lost all track of time for a while, until he realised Vivienne had come and sat down quietly beside him.

What are you thinking about? -she asked, then added more softly: -*your father?*

No, I believe he's part of me now. In some ways he feels closer now than when he was alive. There's not a tribe on earth who don't believe something similar. Not a religion in the history of the planet that hasn't suggested this, until now of course. Our religion of science, handy for opening a tin of soup, but not for making any coherent or useful sense out of the business of life and death, is it?

Pahhh... -Vivienne snorted, -*Science built your jeep and your laptop and your GPS, that's all useful isn't it?*

Only, ultimately, if it makes people happier. Are you sure that it does?

No. Not sure. Vivienne said quietly, after a while.

So I don't miss him... because he's part of me, he's looking out from inside my eyes right now.

Maybe if I knew Leo was dead, I could feel closer to him, maybe that's my problem... -Vivienne looked down at the ground, digging at it with a stick.

The sun seemed to shift a notch lower and redder, the flies rose up in clouds from the marsh. They turned and looked at each other. *And what does your father see through your eyes now?*

Vivienne... Anton looked away into the distance, *you are a beautiful woman... but what's the point in all of this?*

This?

Men and women, animals and plants, wind and water and trees. What does it all want? You've seen it all on this journey: the bears hunt the wolves who hunt the wild cats who hunt the mice... it's all carnage and copulation and child-rearing. But what does it all amount to that's of any consequence? What does God or Gaia want of us? Just birdsong and peacock feathers, reproduction and flowering? Aren't you ever tired of this pointless cycle, what does it all lead to? Just our own extinction or some marvellous future of space travel and dreams? Either way we won't see one bit of it, we'll be dust. So why bother? Just how and why should we keep going?

For the beauty of it of course, Vivienne sighed, *...the ongoing revelation of beauty. Pain, horror, joy, hope... they're all just colours in the palette, light and shade, life and death, the colours without which the picture of life could have no beauty, it would just be grey mist. Leo said these answers can only be felt, not understood...*

Felt, not understood? What does that mean? Where does that get us? And he's not here. Where did it get him?

Vivienne put her hand on Anton's forearm: *He said you must acquire the grace of an animal, the innocence of a child, to understand. A total lack of self-consciousness.*

And how do we do that?

Pay attention... she said and then leaned closer and kissed him.

*

Imelda checked in on the children again and was pleased and amazed to see that they were apparently enthralled in a game of chess. She hovered at the door unnoticed, such was their concentration.

What's happening now? asked Lucia, their two faces lowered like vast moon and sun over the bloody battlefields of their minds.

The Queens have made all their moves and all the pawns are gone. They were in the open, but now your queen is trapped by her defences.

What can happen next? Are any moves possible?

I'm not sure, it might be stalemate.

Checkmate?

No, that's different, that's when we trap and kill the kings, but they're both still free and just wandering about.

Can the knight save the Queen? Make a way out for her?

Maybe... but there are two knights remember, I've been keeping mine in reserve, hidden away out of sight. I might bring him forward to challenge yours.

A jousting match?! -Lucia clapped her hands. *Beheadings?*

*

Running back in the twilight to meet Claudia, Anton fought the rush of adrenalin and endorphin in his veins, the impact of pheromones and oxytocin, the demeaning predictability of his body's reaction to making contact with another.

I hate this, he said to Claudia, smiling strangely, as he found her at the river's edge, light in her hair, turning round to look at him. *It's like some third rate teen movie, where Vivienne and I are supposed to get all gushy now while you play gooseberry and get lonelier. Jesus, why are we so trapped inside our biology, so incapable of being more?*

Anton, what are you havering about?

Forgive my impertinence, but I seem to have got to know you and your family through some kind of divine accident of fate and I can see you're not happy in your marriage…

Her eyes fell. *Ohhh… what has Viv been saying to you?*

Nothing, nothing at all. I'm just talking about what I see with my own eyes, and it feels weird not to talk about it. I think you should, and we should.

Anton, you're very sweet, but I don't want to off-load all my private complications on you.

No, no, what I'm saying is that I've grown to like you, Claudia, respect you and like you very much. I want you to be happy and for things to work out for you. I don't want to be the agent of anything that makes you unhappy.

Her eyes were soft and full of sadness and something approaching love now, as she stood and looked back at the babbling idiot Anton seemed to have become.

Vivienne had caught up with them now, her skin glowing, her long golden hair blowing back over her shoulders, her head thrown back in laughter at first but then unsure whether Anton was joking or serious. Claudia looked half way between enchanted and horrified.

I feel like a character in a novel who's about to punch the author, -Anton said, looking at them both uncertainly. *Fuck it,* he said at last, and grabbed Claudia and kissed her passionately on the lips.

Fuck it, he said again, muttering madly to himself as he turned away from both of them, almost angry, stomping off. *I'm *supposed to be helping you find your brother and your husband. Two married women, maybe one of them a widow, the other one's husband's just saved my sanity a year ago, what kind of a way is this to show gratitude? This is nuts,* he sighed, sitting down on a tree stump to talk to the long grasses.

But he heard a swishing noise and a splash behind him that brought him to his senses. Vivienne's clothes lay hanging from various trees. She had thrown herself into the river.

Jesus, what now... -he said and got up and headed after her, with Claudia following at his side, but they both slowed down as they reached a rock outcrop and saw that she was swimming happily and safely among the water lilies.

He turned to look at Claudia as if waking from a dream and saw that her eyes were kind and mocking, reflecting a glowing blue twilight that now seemed to be permeating everything, as if moving through their bodies, making them translucent like fish.

She stood in front of him and unbuttoned his shirt as they both started laughing. With the immediacy and innocence of children, blinded by the heartbeat of the sunken sun, they moved hand in hand into the pure moment, slipping into the silken water.

The grace of animals! -Anton shouted to Vivienne after the first shock of the cool water had exhilarated him, and she laughed back as they swam to meet her. Silver diadems of light, swaying reeds and lilies circled and brushed past them, enfolding them. Countless unfamiliar textures caressed them in a kaleidoscope of touch. Without clothes, the world changed, they changed. They all three embraced and frolicked in the water in a way that was entirely chaste to them, but which might have aroused a more cynical observer. With their ardour neutralised by cold and tiredness, they were able to fondle each other, even their genitals in a way that was only friendly and hilarious. They were laughing at being human.

They had walked nearly twenty miles that day. When they returned to the glowing embers of their campfire, they were so tired and refreshed and shorn of care that they simply fell asleep naked together, entwined, under one blanket. The question of the logistics of who might be contemplating sex with anyone else would have to wait until the morning.

*

Vittorrio opened his soldier chest and brought out a dozen of his favourites: one to thirty-second scale plastic Romans with tin alloy bases, red fibre plumes and shiny metallic shields. He carefully laid them out on the chequerboard in among the remaining chess pieces.

What rule is this now? -his sister asked, a little sceptically.

When two bishops get taken straight after each other, you are allowed to supplement both sides forces, you know like reinforcements.

But how will we know which ones are yours and mines? Whose black and white?

Surprised by his sister's practicality, Vittorrio reluctantly had to face that he hadn't addressed this issue, and thought on his feet instead like a true politician: *Neither. They're a third force. Like UN Peacekeepers except they're totally up for it.*

We can't have three sides, we'd need to get Imelda in to play for them.

Yes, we can have three sides. There were three sides at Waterloo. There were three sides in the Balkan wars, Daddy said they had Serbs and Croats and Muslims and Albanians...

That's four.

*Well, it was complicated. We'll keep our war simple,
promise. Now, lets throw the dice to see what the Romans do…*

*

The moon cleared the clouds for a moment and revealed a
figure, crouched among the highest branches of a cedar, hunched
and patient, watchful, immensely still. His breath sighed in
indiscernible harmony with the woods around him as he surveyed
the small campsite below him. Such was his camouflage it
would have been impossible to guess his identity now, even to
those who might have known him once, nor possible to tell if
the weapon clutched at his shoulder was a rifle or a spear. The
clouds shifted to clothe the moon once more and he was gone,
returned to the background of bark and leaf like a chameleon, a
dream forgotten by a child waking on the first day of summer.

~

8.

THE DOCTRINE OF SIGNATURES

An (Unpleasant) Interlude of Sorts

The best-known references to the phallic Mandrake root are in Shakespeare, John Donne and Beckett's Waiting For Godot: the ancient myth that they grow where the sperm from a hanged man hits the earth, and scream when they are dug up. This kind of belief is actually part of a much wider and more ancient philosophy that was taken up by the alchemist Paracelsus: the direct father of modern medicine. The herbalist "Doctrine Of Signatures" states that plants have been made by God to bear the likeness of the parts of the human body that they may offer cures for. Thus rhubarb or celery, resembling human bones, might therefore make bones stronger if eaten, and a walnut, resembling a human brain, might be taken to cure a neural disorder. Aspirin, despite centuries of pharmaceutical experimentation, is still made from the bark of weeping willow.

*

June: On my customary early morning walk to work through the Willow Street pedestrian precinct I happened to spot an unusual green plant or fruit lying on the ground. It was about the size of a child's fist, with spiked green petals like an artichoke on steroids. I assumed it was some discarded exotic vegetable from foreign climes, perhaps fallen from the stall of a temporary market.

*

July: In the months leading up to the infamous *Cash-For-Trash Scandal* in the northern European city of *Sylvow*, Mayor Merrick has a recurring dream, or more precisely: a nightmare.

He is chairing a crisis meeting in the City Council Chambers. His mouth is moving but he cannot hear his own words, although everyone else seems to be listening. He can feel tension rising inside himself and in the eyes of his audience as he talks towards some conclusion. Then, and he often tries to wake before this point: there is a flash of white light and splintering glass as the ornate stained-glass windows of the grand-salon are shattered by sheets and fingers of ivy that shoot into and across the room from both sides. These tendrils instantly ensnare many of the counsellors, including himself. Some choke to death before his eyes, but he is lifted from his chair and pinned against the wall.

The double doors at the far end of the room are thrown open and a weird vision steps in: an adolescent boy as white as sapwood or the polished marble of a Bernini sculpture. His movements are stifled and awkward like some demonic Pinocchio. His long fingers touch the blood-soaked meeting table and it crumbles in seconds into rotten embers. The counsellors' bodies blacken and shrivel in their seats, peeling away like rotten fruit.

The boy steps nearer and the closed white eyelids of his statuesque face only now roll open to reveal jet-black eyes without pupils. His mouth opens and he begins to speak in a voice like the rasping of a thousand discordant violins, a cacophony made of the car horns and wailing sirens of the polluted city outside, the noise of hell itself.

The Mayor notices now that the boy is sexless, has neither genitals nor navel, and holds in his outstretched hand a broken Victorian pocketwatch: its springs wavering like an eviscerated bird. His red tongue is long and serrated, like a living sword emerging from his head, as it continues to rasp its indecipherable music. He turns and gestures towards the far wall, as if he wants the Mayor's eyes to follow. In front of a large ornately carved mirror there sits a white chair made entirely of human bones. The mayor awakens as he is overcome with the terror of having to sit in this chair and of what he will see in the mirror. He wipes the sweat from his face, and is troubled for the rest of the day by the nagging feeling that the boy in the dream bears a distorted resemblance to somebody he knows well.

*

August: In the early morning, a rain of unidentified vegetables falls from the sky onto Willow Street. A few passers-by laugh at first and try to kick them, but within minutes it is noticed that wherever they fall the objects quickly fasten themselves to the pavement and become entirely immoveable. By the evening, the newspapers and television are onto the story, and a pneumatic drill has been unsuccessfully brought to bear on the situation. The police intervene and cordon off the entire precinct. The next morning, to general surprise the fruits are gone (now dubbed *"caulinuts"*, meaning crosses between chestnuts and cauliflowers) and only their feathery grey husks are left blowing about harmlessly amid nearby traffic. A full month passes before curious disruptions and anomalies begin to appear in the electrical, water and drainage services beneath Willow Street.

*

September: A petition of protest is presented to the Mayor of Sylvow under the full glare of media attention. The story has now broken of allegations of corruption and malpractice by the administration. In the face of the growing autonomy of the European City States and punitive environmental taxes, the mayor has allegedly taken to secretly buying refuse consignments from neighbouring regions and having these buried illegally, under cover of darkness in unmarked sites. Much of the waste is said to have been hazardous industrial grade and may in some cases have filtered down to pollute the water table. Cases of fatal illness among local children are being linked to the burial sites. A full denial is issued by the Council Offices but shortly afterwards a press conference is forced to be abandoned as the Mayor withdraws under siege. Only days later, details emerge concerning the mysterious death of a reporter investigating the waste, and public opinion is further enflamed.

The Doctrine of Signatures

*

October: Mayor Merrick's 12 year-old son Tarquin is often bullied at school, but has recently found a much-needed source of credibility in his prowess in playground chestnut contests. Driven to seek ever larger and harder chestnuts to feed his self-aggrandising obsession, he begins employing the various ancient and arcane techniques of chestnut-enhancement known only to schoolboys, mostly involving vinegar and furniture polish.

In the local woods a short walk from their house, the Mayor's son has been keeping his eye on a particularly promising chestnut as it develops. He knows it is premature and that he should wait a few more weeks before taking it down with an expert stick-throw, but finally he is unable to restrain himself. The tree is not so far from the public footpath that some friend or rival might not spot it and beat him to it, and then the disappointment, the chagrin would be unbearable. So the deed is done and the gnarled green shell falls into the autumn leaves with a satisfyingly rustled thud. He takes it into his hands and is surprised to find it is even heavier and more enormous than he has dared to imagine.

He hurries back to his bedroom laboratory to begin surgery on it. Opening the shell with a scalpel he soon sees his worst fears are realised. The chestnut is incredibly white and soft, the thought of what size it might actually have attained without human intervention is terrifying. Tarquin focuses on the task in hand. The sweet wood-sap smell is overpowering, the white skin around the soft inner shell resembles the pith of an orange. He places the huge soft white nut into a deep petri dish of vinegar and hides it in the darkest recesses of his wardrobe.

Returning the next day he finds to his disappointment that the nut is so premature that it has started to wrinkle rather than harden up. For a moment he nearly throws it away until he notices a curious detail: several flies and a small spider have all expired in the vinegar during the night and their limbs seem to be dissolving, releasing a strange green efflorescence. A similar green seems to be appearing around the chestnut itself, as if some sort of symbiosis or electrolysis is taking place. Just as he begins to marvel at this, his mother approaches the room and he hurriedly closes the cupboard.

With the intervention of a sleepover at a cousin's house, it is two days before Tarquin next gets to examine the chestnut and then to suddenly understand the nature of what he is really dealing with. A palpable stench is now filling the wardrobe and the chestnut, surrounded by green efflorescence and dissolving insects, has wrinkled and swollen up to resemble nothing so much as a tiny mammalian brain. Tarquin shivers, reminded of newsreels of genetic experiments with human ears growing from the backs of mice. He feels more like a gardener than a schoolboy as he finds himself fastidiously changing the petri dish for a larger one to prevent the "brain" from getting pot-bound, and even throwing in a few drops of plant-food for good measure. He feels unsure as to what material or social benefit this monster is going to afford him but, in the true spirit of human science, instantly quells his moral qualms under the persuasive weight of curiosity.

*

"The American Weekly edition of 26th September 1920 featured a story with accompanying illustration of a young woman of the Mkodos tribe being consumed by a large plant in Madagascar in 1878.

Plant carnivory has probably evolved independently at least ten times; however, some of these 'independent' groups are probably descended from a recent common ancestor with a predisposition to carnivory.

Known carnivorous plants on earth currently number more than 640 plant species from at least a dozen genera. They are almost entirely restricted to habitats such as bogs, where soil nutrients are extremely limiting, but where sunlight and water are readily available. Only under such extreme conditions is carnivory favoured to an extent that makes the adaptations obvious. The archetypal carnivore, the Venus flytrap, grows where soils have nitrate and calcium levels that are almost too low to measure"

-from WIKIPEDIA.

*

November: Tarquin is of that age at which one's first sexual and romantic feelings begin to emerge and, without an outlet, can begin to take on an obsessive, and in some cases guilty, quality. The seed of guilt in Tarquin's case has already been sown by the foul-smelling chestnut-brain he is now concealing in his wardrobe, sealing inside cardboard boxes with duck tape and surrounding with unwashed socks as a diversionary tactic to distract his mother.

By day, in school hours, his own distraction has been brought about by the occasional sight of a schoolgirl two years above him who floats about the classrooms and corridors with a mellifluous air, her blue eyes always seemingly somewhere else. She seems to Tarquin like a dreamer and loner similar to himself, but he never dares talk to her, lest he break his own spell and becomes convulsed with embarrassment. Her long straw-blonde hair and pale white skin are now the basis of his private fantasies, the latter being disturbingly fused in his mind with the white protective pith of premature chestnuts: they seem to share the same texture and perhaps divine origin, and no doubt (though he can only guess) the same sublime aroma of pristine and fertile natural creations.

He has begun to masturbate regularly while thinking about her late at night in bed, and in his mind her white skin always gives way to the thought of the white surface of the chestnut-brain then visa versa. Once or twice, as his excitement is mounting, he is alarmed and puzzled to hear a faint knocking from within the wardrobe, as if the brain itself is somehow aware of his nefarious nocturnal activity. At first he is horrified and gets up to check the hall outside to make sure that his mother isn't prying and knocking on the door, but finds he is alone.

One afternoon after school, he finds himself alone while his mother goes out on an errand and he takes the opportunity to masturbate freely without fear of discovery. As usual, his mind is filled with thoughts and visions of Anne-Marie, as he has heard she is called. Again as his excitement begins to spiral, he hears the knocking from the wardrobe. He desists, and the knocking stops. He starts again, and it soon resumes. Afraid, and yet unable to restrain his curiosity, he opens the wardrobe and unpacks the chestnut-brain. It is now swollen to almost the size of a face, and to his amazement its texture has tightened and unwrinkled as if to mimic the smooth texture of Anne-Marie's skin. The sight both shocks and excites him, and before his rational mind can pass judgement his little member has answered by stiffening and rising fiercely in his hand. Against every cautionary impulse in his body, he finds himself unable to stop his hand from resuming its soothing motion upon himself, and the brain begins to beat in its glass tray, its surface pulsating like a transplanted heart.

Quickly a sharp pain begins down inside him, he knows he should stop, but he is divided evenly between fear and pleasure, and can only continue in utter apprehension. The fire cuts through him and for the first time a white viscous tear appears at the eye of his manhood and dribbles down over his hands. The brain suddenly convulses, returning to its previous wrinkled state and resembling, it occurs to him for the first time, the folds of his scrotum. As his body sags and eases and his eyes now fall over the weird spectacle in front of him, something unexpected happens: the brain twitches and clutches itself for a second into the shape of a rapacious vulva and Tarquin screams and falls backwards in terror, falling over his own trousers. Instinctively, he has put his hand to his face and now to his surprise he finds himself tasting his own semen, licking some of it off his thumb. In tentative curiosity, he rises to his tip-toes and goes over to look at the brain again and sees that it has returned to a state of peacefulness. He holds out his hand and lets a drop of the semen fall off onto the brain. It hisses and vanishes instantly into its folds releasing a small gasp of steam, like spit on a hot stove.

After this incident, he feels compelled to hide the brain in its box in his parents garage. Now, with his growing sense of sexual guilt and the slowly growing size of the brain itself, he finds new physical symptoms manifesting themselves on his body. His perennial skin complaint, which begins as a red itching on his arms and legs, is now solidifying and congealing into scabs that are hard and grey and deeply fissured: resembling the bark of old trees. He tries to keep these patches secret from his parents and classmates but eventually a doctor is called, who surprisingly gives the condition some Latin name and prescribes a lotion for its relief, as if the whole thing is totally unconnected with the chestnut-brain and Tarquin's growing taste for drinking his own semen.

*

" *...we will add a few words about mandrakes and androids, which several writers on magic confound with the waxen image; serving the purposes of bewitchment. The natural mandragore is a filamentous root which, more or less, presents as a whole either the figure of a man, or that of the virile members. It is slightly narcotic, and an aphrodisiacal virtue was ascribed to it by the ancients, who represented it as being sought by Thessalian sorcerers for the composition of philtres. Is this root the umbilical vestige of our terrestrial origin? We dare not seriously affirm it, but all the same it is certain that man came out of the slime of the earth, and his first appearance must have been in the form of a rough sketch. The analogies of nature make this notion necessarily admissible, at least as a possibility. The first men were, in this case, a family of gigantic, sensitive mandragores, animated by the sun, who rooted themselves up from the earth; this assumption not only does not exclude, but, on the contrary, positively supposes, creative will and the providential co-operation of a first cause, which we have reason to call God.*

Some alchemists, impressed by this idea, speculated on the culture of the mandragore, and experimented in the artificial reproduction of a soil sufficiently fruitful and a sun sufficiently active to humanise the said root, and thus create men without the concurrence of the female. Others, who regarded humanity as the synthesis of animals, despaired about vitalising the mandragore, but they crossed monstrous pairs and projected human seed into animal earth, only for the production of shameful crimes and barren deformities. The third method of making the android was by galvanic machinery. One of these almost intelligent

automata was attributed to Albertus Magnus, and it is said that Thomas Aquinas destroyed it with one blow from a stick because he was perplexed by its answers...
"

-from *Witchcraft and Spells:*
Transcendental Magic its Doctrine and Ritual
by Eliphas Levi, translated by Arthur Edward Waite, 1896.

*

December: The services beneath the Willow Street Precinct begin to seriously malfunction. Lighting, electrical, telecom and data become intermittent then fail altogether. Upon digging up the streets, contractors are amazed to find a network of organic roots and tendrils that have strangled and severed, but also partially reincorporated the wires and pipes of human society. It becomes obvious that the process has been secretly progressing unchecked since the fall of the "caulinuts" in August. While some buildings on the precinct have been evacuated, a few remain in use but shortly afterwards the toilets in these begin shooting human sewage out at anyone within range. Environmental Health close the precinct but, weeks later while carrying out tests in protective suits, find the toilets have progressed to firing sulphuric acid, burning through their clothing. The precinct and three city blocks are abandoned and cordoned off and the army move in.

*

Unbeknown to botanical researchers, an avenue of trees in the west-end park have been gradually developing their catkins into small bombs of concentrated sulphuric acid. After presumably biding their time for 30 years, they suddenly drop their cargo on a passing cyclist in a seemingly concerted guerrilla ambush. Half a minute later, a motorist driving at 15 mile per hour through the cross-park boulevard is amazed to see a semi-stripped skeleton ride a bicycle out from the trees and clatter onto the road in front of him. He at first presumes he is witnessing an elaborate student prank. The cyclist's exposed long intestine has snagged on a passing oak tree and been unwinding for the last twenty-two feet before bringing him to a halt.

*

January: While his parents are away for the day, Tarquin goes to check on the well-being of the chestnut-brain now housed in a hidden corner of the disused shed in the garden. He notices to his surprise that roots from the brain have now eaten through the timber walls of the hut and begun digging down into the earth. As he lifts the damp cardboard box that covers the brain, a cloud of acrid white spores are released into his face and he coughs and doubles over, almost fainting.

He finds his eyelids growing heavy, his mind swirling as if the heady fermented scent on the air contains some hallucinogenic properties. As his head lowers towards the ground and the cloud of spore settles, a taproot from the base of the brain threshes around and then, detecting his breath and body-heat, inches its way towards him with the undulating movement of a grass snake. It climbs rapidly up his arms and shoulders then insinuates itself fiercely into his left ear. Tarquin winces and cries out but paralysis soon takes over. A little blood from his punctured ear-drum trickles out onto the fleshy earlobe. The taproot pumps and feeds itself deeper, violating, deflowering him.

Tarquin's mind swims in a narcotic haze. He finds his body is a hundred feet long and stretched out flat under the cobbles of the Willow Street Precinct. He finds he can look up women's dresses at will, and spit urine and faeces out at passers-by from the pipes of toilets. He can switch the lights on or off in entire city blocks just by twitching his nostrils or flickering his eyelids. He is plugged into the *Earth-Brain Root System*, and able to feel the breathing of forests and streams. He feels his whole body become a battleground on which Man and Nature are enacting a titanic struggle. He flexes his jaw and flicks on all the TV sets in the electrical showrooms on the corner of Danver Street. He sees his own face appear on them for a moment and turns the sound up until it is so deafening that customers begin fleeing the shop. The newsreels are talking about the disappearance of Mayor Merrick's son, his suspected kidnap by environmental terrorists. Tarquin sees this is him they are talking about and, with enormous effort, remembers where he might be, what danger he is in, and tries to open his eyes again.

Wailing, but with his mouth increasingly choked with ivy that seems to be rising up from inside his stomach, Tarquin tries to stand and starts to fight with the chestnut-brain. Kicking at its roots, he feels as if he is trying to sever his own fingers, but realises dimly that his very life is at stake and there is nothing left to lose. Struggling wildly, he kicks through the rotten wood planking of the disused shed and staggers out across the garden with the brain hanging and bouncing at his back, its many tendrils and roots entangling him, seeking further orifices to colonise.

With some vague and ill-founded hope that water might put an end to the assault, he staggers through the bushes and into the woods across the street, but falls to his knees again before even reaching the stream. The brain completes its colonisation of his nervous system and paralyses his body where it lies, half-kneeling, eyes-closed, mouth open in silent agony. Now it begins its work of sending roots back down into the earth, of connecting to other trees, exploring and deconstructing its host's body, building new structures for its higher purpose. Leaves blow about his knees and hands as his skin grows grey and dry by the hour, his blood silently redistributing itself beneath the earth, mingling with sap and chlorophyll.

By the time the sun rises the next day and the police search the neighbourhood, Tarquin's body is no longer recognisable to the untrained eye: his clothes have been eroded and digested apart from a few tatters that blow off in the wind. The dark scabs of his skin disease have expanded to cover his flesh like thick tree bark. Already he is just an unusual knot at the base of an old gnarled tree, a freakish natural formation, a distorted stump that only an over-imaginative child would dare suggest bore any resemblance to the shape of a crouching figure with an open mouth, face withered and contorted as if in the last throws of agony or sexual ecstasy.

*

February: The corollary of the caulinuts: "chestflowers" begin as wind-driven spores entering through hospital windows. Once inhaled, they grow within and quickly puncture the human chest cavity, but keep the host alive with arteries and veins interwoven with their root system. Entire hospital wards are reduced to what one nurse memorably calls "fields of bloody daisies" with patients pierced beneath them like compost bags. A national emergency is declared and borders closed. After initial attempts at humanitarian intervention fail, the decision is taken to burn all the victims alive in order to contain the outbreak.

*

March: Heartbroken and desperate for information about the disappearance of his son, troubled by the ongoing environmental turmoil, and apprehensive that the two situations are somehow irrationally linked, Mayor Merrick secretly initiates the *Gaia Gate Project*. Enormous horizontal wind chimes, made from requisitioned gas pipelines are installed on several of the hilltops surrounding Sylvow, under cover of being new wind-turbine prototypes. Their sounds are then recorded and analysed by computers for intelligible messages. The official objective later found noted in confidential documentation is *"to give language to the voice of the wind"*.

In Project *Pagan Bone Solstice*, bones of animals of every species, including humans are arranged on the ground into an elaborate "terminal moraine" surrounding a Neolithic menhir at sunset. Autumn leaves are gathered up from city streets and woven into special suits for teams of researchers to wear in expeditions into the forest. They are to note, among other things, the detail of patterns made on cliff faces by wind-driven rain. The *Gaia Gate* story only breaks when pigeons are found to have had string tied to their feet in municipal city parks so that their movement patterns can be photographed. On closer inspection the string is found to actually be magnetic ribbon with binary-code prayers to Gaia written on it. The Mayor is forced to take compassionate medical leave amid doubts over his sanity, as further stories emerge of goats being disembowelled according to geometric formulae, and circles of standing stones being bombarded with laser beams.

*

April: Anne-Marie Vincent, aged 14, is taking her father's Jack Russell Terrier for a walk in Dryden Woods, when the animal starts to bark at the edge of a curious black bog surrounding a grotesquely gnarled tree. On closer inspection, she finds the dog is pulling at something resembling a human leg bone emerging from the black soil. Before she can even react to this she is lifted into the air and run through in several simultaneous directions at once by thin sharp branches of new Spring growth. There is no time for blood or pain or wounded cries. As each of the branches whistle through skin and sinew, their leaves and blossoms are whisked off to fall slowly through the air in a festive mist like carnival buntings.

The spectacle is both obscene and strangely beautiful, although its only spectator is a small uncomprehending dog. Anne-Marie's golden hair weaves the dappled light beneath the forest canopy, her perfect limbs relax in artistic curves like a ballet dancer, making momentary symmetry with the enclosing branches before she is released to fall into the blossom-sprinkled mire and vanish slowly beneath the surface. Roots move blindly to meet her limbs in the gelatinous warmth below, entwining and caressing them. A tap root brushing over her thighs is aroused at the contact and plies itself with disorientated urgency into her anus. The folds of her pudenda, courted for a moment by a similar protuberance, are breached and plugged by a tendril terminating in a fat thick phallus of sapwood, spitting spores. A specialised array of sepals and carpels open her mouth wide and slide down her throat. When the last of her golden locks is gone beneath the mud, the Jack Russell runs home barking.

*

May: The *Earth-Brain Root System* has now been traced back to its probable epicentre. A clearing in the forest near the Mayor's own house, also believed to be the scene of Anne-Marie Vincent's disappearance. Police tents have been set up around the site between the inner and outer cordons. Into one of these tents, the Mayor is led tentatively by a team of biologists and botanists, his eyes taking some time to adjust to the darkness. In a controlled temperature environment, the scientists have been retrieving and categorising white tubers that have been emerging from the mire around the poison tree. *We've had their structure analysed sir, and they're basically cellulose, starch, water carbohydrate.....* Like potatoes, you mean? *Not quite, we also think they're single-cell organisms... more like stillborn tadpoles, but solidified like branches of dead coral.*

Resembling weird mushrooms still sprinkled with flecks of earth, the protuberances lie out in a long trough under glass with labels below each noting dimensions and gestation time: like museum exhibits. The first are small, the later ones as large as dogs. *Two months: premature tuber. Four months: intermediate tuber.* The Mayor gasps. Like parts of a Picasso painting, they vaguely resemble pieces of human form, but re-imagined, re-configured. Unknown limbs and obscene genitals fuse, building blocks for some life form as yet unperfected, a terrible chimera waiting to be born.

*

June: On my next morning walk to work through the pedestrian precinct I saw a single brown feathery husk trapped beneath a municipal dustbin, perhaps all that was left of the strange fruit I thought I had spied there the day before. No doubt it had been quickly whittled away to nothing by the ravages of the wind and inquisitive dogs. I let out a private sigh of relief. My city had been spared, for now.

*

Adder's Tongue = for mild snakebites.
Black-eye root = for bruises.
Bladderwort = for diarrhoea.
Bleeding Hearts = for broken hearts.
Bloodroot = for blood disorders.
Butterwort = for curdling milk into butter, and throat and skin irritations.
Ginseng = for lethargy.
Gravelwort = for stones in the urinary tract.
Hedge Woundwort = for antiseptic treatment of cuts.
Liverwort = for liver disease.
Lousewort = for anaemia and heart troubles, aphrodisiac, ridding of lice and scabies.
Lungwort = for lung disease.
Maidenhair Fern = for baldness.
Mandrake = for sexual arousal in females.
Milkwort = for stimulation of breast milk in nursing mothers.
Pilewort = for haemorrhoids.
Ragwort = for skin inflammation, ulcers and gout.
Sandwort = diuretic, kidney tonic, relief of cystitis and irritable bowels.
Snakeroot = antidote for snake venom.
Spleenwort = for treatment of the spleen.
St John's Wort = for depression.
Toothwort = for toothache.
Wormwood = for intestinal parasites (and nuclear fallout).

~

9.

"Ah, love, let us be true to one another! ...we are here as on a darkling plain Swept with confused alarms of struggle and flight, Where ignorant armies clash by night."

–Matthew Arnold, *Dover Beach.*

"...but in a battle by night ... how could anyone know anything clearly? ...For the front lines of the Athenians were already all in confusion ... and the two sides were difficult to distinguish.... they not only became panic-stricken but came to blows with one another..."

-Thucydides, *The Battle of Epipolae.*

Vittorrio and Lucia took the carved chess pieces out again and set them up carefully on the marble chequerboard on the table at the centre of their parents' study.

Fifteen miles away, their father Franco Reinwald locked the door of his consulting room, the key entering the lock with stealth, the antiquated locking mechanism turning with an emphatic throw. The door shivered in its frame.

Black and white. The chess pieces were all in place now, when Vittorrio lifted the first pawn with an almost religious reverence, then slowly let the polished ebony touch down on the cool marble.

With silence, almost indifference, Franco's patient and lover Veronika put out her cigarette and knelt down in front of him and unbuckled his trousers.

Seventy five miles north-west in the forest surrounding the city of Sylvow, Franco's wife Claudia and her friends Vivienne and Anton, after travelling for seven days in search of Claudia's brother Leo: would now awake shortly after first light to find they had been surrounded by armed men in autumn-leaf cloaks and bee-masks.

*

Are we interrupting something? -drawled a cynical low voice from behind a mask.

Vivienne and Claudia woke up and screamed, burying their nakedness against Anton, thus greatly contributing to the pornographic impression forming in the minds of the unsympathetic observers.

Widespread laughter broke out, and some of the bee-masks lifted. The revelation of real human faces underneath did little to lift the atmosphere of threat and humiliation, and Claudia began weeping as Vivienne sat up and spat her contempt at them, clutching the blanket to her chest. *Animals!* -she howled, -*Show some manners!*

Sorry to have spoiled your little orgy, what did you expect us to do, knock?

You shouldn't be so greedy son, share your harem around…

What's your secret, sunshine, have you got a big cock or something?

Finally their apparent leader took pity on them and threw Anton some clothes. While everyone laughed, Anton then ran around retrieving various pants, bras and blouses from tree branches and discreetly fed them back under the blankets to the ladies so they could regain their modesty.

Who the hell are you people, and what do you think you're playing at… Anton began, squaring up to the leader, but the man instantly switched from derisory mirth to threatening authority:

Your papers please…

Sorry?

The atmosphere changed, one of his lieutenants cocked his semi-automatic, and everyone tensed up, seemingly worried by Anton's challenge.

Your identity cards, passports, driving licence, all kinds of I.D. This is a designated Civil Defence Area, and if you don't have the correct authorisations to be here then I'm going to have to put you all under military arrest.

Who are you? Anton asked simply, adjusting his tone.

Major Percival DeVroek, sir, Special Operations Commanding Officer, North-West Quadrant.

This is absurd. We're over seventy miles from the city now, and you're talking like you're a ticket inspector on a suburban train, pulling rank. How did you find us? We didn't know we were in any kind of a Defence Zone, we're in the middle of nowhere. And if you're soldiers why are you all dressed like Halloween Guisers? Is this some kind of a joke?

No joke, sir, I promise you. These men are all under my command. Special Forces, soldiers and engineers, engaged on a confidential Governmental Environmental Defence Operation.

G.E.D.O... Gedo, Army Gedo, Armageddon, eh? -Claudia laughed, now nearly dressed -*you couldn't make this stuff up.*

Anton reached to touch the mask that DeVroek held in his left hand and, wrong-footed, unable to think of what particular regulation it contravened, the Major let Anton take it and examine it. It was hard to say if it was real or synthetic, as if a huge bee a foot long had been gutted and flattened and skinned and folded out into a mask shape. Somehow, markings on its back now held two eye holes, with the transparent gossamer of bee wings fixed over them as protective lenses. The various legs and antennae dangled around the throat and crown of the wearer. *Wow...* Anton whispered, *what is this for...*

Just pray you never find out, DeVroek said, taking it back, *you are in considerable danger out here on your own, lucky we found you. Now, your papers please...* The Major spoke with measured patience, but there was a degree of urgency and threat in his voice.

Anton went over to his jacket where it hung on a tree and withdrew his wallet and identity cards from his pocket and held them out to the Major.

These cloaks... Anton said, *are they made of real leaves?*

The Major ignored the question, -*You're a forestry worker I see, are you here on some official business?*

One of his cohorts was sniggering again, eyeing Vivienne getting into her cargo trousers.

No, a holiday. -Anton replied.

Not everybody's idea of fun... but then again... -he raised an eyebrow. *You have violated a Defence Area, trespassed, that is an offence for which we will have to charge you and escort you from the area. You will have to report to your local police station on your return to the city, where you will be questioned and debriefed. If you've seen anything of a confidential military nature then you will each have to sign non-disclosure affidavits. Is that clear?*

We've seen nothing, Anton began, but already Vivienne had blurted out: *...is this about your beehives wired up to batteries?*

DeVroek spun around: *why did you enter the prohibited area?*

Anton took Vivienne's arm to encourage her to remain silent. *We didn't see the signs until we were inside one of the zones, then we made our way out.*

The Major and his lieutenant looked at each other, and Anton tried to provide their thoughts for them: *wolves, foxes, deer, rodents.... any of them could have cut the yellow tape.*

Check their rucksacks for cameras and phones... the Major ordered his men.

I suppose we thought they were forestry grids, demarcation zones for felling, or some weird art installation... which come to think of it is pretty much what you guys look like. What on earth are you trying to achieve out here?

The Major just shook his head, and then Claudia asked: *is this something to do with the Cash-For-Trash scandal, the weird plants that have been appearing in the streets in Sylvow, the outsized insects? Are you acting under direct orders of Mayor Merrick?*

The Major turned to fix her with a particularly malevolent glare that after a few moments everyone present took to mean she had been dead-on with some or all of her hypotheses. *A troublesome woman... your papers please,* he sighed, *and yours too, Blondie...* -turning to Vivienne.

His lieutenant was raking through Vivienne's belongings at that moment and emptied some of her cosmetics out onto the mud. To everyone's astonishment, Vivienne lunged at him and sent him flying sideways with a bare-footed drop-kick. Instantly, an array of semi-automatic weapons swung into view from under the circle of leaf-cloaks that surrounded them, several red laser datums hovering on Vivienne's forehead where she knelt on the ground. *Woahh... Woahh... everyone calm down,* -Anton exclaimed and knelt to embrace her until every red dot covered his back instead. He brought her to her feet and carefully back towards the Major, whispering to her to calm down, and restraining her from spitting at the glowering lieutenant who was also back on his feet again.

There you go, Ginger, -she said contemptuously to the Major as she handed over her passport.

*

I don't understand... Lucia sighed, scratching her head. *Everybody's dead now apart from the two Kings and they can only move a square at a time, so they're just useless old codgers. What are they going to do, head-butt each other to death?*

But just look at all those dead bodies... Vittorrio marvelled, plastic, ivory and ebony strewn across the marble chequerboard, *...as far as the eye can see.* Then he lay his head down level with the carnage.

What was the point, what will the Kings do now?

They'll tell everyone what really happened when the cavalry arrive or the police or the grey aliens from Zeta Riticulae. Explain it was all the Queens' faults for envying each other or wanting to emancipate their pawns or something...

I don't think the Queens wanted a fight, I think you made them do it!

What?! Who am I? I'm just a player?!

You're like a bad demon that whispers in people's ears. You're like that wind that mummy talks about, the one that drove people mad...

The mistral... -Vittorrio said, then noticed that Lucia was now watching something over his shoulder, so turned around to follow her eyes to the door.

Imelda, their parents' housekeeper, had been standing there watching them for the last few minutes. They both exclaimed in unison: *Imelda... why are you crying?!*

*

The soldiers led them several miles south to where they had moored a motor launch on the banks of a wide muddy river that seemed as if it might snake its way back through the forest in the direction of Sylvow. They radioed ahead, but after many long monotonous hours travelling had to stop and disembark at nightfall and set up a temporary bivouac.

At sunset, Anton heard a distant metallic roaring he had heard the night before, now slightly louder. *What the hell is that sound?* -he asked the Major as they sat around the campfire eating army rations. The other soldiers seemed relaxed, and one of them mumbled quietly: *attenuated wind chimes, western horizon azimuth twenty...*

You guys speak a different language, when you speak at all, Anton sighed. But when the Major got up and left, one of them made eye contact with him and gestured surreptitiously for Anton to follow. A hundred yards away in the growing shadows, under a tarpaulin he and a colleague had a laptop open, and were flicking through pages of something that looked like musical or soundwave analysis on screen. It was as if fragments of the distant metallic sound were being recorded and replayed and dissected. Now Claudia had come to stand quietly at Anton's side and she whispered: *are you guys looking for little green men or something, a crashed UFO?*

The soldier bristled at her derisory tone, and stood up and shuffled them back towards the fireside, keeping a wary eye on the distant Major. *It's not aliens, I know that much, it's something weirder, the eco-system is going haywire, The Enemy Within, the Major calls it.*

Now there's a fine cliché, Claudia mused quietly. *Is this about Gaia? The disappearance of the Mayor's son? How long have you people been out here? Have you seen my brother, have you heard of him? Leo Vestra? He lives out in the woods here somewhere, moving about...*

Claudia felt Anton nudging her as if warning her not to say too much, but she could see that none of what she was saying seemed to be ringing any bells with the soldier, who just looked at the ground and shook his head from side to side as they walked.

*

That night Claudia had a short and cryptic dream in which a regiment of semi-transparent soldiers in archaic dress were moving through the forest: their whitish texture like the gossamer wings of moths, their swords glimmering in moonlight. In her mind they seemed both a natural and a manmade force, like mechanical locusts, harbingers of some ancient deity whose meaning was buried deep in her ancestral memory, the stuff of forgotten folktales, erupting from the id.

*

After sunset, the sky was overcast and the night starless and moonless, pitch black. Some time after midnight, chaos broke loose. Anton awoke and the soldiers were suddenly shouting to each other, and dull thumping and muffled cries seemed to be ricocheting between the tree trunks as if a silent army, a ghostly Roman legion, were breaking through the forest like a wave. Claudia found Anton in the dark and they embraced, mouths and ears and eyes straining to make sense together of what was happening. *Where's Vivienne?* -Claudia suddenly rasped in anxiety. Anton felt her fear shudder into him. They thought they heard a female cry, then another one. Perhaps a voice stifled by hands. Energised, they linked hands and made their way, groping, hunched in the darkness, clinging to the terrain, trying to move towards the voice they had heard. Gunfire broke out and bullets whisked by their heads and they dived down onto the ground and lay on their chests with their faces close to the dirt. A soldier ran over their backs, then seemed to stop dead and fall backwards in front of them. They could hear strange gurgling sounds coming from him, and Anton leant forward to search with his hands over the man's body. Flashlights were sweeping through the trees now, turned by unseen hands, throwing complex blades of vision and obscuration, wheeling shadows, that lasted only for a second. In one of these they saw for a moment the wounded soldier in front of them: lying with a large crudely sharpened stick through his blood-soaked chest, to which his twitching hand was grasping as his last breaths gave way.

Instinctively now, Claudia and Anton got up and began to head towards the river. The moon cleared the clouds above the treetops at last and a little light began to filter down to make sense of the scene they were walking through. Several soldiers' bodies seemed to be heaped on the ground at various points around them and another two were wrestling with each other a hundred yards away. Several others seemed to be fighting off some kind of wild animal, a bear perhaps at the edge of a dense thicket, but using tent poles and the butts of their rifles, as if their ammunition had been stolen. Then they heard footsteps behind them and torchlight wheeled across their backs. They expected to see the Major or his lieutenant but it was Vivienne, her face smeared with blood and dirt, her clothes torn. Claudia shrieked and Vivienne put her hand over her mouth and hugged her, then pushed her and Anton both forward: *we have to get away from here, if we get to the riverbank we can follow it west.*

Viv, are you hurt, are you hurt? -Claudia was whispering hysterically, but she made them press on until they made it to the water's edge and began moving at speed, ceasing to question anything until they could feel safe again. Behind them the cries continued, increasingly intermittent, until there was a final long burst of machine gun fire, like an execution.

When they had made an hour's distance and the first light of dawn was breaking, they made a den of bracken and fir branches and fell into sleep together again, intermittent and fitful, lost as orphans, a trio of refugees.

When Anton awoke again, he found Vivienne back down at the riverside, starting to wash herself, and he noticed dried blood on her legs, bruising appearing down one side of her face.

What happened, Viv? What happened back there?

He waded into the river and they embraced, up to their waists. She shook against him, saying: *I woke up and they were trying to rape me, Anton.*

Who? Anton said. *The soldiers? Who attacked the camp?*

I don't know, I don't know... she shook her head and looked vacantly at the water, as if trying to remember. *Everything went crazy. Were they fighting amongst themselves?*

*I saw a guy with a stake through him, a sharpened branch.
What the hell was that all about?*

Suddenly Vivienne got out of the water and ran up onto
the nearest rise and cupped her hands to her face and shouted at
the top of her voice, over and over again: *Leo! Leo! Leo!*

Anton ran to catch up with her and pulled her down
onto the ground and covered her mouth: *What are you doing?
Have you gone mad? Was Leo back there? Did you see Leo?
The soldiers will hear us and come after us, blame us for what
happened, are you fucking crazy, Viv?*

She rolled her head back and forth, gibbering incoherently,
moaning, then kissed Anton full on the lips and nudged into him,
increasingly passionately.

She was reaching to unbuckle his trousers when Anton
felt a bare foot kick his backside.

*Get a room for pity's sake, you dumb fuckers. Look at the
pair of you rolling around in the mud like pigs. Pull yourselves
together... and I don't mean mutual masturbation. Get up.*

Shame-faced they returned to their senses and stood up as
Claudia shook her head and eyed them ruefully. They returned to
the riverbank as Claudia addressed them like two misbehaving
children: *I don't know what the hell happened back there, but
correct me if I'm wrong... we need to go back. We have no maps,
no compass, no GPS, no food, no knives to kill food, no identity
papers... so we need to go back.*

When they retraced their steps and arrived back at
midday they found their rucksacks and equipment lying around
the clearing, their identity papers and belongings in one pile
at the centre of it, as if someone had gathered them up and
examined them. The motor launch was gone and there were
signs of a struggle, fragments of bloodstained clothing. Where
the soldiers bodies had lain they found track marks as if they had
been dragged, then the remnants of a fire, piles of black ashes

as if each body had been carefully burned with petrol, no bone fragments bigger than a penny left behind.

In the ashes of a separate fire, Anton found some fragments of a map which he retrieved and laid out carefully on the ground, then placed them next to his own charts, while Vivienne and Claudia looked on.

Here, he gestured, comparing two zones on the map, *there's the area they had cordoned off, the one we stumbled into, and here's another one, closer in, a clearing, an open plain, it's on our route back to Sylvow, or one we could take, we could skirt around the edge of it and try and find out what these guys were up to.*

Were you hurt, Viv? -Claudia was leaning close to Vivienne now, taking her in her arms, tears coming as the shock wore off. *You could sue those guys or the government, a scandal, a breakdown in discipline.*

Well, by the looks of things at least half of them are dead now, Anton reflected, *and I don't think anyone's going to be suing them. I saw their insignia, they were special forces, a black operation as they call it. I think you'll find they were all officially ghosts. As far as the government is concerned, none of this happened, probably.*

It fucking happened alright, Vivienne said, *I gave some bastard a rock on the head to prove it.*

*

When Franco got home, he embraced both the children and marvelled at the chaotic mess they had managed to make in the study. He and Imelda helped them clear it all up then they went out together to a restaurant. It was peculiar to have Imelda acting as a surrogate parent, but Vittorrio and Lucia loved the novelty of the situation. Dropping Imelda off at her house afterwards, he got out to have a word with her while the children waited in the car.

She is coming back... Mrs Reinwald... isn't she?

Franco closed his eyes. *Of course, Imelda, although I won't pretend we've not had our problems of late, but she will be back next week, hopefully refreshed and rested.*

I'm sorry, I just felt I had to ask. You know, I care about you both and the kids after these last four years.

For a moment Franco looked at her as if he had never seen her before in his life. He shook her hand then embraced her. He loved that she was small and slightly overweight, modestly even shabbily dressed and happily married. He loved that there was money involved in their relationship, but not in a seedy way. Money could be purifying and simplifying of human interaction, did anyone ever think of it that way? He loved that he and Imelda could sit and talk in a bedroom for hours without the slightest flicker of sexuality. He loved that he didn't love her.

Next day he took a long lunchbreak and took Imelda and the children out to the countryside. They sat by a lakeside and ate sandwiches, on a red and white picnic cloth spread over the ground that Vittorrio and Lucia immediately wanted to play with as a chess board. Soon they were babbling about *rook to pawn four* as they shuffled jam jars and flasks around, giggling, while Franco and Imelda watched from a short way off.

What's got into them? -Franco asked, bemused.

Chess... Imelda smiled, *it's their latest discovery, they've been playing at it all week.*

Do they know the rules? Can they actually play it? -Franco asked, impressed.

Imelda shook her head and whispered: *well, they're certainly playing something... but they're not playing chess.*

*

A day and a half later, when they reached the edge of the Inner Experimental Zone, the metallic droning had started growing louder again. At last they stumbled upon its source: at the edge of a valley, on a long outcrop of rock from which the city of Sylvow could now be seen in the distance, they found six long steel tubes each perhaps fifteen feet in diameter by sixty feet long, angled into the prevailing wind, resting on rough concrete bases.

Wind chimes... Anton muttered. *That soldier said they were wind chimes...*

Among the gravel at their feet, they found wires leading to hidden microphones, recording equipment.

This is nuts, he said. *Somebody's trying to record the wind, like it's a language or something.*

And what the devil is that? -Claudia asked, facing the other way, gazing down into a small hidden valley where white shapes formed odd patterns on the grass.

Let's go find out, Anton said.

Darkness was falling again, and a full moon rising high above them in the pale blue summer sky as their three figures sauntered down into a hundred foot long installation of animal bones, arranged over the hillside as if leading from the wind chimes down to an ancient circle of standing stones. Claudia paused and knelt and identified some of the bones: *goat fibia, horse ulna, sternum, humerus, tibia, scapula. I don't believe it, those are whale bones, and that's...no, it can't be... that's a rhinoceros skull I think. There must be over sixty different species of animal bones here from all around the planet, what are these doing here laid out like this?*

Vivienne had gone ahead and stopped short at the edge of the installation, in front of the standing stones. The others caught up with her and Claudia brushed past and knelt down before what she had found. She lifted up a grinning skull in her hands. *This is human,* she whispered, *placed here like the last in a sequence.*

How old is it? -Vivienne asked in an unsettled voice.

Difficult to say for sure, she said, *but relatively recent I think. In fact I've got the feeling I don't want to know. There's something sick about all of this. What kind of research project is this?* -she turned and looked at Anton.

It's more like art than science isn't it? In fact... it's paganism, that's what it is, isn't it? -Anton turned around and looked back up the hill and all about, rubbing the hairs on his chin. *This is some weird kind of pagan or occult ritual don't you think, but given scientific trappings?*

It makes me shiver, whatever it is... Vivienne said at last, pulling her jacket up around her neck as the evening breeze picked up. She took Anton's hand. *Let's get out of here, who knows how many hidden cameras could be recording us as extras in this creepy government freak show, let's go before we get arrested again.*

Taken prisoner, Viv. -Claudia corrected her, *-that was like no legal arrest I've ever heard of.*

The blown and woven patterns of summer evening cloud above them suddenly struck Anton as rib-like and the glowing moon itself like an emblematic skull with the texture of weather-beaten stone. Valley and sky inflected and echoed each other, recalling Jonah and the whale. Dwarfed by these obscure designs that seemed neither wholly manmade nor natural, they made their retreat back into the trees before night fell. The installations seemed like the product of some new and higher dialogue between Man and Nature, and they felt small and vulnerable next to them, like swallowed white morsels in the gut of a monster.

The air was chill and heady as red wine to their exhausted bodies glowing red in the sunset. They felt that they had glimpsed some blasphemous and unnatural communion. In contrast, the darkness that soon flowed about them was strangely comforting as they sought a bivouac for the night among the velvet pines. By moonlight, the fronds of the forest closed about them, both silken and harsh, enveloping them like the silver chainmail of an ancient army, resigned and war-hardened, armour glimmering in night.

*

Travelling as directly as possible, it took them a further two days to return to the outskirts of Sylvow. Claudia's heart was heavy that she had failed again to find any trace of her brother, but to Vivienne the journey had been cathartic. She realised she no longer dreamt of her husband Leo's return, but had even come to dread it. She hadn't entered the forest to find him so much as to find his body, to put a full-stop to this so-long-unfinished life sentence he had subjected her to, and to start a new one.

Anton called round to see her the day after their return and she had been like a coiled spring all morning, full of undirected anger and frustration with the world. She slapped him in the face, slammed the door behind him, kissed him, unbuckled his trousers, then mounted him on the hall floor. She half-hoped her staid neighbours could hear their distressed and confused moaning through the door, as if they were struggling to put out some mysterious forest fire that had broken out on their carpet.

Claudia returned to find Franco and the children watching television with Imelda taking her place on the other end of the sofa, as if balancing a see-saw. His face was uncomplicatedly happy as the children hugged her as if she were a giant redwood.

Later as they undressed for bed, Claudia found herself saying something sour and bitter that she had rehearsed for two weeks, but to her surprise she now found her voice delivered the line with a tone of warmth and compassion: *So, did your little tart throw you out then?*

Shot through like an albatross, Franco sighed and slumped down on the seat in front of the dressing table, staring at himself in three mirrors, like a triptych, front and side profiles the shards of a fragmented self. Then over his shoulders, he saw Claudia was already under the covers and smiling sadly at him. *Oh what am I to do now?* -he despaired, head in his hands.

With a light and youthful gesture, Claudia removed the nightdress she had only just put on, and jettisoned it out from under the covers with a carefree hand. She brought her knees up to her chin and the duvet cover shifted with her; its whole pattern slipping and shifting like a distorting universe.

The world hasn't ended yet, -she laughed. *Just come over here and use me, you dumb cluck...*

*

Leo collapsed on a bed of bracken, bleeding heavily from his left side. The bullet that had grazed his chest had not hit any veins or arteries, but his left leg had required a willow tourniquet and bowie knife to dislodge the bullet. He braced himself for the impact of fresh water that he had gathered from a stream to cleanse the wounds.

Franco gasped as Veronika moved her indefatigable mouth. He sagged over her freckled back, shaking at the knees and stroking her hair and ears. He was beyond care, deaf to the knocking on his door as his secretary Rosemary sought to inform him of a change to his next week's appointments. *Yes...*

he sobbed, between gritted teeth, ...*I'll be with you in just a minute.*

Leo howled like an angry bull, content that at least he would remain unheard again now for a while in his own wilderness, as the heated blade from the fire cauterised his skin and he bound clean bandage around his leg and side. He might need a splint made of tree branch, even a makeshift crutch to help him for a while, but at least he had guns and ammunition to make hunting game easier for the next few weeks. The wood smoke took the smell of blood off the wind before the wolves would wake at nightfall. Meanwhile, upstream and out of sight: a dead sheep lay in the water and the million tiny microbes that had leached from its skin now entered Leo's system.

*

Who won then? -Imelda asked, leaning in the open door of the study, impressed that the children had nearly finished tidying away all the chess pieces and soldiers without even being asked.

Surprised, Vittorrio paused and stared back at Imelda for a moment, watching the racing white clouds in the blue sky in the window over her shoulder, his eyes far away, a weather change on the way. *Oh... we did.*

Imelda's brow furrowed, puzzled.

But we might not be so lucky next time, his sister added.

~

Lenni stumbled on all fours through the long grasses, away from where the adults sat talking. When they started shouting on him, he learned that by keeping silent he could evade detection and prolong the game. Shuffling down the steep bank, he noticed the human voices fading, to be replaced by sounds of wind and silence and distances, the whispering of the wilderness.

He felt the far horizon call him, the exquisite junction of sky and land. He moved forward again on all fours like a little fox, confident and nonchalant, unafraid of anything.

High above him, a wheeling eagle spied his clothed back and was puzzled by this new rodent. Ahead of him, a she-wolf paused and hovered by a riverbank, the fragmented sounds and smells of Lenni reaching her for a moment as the wind changed. She rotated her ears, flaring her nostrils, trying to make sense of her mental pictures while the hidden child, pink among the cool green grasses, moved invisibly towards her, knees and palms beating the ground.

The grass parted and Lenni knelt at the edge of a clearing, and less than three feet away the wolf gazed back at him. Surprised and bemused, they froze and stared into each other's eyes for an eternity. The breathing of the child was slowing and relaxing now, beginning to turn into laughter. The wolf's tongue was hanging out in the heat, her eyes blinking in the sunlight. Their breathing was reaching equivalent pitch and frequency, their eyes yellow and blue, pupils dilating and focussing, both creatures taking stock of each other.

*

Anton and Vivienne had only been living together for a month, when Vivienne announced that she was expecting their first child. Anton was stunned and then quickly overjoyed, and waited for the look of panic and bewilderment to fade from Vivienne's face and be replaced with the rosy glow of maternal pride. But it never was. It was too late for a termination, the doctors had told her, she said. Then Anton felt numb and dumbstruck by an invisible wave of horror. She had discussed it with them, whoever they were, medically-trained strangers, before him, the father to be. So what was he to her then? The pet dog?

But of course they couldn't marry, she explained, since her estranged husband Leo was still technically only missing and not presumed dead, and an annulment without his consent or known whereabouts would only offend his family.

Anton felt as if this mythical man Leo was casting a long and unreasonable shadow over his own life. Part of him wanted to seek him out and find him himself in the woods and throttle or shoot him. Indeed, as an increasingly experienced woodsman now, the notion was not entirely far-fetched. But these were twisted, embittered thoughts. Soon he would be a father and would be called upon to show a more positive standard of behaviour. He would rise to the occasion, be a better man such as his only recently departed father might have been proud of.

These were troubled times, after all. There had been a spate of child disappearances that year, including famously: the mayor's own son Tarquin. Environmental terrorists had been blamed, animal rights activists, even wolves and foxes. But the explosion of new plant life in the streets, the choking of human wires and pipes by new roots and tendrils, all pointed to a stranger explanation.

After the breakdown brought on by his working long hours, Anton had sought a career in forestry, imagining it as something more peaceful and slower paced. But how could he have anticipated that forestry was about to become the most political profession on the planet?

Sylvow's eco-system was changing. Bee population and behaviour had inexplicably altered, resulting in the decline and devastation of thousands of suburban gardens, whose pretty and pointless flowers and ornamental borders the bees were steadfastly refusing to pollinate. More worrying than this unsightly inconvenience however were the signs of similar pollination failures amongst industrialised food crops like maize, tomatoes, fruit trees and field beans, one third in total of all human food being bee-dependent. The threat of widespread food shortage and collapse of the world economy were obvious. World markets, share prices, stocks and commodities, all grew twitchy while consumer confidence nose-dived.

Instead, the price of tarmac soared as the City Council found themselves called upon to patch-repair damaged roads every week. A plague of Japanese Knotweed and Rhododendron groves were splitting through the central reservations of dual carriageways with supernatural ferocity and speed. The bees and birds were being blamed for spreading and sowing the seedlings by confused scientists, but how could you reason and negotiate with a bee hive? Indeed, it was increasingly difficult to find them. Where had they retreated to?

The long-standing theory that mobile phone transmitters had been damaging bee navigation systems had been loaned bizarre credence recently by the receipt of an increasing number of unexplained calls to mobile phones which consisted of neither human nor computer voice, but of the sounds of the buzzing of a vast conglomeration of bees. Research was being undertaken, the signals traced, the hives sought out.

Anton was increasingly drawn into these expeditions, initially as a guide, but later drawing also on his architectural experience in setting up temporary encampments for scientist and soldiers recruited onto the studies.

*

This is ridiculous... -Claudia was saying as she read through her Sunday newspapers. *It says here they want people to start recording all their mystery beehive calls and sending them in to the Department Of The Environment. They've got some team of computer programmers working on a sub-routine to try and find recurring patterns and see if they can de-encrypt any messages contained within it. That's madness. It'll just be bees buzzing. What are they expecting?*

They don't communicate by sound anyway, -Franco said, standing at the window and thinking that it was somehow significant and symbolically important that their garden should have died off this summer out of all the other ones. *They communicate by dancing, the waggle-dance or something it's called, strange but true...*

Oh yes, that rings a bell, you're right. Maybe they should send the National Ballet Troupe out to perform in front of a hive, you know the Nutcracker Suite or something, see what the bees make of that.

Franco laughed. *They say a little bit of knowledge is a dangerous thing. Speaking bits of a language you don't understand can only end in tears. Reminds me of the old joke about buying a blind friend a cheese grater for his Christmas.*

Well? -Claudia asked, bemused, eyebrow raised, over her newspaper.

Most violent book he'd ever read.

The phone went and Claudia sighed, put the paper down and walked out into the hall and returned only a minute later.

The local beehive asking us to keep the noise down? -Franco asked.

No... Claudia said, eyes wide. *Vivienne went into hospital a couple of hours ago. She's just had a little boy.*

*

The baby's tiny finger was closing and opening around Anton's comparatively enormous thumb. Both he and Vivienne's faces were flushed and purged and refreshed as if some astonishingly powerful force had just swept over and through them. As though a tidal wave had just come from the horizon and swept into this hospital ward and left again by these swinging glass doors, leaving everybody wet and wide awake and crying. Their brains had been rebooted. They were parents now, magically and momentarily at one with every other motherly or fatherly creature in the universe, from mice to birds to whales. Anton could feel his own father's spirit inside him again. Maybe this was what everyone felt at such moments, whether they felt able or willing to literalise it or not. Were a

183

veritable choir of ghostly generations of ancestors sitting on their shoulders and holding forth with hymns of heavenly music at the sight of yet another new human? It was such a blinding moment of insight, lasting only a second, it was hard to dissect it. Anton saw why birds sing, why dogs run and roll in summer meadows, why dolphins play, why children giggle, why the mouth of life is forever brimming with laughter. Bird cry, baby cry, breaking wave of life and need. His father's death had only been a trough of that wave, and now he was being shown the crest. They were the same wave, one of millions in a boundless sea, and the power and progress of that sea were inexorable. Nothing could oppose or defeat it. You must simply ride the wave or be destroyed by it. But even then, broken as flotsam and jetsam, you would be riding the wave again until you became it. Yes, that was it: one day you would be dead and you would have become the wave.

*

The few flowers that hadn't been finished off by the pollination crisis seemed to be getting killed by other means. It was a depressing thing to watch. Claudia's rosebushes were being consumed by red spider mite, her hostas by slugs, her chrysanthemums by aphids, millions of them, more than any year before. The insects were on the march, tiny metallic armies acting on obscure orders, their armour glinting menacingly in the noonday sun. Where once the living room floor might have contained the occasional dead slater or two every week, now Claudia would find twenty or thirty a day, very much alive and moving in different directions at once like a commuter crowd at Grand Central Station.

The harsh and mocking call of a magpie rang out behind Claudia and she dropped her rake and turned to face the thing:

she had always found something demonic in their behaviour, as if their whole species had had orders to taunt her since childhood, and now to drive her from her own garden.

The bird looked at her then rotated slowly on its branch, as if inviting her to follow its gaze.

A group of starlings dive-bombed the neighbours rear windows, setting off their burglar alarm. They then sat back on their branches and began impersonating the alarm sound, copying it and blending it with slowed-down and pitch-bent versions, turning it into an avant-garde concerto. It was both sinister and hilarious.

The phenomenon of birds imitating car and house alarms had so far gone largely un-remarked upon in the media; apparently nobody knew what to make of it. Did these birds hope to mate with a burglar alarm? What would their offspring be? A bird you couldn't steal?

*

Everyone fawned over the baby, a few people said he bore a striking resemblance to Vivienne, but only Claudia said he looked like Anton, and he could tell by her voice she was lying. When Vivienne had said she wanted to call him Leo, Anton had seen red, as if a forest fire were taking hold behind his eyes, then he had gone to the back door for fresh air for ten minutes before he could carry on. They settled for Leonard, in honour of Bernstein and Cohen, but little Lenni's cries would soon become decreasingly musical in either of their ears.

Waking continually throughout the night, they were tested by the stress and strain of sharing the duties of ferrying food in and excrement out of their defiant little bundle. Anton loved the child but found himself transferring the force of his nocturnal frustrations and deprivations onto Vivienne, who became similarly antagonistic in return. Had they really wanted to become parents? The baby had been an accident of course, but from the very day of the news there had been some sort of tacit conspiracy between the two of them not to discuss this fact. Its implications had seemed too troublesome. But now as they struggled with the reality of being parents, it was as if this secret had become a seed of resentment between them, as if each might ultimately blame the other for what their lives had become.

Anton needed to leave to go to work, leaving Vivienne to do all the child care, meaning that when he returned at nightfall: both of them were exhausted, one resentful, the other poised to be resentful of the slightest hint of the other's resentment. Sometimes Anton would find Vivienne crying with despair in the middle of the night, regardless of whether it was she or him who was holding Lenni and rocking him to sleep, and Anton could only wonder to himself if such desperation was normal in new parents. Who could he talk to about it? There seemed such societal tribal pressure to regard childbirth as the happiest thing that could ever happen to anyone. It was hard to find the strength or daring to spoil the barrage of friendly smiles and jokes from friends and relatives and colleagues with even the tiniest of sour notes or *Maydays*, the faintest flags of disquiet that might have alerted people to their distress.

Claudia was the best bet. A strange bond now existed between the three of them. He could feel it when they were reunited, a mutual yearning and sympathy, which was probably invisible to Franco and to everyone else on the planet.

When Claudia took Lenni from Vivienne and held and soothed him it was with a supremely experienced and motherly air that at once reassured Anton then filled him with concern at the way Vivienne looked on nervously at the scene. There was something in her body language that was about reluctance and rejection, Anton found himself admitting inside the solitude of his own head.

Some whispered argument at three in the morning finally boiled over into such clumsy insinuations and Vivienne slapped his face, nearly waking him up. They both jumped as the phone rang, and Anton was bemused to discover it was just the unintelligible sound of the humming of bees.

The following day, he was almost relieved to hear that he was required to accompany the next scientific expedition into the forest in a few days time. He could have pled paternal leave but secretly thought both he and Vivienne might benefit from being apart, provided she could get some help with the baby from Claudia.

*

One of the research scientists had gone missing and Anton was enlisted to lead a search party out of the designated study area and into what had been mysteriously labelled on his government-issue map as a *Restricted Biological Transitional Zone.*

For many miles and hours, Anton led three researchers and four soldiers through ostensibly normal forest vegetation until he began to notice unexpected die-back and fatality among the trees. Some kind of air-borne disease or perhaps a poisoning of the water table might be possible causes, Anton mused, since no sign of human intervention or sabotage was evident.

Then as they walked on, the trees thinned out until they found themselves at the edge of a broad shoulder of grass and moorland. They climbed and crossed this horizon until they stood and looked down on a forest clearing perhaps two miles across: filled with a self-sown orchard of odd plant species which Anton was unable to identify.

They vaguely resembled pitcher plants, the carnivorous *Sarracenia* of the American savannah, but much larger and of stranger shape and colour. They were like swaying green vases with drooping purple tongues, taller than their heads as the members of the expedition walked tentatively between them. Looking up, they could see the snaking veins of the leaves, disturbingly alive like the human venous system, resembling anatomical diagrams of hearts and lungs. Translucent, the light filtered down through these leaves in odd hues of green and orange. Somehow, Anton sensed they had grown there very rapidly, and were growing still. Some of the soldiers touched and rattled the swollen vases, trying to peer through their skin to where some slopping sap or accumulating spores seemed to be in the latter stages of gestation. The tip of the protuberances were each tightly sealed but had the puckered and wrinkled appearance of prunes swelling in preparation for some as yet unknown purpose. One soldier joked about the resemblance to his wife's genitalia, but his mirth was silenced a few yards later when a pint of yellow acid dripped onto him from the swaying head of a vase he had struck, and he had to run to wipe the smoking residue off his hands onto the grass without showing his childlike panic to his comrades.

*

The picnic should have been a perfect idea. Claudia and Franco with their children Vittorrio and Lucia with Anton and

Vivienne and Lenni now tentatively trying to take his first steps: running but mostly crawling around at everybody's feet.

But trouble was brewing between Franco and Claudia. A sense of silence and discontinued arguments seemed to fill the air despite the beautiful setting: a wooded hill several miles to the north of Sylvow, the whole cityscape laid out down below them in the muted afternoon light after a morning of intermittent rain.

Vivienne tried to fill the air with anecdotes about Lenni until Franco finally started a new line of conversation with Anton: *Tell us, if you're allowed to that is, Anton, about these expeditions into the forest you've been involved with...*

To be honest, Anton sighed, *I don't know much more than anyone else, so it should be easy for me to not give away any government secrets since I don't know any yet.*

But the change to our plants and trees... is there some kind of virus affecting the forest, some symptom of global warming or acid rain?

Maybe all of the above plus something more, something nobody understands yet. So far, and by that I probably mean for the last several million years, our eco-system has been responding passively to external stimuli and to us, that's to say it has been re-acting.

And now?

Well nobody knows for sure yet, and I'm out of the loop in terms of the confidential findings of the top government scientists, but it's as if... Well there are certain signs that may suggest...

Even the birds seemed to have stopped singing, and Anton found everyone looking towards him, even the children, as he picked Lenni up and rocked him in his arms.

He laughed. *Well, you won't believe me, but the signs are that Nature may be becoming pro-active, dynamic in response to or in anticipation of some unknown future event.*

In plain English? -Claudia laughed, wiping chocolate from Lucia's mouth.

I get it, Franco interjected, *you're saying Nature is fighting back against us, against our pollution and over-development.*

Or... Vivienne said, *that some kind of global event like an Ice Age or a deadly virus is imminent and Nature is taking steps in preparation? Just liked Leo predicted in his letters from the forest.*

More like both of these at once, somehow, Anton said.

You mean Man is the virus, Man is the cataclysm and Nature is battening down its hatches in order to survive us? Franco mused.

No. The opposite of that, Anton answered. Everyone looked at him, puzzled.

What on earth is the opposite of that? -Claudia asked finally.

That a natural disaster is coming which, in conjunction with our burden on the planet, could extinguish all life, so Nature is going to manage the situation by removing us, or at least by promoting other life forms which will stand a much better chance of survival in the new climatic conditions that will prevail.

Destroying the human race? -Franco asked.

Why not? -Anton sighed. *It happened to the dinosaurs when a meteor hit the Yucatan peninsula, and alternative species got promoted: like the little mice they say we eventually evolved from. It was all change, and something else took over. Maybe we've had our innings now so out we go. Or maybe we'll simply be drastically reduced in number, like our wings being clipped, put back in our Pandora's Box.*

Those are hackneyed metaphors, Anton... comical even, but why do I get the feeling they stand for something very sinister?

Damned right, Anton said. *The Four Horsemen of the Apocalypse probably, failures of harvests, flooding, famine, disease, widespread displacement of populations, every disaster movie you've ever seen and a few more that haven't been made yet.*

Well, this is cheery! -Vivienne sighed, and set Lenni down to trot around among everyone's legs, chasing after Vittorrio and Lucia.

Is the world ending, Daddy? -Vittorrio asked when he came to a halt, and Franco laughed.

You took the words right out of my mind, son.

Your mouth, you mean... Claudia corrected Franco.

But can't all this be stopped, Anton? Isn't it still sheer conjecture after all. Isn't the only evidence still just some unusual plant deaths and the arrival of some weird new species that chew streets up and interfere with sewers and datacom?

Yes. But sentient plant-life, if that's what we're talking about, would be just about the most major evolutionary development on Earth in the last billion years.

Meaning?

Meaning something big has to have triggered it, and its outcome has to be...

Something even bigger?

Franco's mobile phone rang and everyone jumped. Franco made to take it out of his jacket but Vittorrio picked it up and ran off with it, pursued by his father. *Is it the bees, Daddy?* -he was laughing, *Can I answer it and talk to the bees?*

Vivienne and Anton were laughing but Claudia didn't seem amused.

Is this another sign of the End Of Days then I suppose, Anton? All these weird phonecalls everyone's been getting? -Vivienne asked him.

It's the radiation you want to worry about, Anton started to say, but simultaneously Claudia was saying with a black look in her eyes: *...some phonecalls are weirder than others.*

Vittorrio had answered the call now before Franco had caught up with him and said: *Hello Veronika, how are you? When*

191

are you coming over to the house again to play with Daddy and Lucia and me?

Claudia jumped up and ran over and punched and slapped Franco so hard that he fell over and landed on Vittorrio. Suddenly Vittorrio was crying and Lucia was screaming and chaos and confusion was breaking across the whole situation like a tsunami. Vivienne and Anton, without taking a conscious decision, found themselves running to the assistance of the children, to shield them and break up the inexplicable outbreak of violence between their parents.

Claudia had gone berserk and Vivienne almost had to grab her by the hair to restrain her. *You bastard,* she was wailing. *You filthy, dirty, two-timing shit, you said, you promised, you lied, you shitbag. How many times has that whore been at our house? Did you fuck her in our bed? You filthy piece of shit, you're a monster, you're not fit to be a father...*

When all the maelstrom of anger and lamentation had subsided, the group huddled together for a moment like the fragments of a broken vase. Then Vivienne suddenly darted her head sideways and squawked like a startled crow: *Lenni! Where's Lenni!?*

After a moment the tension snapped and the group exploded in different directions, everyone searching for the baby, running into the long grass, trying to find where he could have crawled in so short a time.

*

When Anton and the soldiers found the missing researcher, they presumed at first that he had tripped and broken his neck or been bitten by a snake, a freak accident. Only when they got closer did they realise his head was covered in drowsy bees. With the aid of smoke from a log they carefully shuffled the insects off and dragged the body clear. His eyes were closed, but his mouth, nose and ears were streaked with blood. An autopsy would later reveal that his brain tissue had been consumed or removed in its entirety through his punctured ear drums.

A day had passed since they had first traversed the field of pitcher plants and now their return route would require that they cross it again. They noticed that the plants had swollen considerably in the intervening period, some almost doubling in size, their main stems now obscene vessels resembling phalluses with bulbous testicles at their base.

Before they had crossed the field, the first of them burst open with a deafening explosion and the soldiers threw themselves to the ground, their trained reaction to gunfire. As if they were triggering each other, other plants then began exploding, a wave of activity across the enormous field. The party cowered and ran at speed, passing between the quivering stems and bursting vessels as they began to see that rainshowers of black seeds were being fired high into the sky, as if on some precise and co-ordinated trajectory.

Reaching the crest of the hill, all the eyes of the party, soldier and scientist alike, were filled with the same foreboding and confusion.

A black cloud was forming over the distant city as the last of the pitchers fired off its salvo and the million airborne seeds they had launched somehow met and coalesced then continued on their slow and menacing descent onto the streets below.

At some subconscious level, Anton found himself thinking of Agincourt and the first deadly rain of English arrows, those strange moments in history when armed conflict notches up a gear and passes onto some new and more deadly plateau. He thought of Vivienne and the baby and prayed they were indoors and sheltering from this uncanny rain.

What are they? -somebody asked, unable to suppress the revulsion in their voice. A soldier stretched out his hand until, as if in answer, a pitch-black seed with wings fell onto his palm and bounced there. It was like a strange sycamore seed or a tadpole at the moment when it first sprouts legs and takes its first steps at the muddy edge of a pond. The foul thing twitched and rotated on its host's palm in a way which suggested that although blind, it wasn't the afternoon breeze that stirred it but some obscure internal force.

The soldier tilted his hand and let the thing fall onto the ground then crushed it under his boot while the scientists held their tongues. It emitted a short high-pitched sound, and nobody was sure for a moment if it was a cry of despair or triumph, if he had killed or merely obliged it by planting it in the rich and virile earth.

*

The she-wolf had lost her cubs in the spring. She had been too weak after a hard winter, her milk too thin when the litter arrived. Two had died almost immediately, two had struggled on for a week, the fifth had been seized and eaten by a golden eagle.

Too late, she found the memory of their touch and smell enchanting her, the pang in her breasts now grown full with the progress of summer.

When the pink human child emerged unexpectedly from the long grass, the wind had been blowing in the opposite direction. Caught off-guard, the she-wolf stood transfixed and let the curious pink creature draw nearer until she saw how defenceless it was, how little threat it posed. She sniffed its back and the little creature pawed her and nuzzled her underside. For a moment her claws flexed, flinching, ready to instinctively repel the child's clumsy prodding and flee the scene. She wasn't hungry, but the child was.

To the wolf's astonishment, the child grabbed her teats and sucked on one of them, the little pink hands caressing her side. Her legs twitched in alarm, then the endorphin and dopamine flooded through her system. She sighed, felt sleepy and leant down tenderly to lick the child's head. Inhaling the strange human smells, she felt for a second the frisson of some deeper fear. Then a sudden wind blew through the grass and stripped human and wolf of all their smells and memories, and both blinked and knelt in symbiosis, relieving mutual necessity, united as servants of a larger world.

The she-wolf picked Lenni up by the back of his grow-suit, the garment bearing a fortuitous resemblance to the loose fur on the backs of her beloved cubs. The child giggled rather than screamed, enchanted by the rapid flight over the ground, the whistling grasses beneath him, the drumming of the miraculously adept paws as they pushed the fragrant earth out under them, gaining phenomenal speed.

At her burrow that night, she brought Lenni dead field mice and sparrows which he played with like toys. A week later, starved almost to death, he wouldn't be so choosy. Soon, the enzymes in his stomach would begin their short counter-evolutionary journey back to safely digesting raw meat. The vestigial cord to his appendix would re-open and eventually allow him to partially digest tree bark and grasses. Until then, there was his new mother's milk and the mysterious fraternity between all the orphaned and bereaved creatures of a God-forsaken world.

~

11.

THE WARLIKE MUSIC OF RAIN

"If there is a universal mind, must it be sane?"

-Charles Fort.

Spider! Vittorrio shrieked and his sister followed suit, as they emerged from Franco's car and saw his girlfriend's dog, a chocolate German Shepherd running to meet them.

It was the second weekend of the month, when lawyers had decreed they could stay with their father, and Veronika was on best behaviour, her recreational drugs and death-metal albums tactfully tidied away into the hall-cupboard by Franco.

There was something exquisitely uncomplicated in Spider's love and affection for the children, unlike all the trials and tribulations of their bitterly bickering and now separated parents. His big tongue licked them and he turned and gazed back with that enthusiastic look of entreatment in his eyes as the children followed him for a good chase around the garden.

Franco looked up at the sky as Veronika hovered smiling on the doorstep: *Do you think it's going to rain soon?*

God I hope not, Veronika sighed, thinking of all the mud Spider would bring into the recently tidied house, *The weather's really been from Hell this month.*

*

Of the altered states that can befall a human being, bereavement is surely the strangest, and the most dangerous. For weeks then months Vivienne's sense of time was completely suspended, her memory of what took place each day immediately clouded. Those around her who spoke to her seemed to be only voices echoing from some high brim at the edge of perception, spectators looking down at her from the ragged edges of a hole through the earth's crust she had fallen into, a freshly-dug grave. Touch became strangely important, also smell, resulting in her frequent urge to vomit and consequent rapid weight loss.

Lenni was gone. Her son, her baby, stolen from her by God knows what: wild animals, child rapists. And now Anton, her only hope of comfort, driven wild by grief and guilt, driven apart from her, had gone out into the wilderness in search of their son. A hopeless task, probably never to return, a modern-day Don Quixote, shadow-boxing with an unreasonable God. Where so many search parties had failed, what chance that Anton should ever succeed?

Through this daily fog of loss, a haze of sleeping pills and anti-depressants, the only thing of substance that seemed to emerge was the smell and touch of Claudia, her estranged husband's sister. It was with surprise, some four or five months after Lenni's loss, that her eyes seemed to open one night to find herself kissing Claudia and wondering just how long this strange short-circuit had been going on for. She noticed with surprise and detachment that every sense except sight seemed already acquainted with the idea: here was a seemingly integral part of her fractured but newly recuperating world. She found she kissed and made love to Claudia as a baby would suckle at her mother's breast. Nourishment, comfort, consolation all seemed dispensed from Claudia's body, her pouting lips, her soothing words like the clucking of doves. Claudia had become like some well of femininity from which Vivienne was trying to renew herself, to heal the invisible gaping wound in her heart where her child had been torn from her.

*

Franco stood at the window of his surgery and watched the first raindrops fall, strangely black and gelatinous he thought, as if the pollution of the city was finally at saturation point and coming out of solution. He had ten minutes free before his next patient, and increasingly he found himself grasping these moments to try to analyse himself and make sense of where his life had currently taken him to.

Temptation, devils, demons and angels: these were antiquated concepts of a former generation to Franco. He had seen enough chimpanzee documentaries to know that the urge that had attracted him to a younger woman was simple anthropology, the passing on of genes to the healthiest host. But it disturbed him to think that his free will might have been overthrown by pheromones and hormones. The concept of duty had its underpinning with love: what he felt for his children and would go on feeling. Then why was his affair necessarily a threat to those bonds? Franco's knowledge of the myriad societies and species on Earth told him that multiple wives and shared child-rearing were probably more common models than the strict Christian monogamy he had been brought up to believe in, but such knowledge was useless. He knew that his and every other society's shared value-system constituted an all-encompassing *mythos*, and that to step outside it would always render you instantly a lunatic or outcast.

He moved away from the window and rubbed his chin. He had recently shaved off his psychiatrist's goatee beard in deference to Veronika's wishes, so that he could "hang-out" with her "young crowd". He hoped hair-dyeing wouldn't be next. He winced. Was Nature using him like a puppet, when he and Veronika made love? They seemed like sporadic attacks from an unseen virus, leaving them thrashing against each other as though putting out a fire, wailing in distress, fatally wounded.

It was hellish but also heaven sometimes, it had to be what Nature wanted. But where did all that leave him? The intellectual, rational side of his mind was appalled at its loss of a foothold in the previously crystal-clear moral landscape of his life. He was lost, cast adrift. He was having an affair, he had abandoned his wife and nearly his children, demolished the moral constructs of his parents and grandparents. Where once he had stood on the top of the white alpine peaks of his imagination in his suit and tie, in conversation with Nietzsche and Freud and Jung, filled with lofty concepts, now it was as if he stood alone in exactly the same place, but with his trousers at his ankles, weak at the knees, exhilarated, red-faced and frightened, while a red-haired child knelt in front of him and sucked the life out of him. He felt heart-sick to think that where once he had gazed upon the truth of the world, now he closed his eyes and trembled at how that truth might look back at him.

The Warlike Music of Rain

*

Claudia didn't need Franco to tell her the psychological implications of what was going on between her and Vivienne. Since their separation, the children spent every second weekend it seemed at Franco's, and the confusion and instability this brought into Claudia's life was like a gaping puncture through which security and peace-of-mind were leaking daily like a trail of gasoline. Her position as a mother seemed strangely vulnerable suddenly, under threat, and Vivienne comforted her in her new independence. The children were getting older, adolescence beckoned, Claudia was worried. How would they orientate their moral compasses when they came to realise their father was an adulterer who had cheated on their mother? And as for their mother... well now.

Claudia turned away from her own reflection in the night window, leaving the million lights of Sylvow to pulse and vibrate beyond the curtain of mournful rain. The children were off to bed. She sat down with Vivienne and they embraced then began kissing. She unbuttoned Vivienne's shirt and kissed her breasts. Sometimes she caught sight of herself in the window's reflection: Vivienne's naked back with her own hands pressed passionately around her. Was what they were doing wrong or unnatural? The hallway from the children's rooms was long enough for any advancing footsteps to be heard, they could remain discreet. Sin was a concept her Roman Catholic mother would have brought to her attention were she still alive. Was she answering Franco's sin of cheating on her, with this new, more dazzling sin of her own? Two blacks to make a white. Old-fashioned talk. Who was to say what was natural or unnatural? If an urge was in one's nature, was it not natural by definition?

Franco was useless to her now, and maybe all men tainted with the ineffectual weakness he represented, their tedious need to endlessly conquer and dominate and penetrate. Such children. Vivienne and she were equals, supremely alike without conflict of roles and status. And as such, there seemed an illicit charge of excitement to their every caress. She never wanted to be bored or sober or subordinated again. When Vivienne came, her cheeks flushed, her eyelids closed, she was like some marble statue, an ancient goddess melting like ice in her hands, sublime and otherworldly: a force of nature summoned by a lightning strike. Scintillating transgression; a deer brought down in a forest with an arrow through her side.

Compared to this, what had every night with Franco ever amounted to? Hair and sweat and gritting teeth, the putter and spatter of that sordid juice of theirs, like little boys wetting the bed. Every man was just a child in the world, demanding and reprimanding, demonstrating and remonstrating. Empty rhetoric.

*

Sky's been looking weird recently.... Sighed Doctor Nikolaus Saltiere, catching a glimpse out of the window before bringing two glasses down to the table to sit with his old friend from medical school. He hadn't seen Franco Reinwald in six years and, despite the occasional email and letter, now felt uncomfortably distanced from the man sitting in front of him. He seemed to remember Franco as something close to a tee-totaller even in his youth, but here he was now knocking back large whiskies with a shaking hand, as if he really needed it.

What's up Frank?

What? -Franco asked, brow furrowing above his glasses.

You look in a bit of a state old man. Reminds me of our college days actually, not at all like the sober stable patrician I thought you'd become in the intervening years. Has something happened?

I've separated from Claudia, he said, just spitting it out, then broke into a cough a moment later as if the power of the whisky had just hit him like a delayed ricochet.

Jesus... Nick exhaled, producing a white pressed hankie from his immaculate blazer lapel and leaning forward to give it to Franco to mop his face and the table, then was alarmed to see him do this in the opposite order.

What happened? Nick asked, clutching the table for stability, as if by transference he too was starting to feel at sea.

Another woman... Franco muttered quietly.

You mean Claudia's a lesbian? -he asked astonished, his eyes wide.

No, you clot! Franco nearly shouted then checked himself, then both he and Nick unexpectedly started giggling inappropriately, some weird release of tension defusing the air between them.

I... have taken up with another woman. Living with her now. Jesus, Nick, is that harder to believe than Claudia being a closet gay? Give me a break!

I'm sorry Frank.

God... they both laughed again. *Am I that stiff? Is that how you saw me for all these years?*

Frank, it was just a silly... you know.

Back to the old days... I see it now. You always had more luck with the female of the species. You always thought you were so superior to me, so socially adept.

Frank, I don't mind being insulted by you, not at a time like this at least, but would you rather I left now?

Shut up and sit down, Nick. You'd leave me here alone to finish my drink? Let's stay and talk, can't I talk to you?

About women and affairs?

I'm not remotely proud of what's happened.

Didn't say you were. What about your kids Frank, can't remember their names, how old are they now?

Six and eight, Nick. Lucia and Vittorrio. They're fine I think, they're with their mother right now. Our lawyers are going to sort something out, I should be able to see them half the time hopefully, at weekends maybe.

How's Claudia taking it?

Could be worse. Terrible at first of course. Unimaginable, actually. Look, has anything like this ever happened to you Nick?

Nick let out a long sigh and leaned back in his chair, looking around at the other pub-goers, younger City-types mostly. *That's a big... personal question, Frank, after all this time, but no. Contrary to what you might think from knowing me back then, give or take a few discreet indiscretions and so forth which never came to anything or never came to light, I have been more or less faithful to my wife. Were you caught out, Frank? Caught in the act?*

Not flagrante delicto for Christ's sake, Nick, not that bad, but bad enough, a phonecall intercepted, my son repeating something to his mother...

The mobile phone is a classic one, Frank, but your son?! That sounds unsavoury.

Never mind, Nick. It wasn't anything like as bad as you're thinking, let's just drop that please...

What do you want from me, Frank? What do you want me to say?

I thought you'd understand. I thought you might have been through something similar...

You thought I was a two-timing bastard?

Nick, please.

The sick thing is, I'm impressed Frank.
*You shouldn't be. Shit. You shouldn't be. How ironic is
this. Now I'm here telling you, old Nikolaus Knickers-down
about what it's like to be a womaniser....*

They both looked out the window of the bar in
embarrassment for a few moments, watching all the legs of the
passers-by, so many skirts and trousers, the humdrum absurdity
of it all, before their eyes returned and locked again, bloodshot,
antagonistic, awkward.

Go on then... -was all Nick could think to say
eventually.

*You only think it's clever and funny if you've never done it,
Nick. Adultery is something that happens to people. It begins with
pheromones and hormones, an embrace or a handshake. Touch
and smell. You think people like us are minds and intellects don't
you? Educated people? Well, the bad news is we're not, Nick.
We're governed by chemicals, chemicals that tell us when to be
hungry, when to sleep, and who to copulate with. A kiss or a hug
is all it takes to start the slide, a half-decent conversation thrown
in and you're really lost. And you know the worst thing?*

Franco was starting to sound demented, and Nick shifted
in his seat, becoming uncomfortable.

*No. That's a Hollywood cliché. There is no worst thing,
just lots of bad things and maybe a few good things. Want the
good things first, Nick? The three good things? First the sex
obviously...*

Please, Frank...

*Two, there's how bloody easy it is. Human beings are
hardwired to believe what they want to believe. You think people
want truth? They don't, they want security, like children do. If a
woman really wants to believe that her marriage is happy and
secure and her partner isn't cheating on her, then all the other
information, all the clues to the contrary can be swept out of the*

corner of her eye with the flick of a wrist, her wrist. **Elision**... *might be the right word for it. When the truth of a situation is just too monstrous to contemplate, people blank it. We are machines for keeping going, not machines for mapping every landscape we walk through. This is what Goebbels meant by the big lie: make people choose between truths and they always take the easier truth that changes their current life least. It's possibly the single most dangerous things about human societies.*

Three, and here's the surprise: it makes you realise what you've got and to enjoy that too. You don't go off your wife and become so racked by guilt you can't lay a hand on her, not at all. The contrast actually makes you appreciate both women more, and your kids. There, bet you've never seen that in a book or film before, have you? You begin to have two lives at once, and both are better, more exciting than the one you had before. The danger of being caught makes you hyper-aware, ultra-awake, and every experience becomes more charged and poignant as a result. There's guilt, sure, but not the real big bad guilt, because here's the rub: you only feel that when you get caught out later. In the meantime it's a kind of bitter-sweet semi-guilt, it kisses as it bites, to paraphrase Nietzsche. So here's the scary insight Nick, because maybe this doesn't just apply to adultery but to every other human sin or misdemeanour, however you want to label it: it only becomes fully real when we are found out. Maybe this is why there can be rapists and serial killers in the world and the rest of us can be so puzzled by their actions: their deeds are real to us, but at some level they remain unreal to them. This is why previous generations to us invented Gods and angels to sit on our shoulders and watch our every move: because they knew, they'd worked it out, they'd observed it; that for most people a sin is not a sin without a witness to a sin.

But what about integrity, Frank? Moral standards. I'm not religious, but I think I have a code of noble behaviour that I adhere to...

*Do you Nick? Are you sure? Because if it's just what
everyone else is doing how can you be sure it is always morally
correct? The citizens of Nazi Germany who handed Jews over
to the authorities believed they were being model citizens, they
were comfortable in the mythos of the society that surrounded
them. Imagine if you were a car mechanic and feeding your wife
and kids depended on how many cars came into your garage for
repairs and services and you saw there was a recession coming
and your money was running low. Would you be a good or a
bad person if in order to feed your kids you started repairing
those cars just a little bit less effectively, calculating that your
customers would have to return a little more frequently and make
you more money? Now imagine if you heard that all the other car
mechanics were doing likewise, that it was tacitly accepted as
normal? Now remember you are a psychiatrist, and ask yourself
what might happen if all your patients were suddenly cured.*

Very clever, Frank, but I...

*What I'm saying Nick is that the sordid little arrangement
that had evolved between Veronika and me and Claudia only
became sordid the moment we were discovered. Then came the
cataclysm. The whole world rips in two and falls over. You know,
like the natural disasters you see on television that always happen
to someone else on some other part of the planet: earthquake or
tidal wave, a societal breakdown where one week people are
dining in sushi restaurants and driving jeeps and the next they're
stealing tinned food and eating the neighbour's dog.*

Frank, are you going out of your mind...?

*What I mean, Nick, is that the whole façade comes
tumbling down. A person you've lived side by side with for
fifteen or twenty years suddenly becomes like a total stranger,
an enigma, an unreasonable mystery. You realise you hardly
knew each other at all. That's the real bombshell, and then the
trapdoor opens up in the ground between you and you realise
you've been living on the edge of a cliff. And I'm not just talking*

about me and Claudia here, Nick, I'm talking about everyone. We skate along a thin veneer of ice most of the time, a currency of courtesy and decency, but it's wafer-thin and, if and when you stumble down through it, you find we're just savage little chimps, lips twisted, nostrils flared, screaming and wailing at each other hysterically. You think you're still in love Nick, or in a marriage at least, in a family, but I've got bad news for you: you're in a dream. Just pray you never wake up, or you'll find the dream becomes a nightmare.

You're in a mess Frank. That's one thing I know for sure, I can see it.

Just fallen through a hole in your fragile reality, that's all, Nick. Don't look down.

Are you done yet?

Probably not. I haven't really covered the sad things yet. Like the loss of innocence, no, worse than that: watching innocence play in the sunlight the day before you destroy it. The happy look in your wife's eyes about some affectionate gesture you've just made while she's blissfully unaware how inside your head she has lost you already, the game is over and she's lost. God must feel that when he watches us every day, the bastard. There is nothing sadder than the innocence before tragedy, but there is one thing sadder than guilt: the absence of guilt and how that vacancy take us closer to the vacancy of God. Nick are you understanding any of this?

Go on.

The sad things. Like how from your partner's point of view you would be better dead. If you die, your partner gets to own you forever and idolise you and turn you into lots of useful things you weren't. You become a household appliance of sorts: an all-purpose projectable-onto foldaway Godhead, to be taken out at all sorts of moments to inspire yourself or your children. But if you're still alive… oh God help you. Damn, that's inconvenient. News of anything and everything positive that might be happening to you becomes a slight, an indictment, a remotely-controlled insult to your cruelly abandoned partner.

Each man kills the thing he loves.

Oscar Wilde.

You still love Claudia then?

Yes of course! And there's another very commonplace misunderstanding. It is perfectly possible for a man to love two women, maybe three women, maybe ten, how the Hell would I know? Love doesn't switch off or switch allegiance on a whim. It's like a searchlight, it catches everything that crosses into its path. We spread it across all our children and relatives don't we, it's the glue that holds families together, but families used to be much bigger and looser when we lived in caves. Maybe it's all this modern bricks and mortar that's the problem. Look at wolves and apes and all the other complex social systems in Nature and in other human societies in tribal culture: multiple wives, shared child-rearing. The nuclear family is just our own little modern project, which fills Nursing Homes and Orphanages with all our debris while we persist in hammering a square hole into a round peg.

Frank, aren't you just trying to justify having had an affair and having been caught out? You're sounding like a free-love sixties hippie…

No. I knew what I was doing and I accept responsibility. I was a deceitful shit. But at least I'm living with Veronika now. I've had the courage of my convictions.

How old is she? -Nick asked.

Franco paused. *Twenty-two.*

Jesus! Nick sprayed his drink all over his shirt and table and this time Franco had to produce his immaculate white handkerchief and offer it to him.

By the time his vision cleared, Nick was amazed to see a vivacious slim red-head in black tights and mini-skirt enter the bar and swing down to sit beside Franco and stick her tongue in his ear.

He rubbed his eyes as if he was hallucinating, and Veronika turned to look at him, fixing him with her harsh green feline eyes, flashing and hard as dazzling emeralds. *Hey daddy-o, who's the dork with the drink problem?* -she exhaled in a smooth dark voice like velvet.

My friend, Roni. This is my old friend Nick from my student days, we go back a long way as they say. Nick, this is Veronika.

Hey Nick, she purred, throwing her head back and offering her hand, *D'you fancy a threesome?*

Franco bared his immaculate white teeth in a sudden smile Nick didn't remember ever seeing before during their friendship, as his eyes widened in alarm. *Joke, Nick, joke...* Franco sighed.

Veronika sucked on her straw and turned to Franco, *-Big boy just took a hard-on, Franky Wanky...*

You're not her type, Nick..., Franco laughed as Nick stood up and excused himself in a flurry of embarrassment.

Try telling his cock that... Veronika sniffed, gazing absent-mindedly after him.

Roni, you are terrible, the poor guy's so embarrassed.

Made his week more like, Frank, his month, his year, his life. Be jerking off for a fortnight.... She sighed in a bored, spoiled tone.

Honestly... Franco smiled sadly and pawed the wet table with his thumb.

What, hun?

Humanity's not ready for you yet, he said, squinting at her like a dazzling enigma.

*

Hey check out the old dude! -tittered one of Veronika's friends, eyes narrowing as he passed a spliff to his best mate and changed the music over.

Veronika led Franco through the thumping darkness of the party. Stepping over the darkened forms on the floor like a scene from the London Blitz or Dante's Inferno: surveying the souls of the damned in Hades. Franco wondered what neighbours, short of deaf-blind mutes, could put up with such a maelstrom.

The mixture of Czech beer and Russian vodka was already making Franco's head swim when Veronika tried to pop some suspicious-looking pills into his bottle. He felt as if the pulsing, deafening music was somehow fusing with the darkness, hitting him with waves of sonic intoxication that washed and blasted the room, distorting his features like G force, flattening his skull back against the hard wall where they now sat on the carpet.

Franco had been at parties when he was a medical student, some of them wild, but he didn't remember anything like this. The couple sitting a few metres away from them were kissing while the girl moved her hand around down the front of her own trousers. Franco shook himself and realised he would have been less shocked had the hand been in her boyfriend's trousers. His eyes popped and he dimly remembered to correct himself and try not to stare. There was something weirdly different about all this and he wondered, mostly in fear, if he hadn't stumbled in on the prologue to an orgy. He looked back at Veronika and saw she was fellating a vodka bottle, until he rolled his eyes and they dissolved in laughter.

Franco noticed with a further double-take that the walls of the apartment were covered in expensive-looking black damask wallpaper, a pattern like Victoriana leaves, and that old-fashioned oil portraits in elaborate frames hung everywhere with the creepy alteration that every face had had its eyes painted out with black or silver paint.

Dragged onto the floor, someone stripped off his shirt. He thought it was Veronika at first, then was vaguely perturbed to see the hand caressing his neatly toned pectorals was covered in rings and tattoos he didn't recognise.

Old dude! -some young bucks were toasting him from a clapped-out sofa, bottles raised in salutation, cheesy mocking grins from ear to ear, like they were sitting in the driver's cab of a passing lorry. He looked closer and saw the sofa really was the front seat of a lorry, some kind of avant-garde design classic. *Check out the old dude with bleached hair and contact lenses! He's got a body like a porn star!*

Turning around in a daze, Franco found Veronika disengaging from a French kiss with a butch lesbian, not necessarily in jest. Franco wasn't sure whether to be relieved that it wasn't another man. *Hey wank shot!* -Veronika meowed back at the sofa dudes, -*He shagged your mum and she was shite. I was there. I made the dog watch.*

My mum doesn't have a dog! -One of them laughed back, not entirely good-naturedly.

Veronika leaned over him and stubbed her cigarette out on the wall behind his ear; *I'd say one had her the night she made you, judging by your looks... and your breath.*

His jaw dropped, while his friend fell over laughing, -*She's dynamite, man... femme fatale with stiletto patter!*

Mickey Mouse has a watch with your face on it... -she drawled before she turned away.

Trying to find their coats on the way out, Franco stumbled into a bedroom in which someone was violently taking their partially-clad girlfriend from behind, kneeling on the bed, his hand in her hair. Franco winced, and then tried to retrieve his jacket from under them anyway. With a start, he realised the girl was actually male. He paused and wavered in the hall as he re-emerged, looked at Veronika's laughing face for a moment as she smiled through a miasma of Lebanese smoke, then lunged into the bathroom to throw up.

*

Veronika's fellow party guests had mocked Franco to an extent he scarcely understood. He was thick-skinned and used to being seen as stiff and boring in the eyes of the young. But the scene had enraged Veronika. Next morning she slapped him hard and put *Spider* out so she could embark on a further campaign of violence.

You fucking wooss. Why did you take shit off them? You're so fucking soft, why don't you ever do anything hard or violent or... manly... Hit me !

What ?!

Hit me Franco. Slap me about. Throw me across the kitchen sink and fuck me up the arse for Christ's sake. Be a man. No, don't be a man, be a wild animal, be a demon, a devil for God's sake !

She punched him in the guts then kicked his knees until he crumpled over then dragged him across the floor and took his belt off and tied it around his neck to lead him like a dog.

*

Three minutes before the black rain fell, the telephone in Vivienne's hall began ringing. It was Anton, and when the answer machine kicked in he spoke onto the tape in an urgent voice, that rose steadily towards alarm: *Viv, it's me, I've tried your mobile but it's off. Wherever you are, get inside. Some kind of weird rain is about to fall on the city. I'm twenty miles outside the outskirts and we've just seen it moving in over you. Viv... get indoors! If you're with Claudia tell her the same, tell her to get the kids inside. Get out of this rain, Viv, save yourself. There's something really bad about this, I mean it, I mean this is the end starting, Viv...this is the end of the fucking world. Get indoors.*

Vivienne didn't hear the details of the message until she played it back later. At that exact moment, she was moaning softly on her back in bed, her hands playing through the curls of Claudia's hair as she let her take her slowly closer to climax, her legs trembling. Claudia clutched Vivienne tighter as if she were writhing to escape her grasp, enflamed by her fragrant musk which filled her senses. Vivienne came in a hot wave of guilt and confusion as the skylight overhead exploded, showering glass on both of them.

As they screamed and leapt up they saw that in between and over each of the glass fragments: hundreds of black tadpole-like seeds bounced and squeaked and writhed, some exploding and sending hissing tendrils out to scrape at the surrounding carpet and bedsheets.

Pulling on her dressing gown, Claudia dashed along her hallway, pulling open the French doors to look down to the courtyard below where she saw Vittorrio and Lucia were caught out in the rain, crying in a doorway, pressed back against the glass, looking down in terror at the bouncing, dancing seeds at their feet. She could see that some of them had succeeded in breaking through cracks and joints in the paviors and were taking root and growing in accelerated animation like timelapse photography. Panicking, Claudia pulled up one of the windows and shouted to the children below: *Stay where you are! Don't move until the rain stops!*

What the hell is it? -Vivienne asked, getting her breath back, running from the bedroom.

I don't know, it's like some kind of alien rain....aghhh! -Claudia screamed as a black seed pod impacted on her arm and then a second one landed and made a puncture and began trying to burrow into her flesh. Vivienne pulled her back inside as she screamed hysterically, and punched the thing off Claudia's arm with a newspaper, blood spurting in a little jet, then crushing it repeatedly underfoot.

Downstairs Vivienne took control of the situation, driven on by the grotesque spectacle of the children beating helplessly against the glass. *Turn around and cover your eyes...* she shouted, then smashed the glass panes with an ashtray, turned the handles and brought the children back in.

Kneeling there, still almost naked, holding both children in her arms, tears of relief filled her eyes. Her own sense of loss for her own son ebbed and healed just a little as she gazed in forlorn hatred at the bouncing and hissing seeds beyond the shattered doorways.

*

When the black rain began falling, Franco had Veronika over the kitchen worktop with her head pressed up against the glass. It would be hard to say later if it was one final thrust or the fall of the seed bombs that shattered the window. But the net effect was Veronika's flame-red hair and screaming face smashing through the glass and out onto the stone sill as the black seeds bounced everywhere around her shoulders and her sexual exultation transmuted instantly into uncomplicated horror.

Franco had to restrain Veronika from going outside, as her dog howled and writhed as it was punctured by a hundred black bat-like stamens. As they watched from the door, darkish green shoots and stems hissed and spread out rapidly from within their still-living host, and by the time the rain ended a grove of something like giant hogweed had taken root from the twitching corpse: but with leaves the texture of brown-bruised leather, reeking of necrotic tissue, and drawing buzzing flies. Beneath their densely tangled roots, now only a spread-eagled collage of dismembered bones, sinew and fur lay about in disarray, where only a few minutes beforehand a living animal had played and barked.

~

12.

FIRST DAYS OF THE DOG REBELLION

New and unexpected seed-bombs were falling from the sky daily. Some of them would rupture the pavements and replace whole streets with tangled groves of trees within weeks. White blossoming penumbras, gossamer wings: these showers of parachutes in the sky overhead soon became as common a sight as snow or aeroplanes had been once, before global warming and the fuel crisis had done for both. The city was being slowly invaded, reclaimed by the forest which surrounded it, and all but the dumbest of observers could see that humanity was on the ropes.

Foremost among these dumb observers were the dogs, Man's so-called best friend – but maybe the dogs weren't so dumb after all. They had started biting and scratching their masters, trashing their owner's homes, escaping regularly into the forests and parks. They knew the score well enough: that their two-legged friends were past their sell-by date and becoming a liability.

But for most people as ever, life was just about keeping on keeping on. The third human blind-spot of *timeblanking*, as defined by the errant woodsman-philosopher Leo Vestra, ensured that a few seed-bombs landing on your street today were easily disassociated from the concept of a complete societal breakdown tomorrow. Nonetheless, the gradual accumulation of thousands of these events, unchecked, would irrevocably lead to this bleak outcome. It was only a matter of time.

Claudia had read Leo's intermittent letters from the surrounding forest for the last ten years, she had even posted some of them off to the local newspapers. The letters had predicted these calamities in detail, and yet she had been powerless to stop them. Perhaps it was under the emotional pressure of worrying about her errant brother that her own marriage had failed and now she found herself living with Leo's estranged wife, for mutual commiseration. Incestuous though this arrangement nearly was, Claudia finally felt in love. Maybe she had always been secretly attracted to Vivienne.

On the weekends when the children went to stay with Franco and *His Tart*, as Claudia charitably referred to her, Claudia could at least cosy up with Vivienne in front of the fire, although it was no longer a gas one of course, due to a string of bad results in the last round of Presidential Oil Wars.

Tough times can get you to thinking of happier days. One of Claudia's earliest memories was of playing on the beach with her dog *Midas*. Loving the animal had been her first and hardest lesson, as for many children, that to love a thing was to risk the pain of losing it, especially since the damned things lived so short a time. Somehow, despite becoming a vet, she had never thought to seek a replacement for Midas, perhaps because she saw so many animals every day at work. But now her children were begging for a pet, some confused story about The Tart's dog having met an untimely end, and the solution was obvious.

If there turned out to be anything untoward about the animal's behaviour then at least she was well-qualified to diagnose it.

So many poor pooches passed through her hands on a daily basis, it would have to be a rescue dog. Claudia took along Vivienne and headed out on her day off to the local cat and dog home and asked to be shown the most forlorn and desperate specimens.

There were the usual embedded collars, heartworm invalids and mange veterans, all of which Claudia knew how to treat, within reason. But this time she spotted something that intrigued her: two West Highland Terriers with curious scars on their sides and extensive hair loss.

What happened to these guys? -Claudia asked the keepers while Vivienne reached her hand through the bars to stroke and console them.

Nobody seems to know... came the surly and disinterested answer, *...Maybe some head case on a sink estate took his bad crack day out on them with a Stanley knife.*

I don't think so... Vivienne said, rolling one of them over and examining its stomach, *check this out. I'd say a surgeon did this or a space alien, is this an abductee dog or something?*

On both dog's stomachs, hidden among the bedraggled hair like a little cattle brand, was the caption **K10**, formed in tiny sutures flecked with blood.

*

Vittorrio and Lucia were immediately delighted with their new furry friends and their new favourite game, chasing the dogs around the sofa, would hopefully surpass any form of entertainment imaginable at Franco and Veronika's. But another peculiarity soon emerged, after the dogs had been groomed and vaccinated and a few days recovery gone by: they were entirely silent. They would look at each other and open their muzzles and gesture as if barking or whining, but not a single audible sound would ever emerge.

It was bizarre certainly, but it was far from inconvenient. How could the neighbours complain about two new hyperactive dogs when, apart from the drumming of their tiny paws on the polished wooden floorboards, they were without aural imprint, indeed who could even guess they were there?

*

The dogs are talking to each other, it's obvious... Lucia was saying. Her brother and her had been listening to their little high-pitched voices for the last half hour they claimed, and Claudia was sceptical. She followed them back to their room and sat down for ten minutes, feeling like a fool, while she and her children watched the two silent terriers opening and closing their muzzles to make supposedly audible sounds which Lucia earnestly translated for her as: *Where did our mother go? Someone took her away and I want to find her. Do you think the Uprights ate her? I don't trust any of them. At least they're not White Coat Uprights. The White Coats always make us sleepy and make us watch pictures and put the bad lightning through us again...*

*

Claudia found herself telling Vivienne about this a few days later, after they had made love. Vivienne threw her head back and laughed like a drain, sitting up cross-legged on the bed, her long blonde locks falling over her breasts. She struggled to hold her hands steady enough to light herself a cigarette, shaking with mirth. *Jesus... you're serious though, aren't you?* She exhaled a long cloud of smoke, her eyes going far away.

Well, the children are certainly serious... that's what concerns me, I suppose.

You know what? -Vivienne said, becoming animated again, *...maybe they're telling the truth. Haven't you heard that there are certain high-pitched notes that only children and teenagers can hear? Didn't some guy patent a device on that principle a few years back, so shopkeepers could have this terrible siren going on outside their shop to scare off the hoodies while the rest of us would walk by oblivious? When I was a kid, we used to make the neighbour's dog open and close its mouth using the TV remote control, they can hear all sorts of sounds we can't, so why not?*

*

Meanwhile, Claudia's request for information about the branding on her dog's stomachs, posted on her Veterinarian web forum had brought in a mysterious reply:

>>*Project K10 reference. I found this on Google. Be very careful, Dr Reinwald, -Benson.*

>>Hello. Mister (?) Benson. What do you know (if anything) about K10? I'm just trying to get any useful knowledge I can about the health and history of my dogs. -Dr C. Reinwald.

>>*Hi. Suggest you stop using this term, I mean the K word. I'm not the only one monitoring the web for references like this. Can we continue this by direct email? Benson@wannabone. com*

>>Hi again. I repeat what do you know about "K"? Tell me something useful if you want me to shut up. -Claudia.

>>*K is big, still ongoing. Classified and dangerous to stumble on, even by accident. Governmental, Military. Back out and stay low. Keep off the airwaves with this. The Suits will kill you. Not an idle threat.*

>>Who are The Suits? Are you with them?

>>*I will escape their clutches soon. But they will always hunt me down.*

>>This could be bullshit. Tell me something useful and I'll meet you and help you out. Promise.

>>*Nobody can help me. If you meet me you'll understand. They messed me up real good. Broke my legs and reset them the wrong way. Sick fuckers. You want something? X-ray your dogs. The plates will show alloy tags hidden inside their large intestines: you should be able to read the serial numbers on them; they will begin CRBRS then four random digits. You'll also see a small shadow on their esophagus/ larynx. Magnify it and you'll see it's a microchip and amplifier. Don't try to remove any of these devices, or even with your surgical skills the dogs will die.*

>>Jesus Christ. The plates came back an hour ago. They're here on my desk in front of me right now. You have my full attention now, Benson. Who the hell are you and what do you want? What's this about?

>>*Meet me.*

*

Claudia took along Vivienne for moral, not to say physical support. Her pepper spray and occasional classes in Karate might prove useful if *Benson* turned out to be a slavering perv with a hard-on and a switchblade.

They waited at dusk by the old wrought-iron gates of a decaying park on the poorer side of town. The district had been a well-to-do area once, all high ceilings and ornate plasterwork, carved Art Nouveau maidens holding up flowery door pediments but now dilapidation was everywhere. Poor Slavic and Arabic immigrants had taken over, fragments of strange music and cooking smells wafted from broken windows, discarded mattresses and rotting garbage lay in the streets. Buildings cracked and leaned like arthritic old men on sticks, the smell of broken gas mains hung in the air. Streetlamps flickered intermittently, throwing a clouded sort of light, yellowed and dust-choked, fraught with age and uncertainty. Weeds were patiently starting to make their way through every crack in the pavements.

Vivienne ran her hands over the beautiful curving finials of the old railings, flakes of paint coming off on her hands. *Do you really think he'll show?* -she asked, looking up, then her eyes followed through to a distant figure over Claudia's shoulder.

Keeping to the shadowy side of the cobbled street, a tall thin figure in a long raincoat, baggy trousers and broad-rimmed hat was making his way towards them. Vivienne's hand tightened over her pepper spray. *Make sure your mobile's on I don't like the look of this guy...* -she whispered.

He reached the pavement on the opposite side of the road from them then hung back in the shadows, face tantalisingly obscured, avoiding a pool of light from a streetlamp that creaked and swung in the night breeze overhead.

I said come alone... -the voice emerged from under the hat, a low whispering rasp like an invalid, with something whining and whimpering about it, insidious.

You're Benson, right? It's ok, this is Viv. She's my girlfriend. She's cool, don't worry about her. One of us, all the way, you can trust her.

Benson hovered apprehensively for a moment, then moved forward: *Let's go into the park for a walk. Trust me. It's safe, no one goes there anymore, and we'll be out of reach of the CCTV cameras. Everywhere is watched these days you know. The damned suits are scouring every corner for me. Maybe it's good there's two of you. You have the advantage so you don't have to be scared. Just trust me and we'll go into the park...*

Who are you, Benson? -Vivienne asked nervously, as they followed him cautiously, noticing at close quarters the strange way he walked, as if floating on skates or stilts.

I'll show you, -he said cryptically, -*when the moon clears those clouds. Do you have your dogs with you?*

Contralto and Soprano we call them. They're in the car, a block away. -Claudia said.

Ah Good... Benson sighed longingly, -*I'd like to talk to them again... I'm sure they'll remember me.*

*

When Claudia and Vivienne had got over the shock of Benson's deformities, they persuaded him to come back to Vivienne's apartment where they could give him some food and medical attention. He was extremely thin and tired, having been on the run for a week. All the way back he played with the dogs in the back seat of Claudia's jeep, rolling and tumbling around and growling with them, then silently flicking their muzzles as if using a secret language together.

Why did they do this to you? -Claudia asked, running Benson a bath and tending to his many cuts and bruises where he had scaled the barbed wire fence of a military compound.

There is no why... -He sighed, *Human beings love experiments, scientists particularly, they're like a dog with a ball. They got me as a baby. Stole me from God knows where, or grew me in a test-tube. Maybe I'm only one of a thousand. You have no idea of the cruelty perpetrated against defenceless captives every day by every government on this earth. They injected me with hormones, broke my bones, messed with my vocal chords, wired me up to a computer keyboard and made me do tricks all day, gave me electric shocks if I answered any questions wrong. Endless psychotic challenges like they were training me to be some kind of super-soldier some day.*

How did you finally escape? -Vivienne asked, stroking the short hairs on Benson's head, and bringing him another bowl of food.

I bit the hand that fed me of course... he grinned slyly, *... then the throat that gave me orders...* he added darkly.

*

Benson slept like a log until noon the next day and, without having to beg, was treated to most of the contents of Vivienne's fridge, predominately the cold meat. He was on a high protein diet now to recover his muscle tone and continue his escape plan.

But where will you go? -Claudia asked. *You can't keep running forever. You've told us something, but we need some more facts. Get us some evidence and we can take your story to the papers, get people to believe us and start to fight back against the forces behind this. Tell us how to help you...*

Benson knew he could never venture out in broad daylight. So he and Claudia and Vivienne sat under her skylight windows in the attic all afternoon and watched the summer clouds racing by like white rabbits. They folded out maps of the city and marked over them with red lines and pins the locations of governmental research compounds where Benson said both humans and animals were regularly tortured and experimented on in the name of anti-terrorist legislation, in detention without trial.

From time to time, his nails would bleed and Vivienne would bandage them. He eventually demonstrated, to the ladies' horror and amazement, how he could retract and extend them at will and how he had lost one of them that had snagged on the security fencing.

Here's the deal, Benson said at last, thumping his bandaged paw on the map in conclusion as the sun started going down at last: -*You infiltrate these compounds with television crews in tow while I get to a safe house and lie low until the heat blows over.*

What an impressive string of clichés... -Vivienne marvelled. *Did they teach you to talk like that in Military Bastard School, make you watch Sly Stallone movies?*

That was the only punishment worse than the water torture, I seem to remember. Look, tonight I want you guys to do me a favour. Let's the three of us head across town and do something very special that I've been planning for a very long time and now at last, with your assistance, I've got a chance of following it through...

*

Claudia's government-assigned petrol ration for a month was nearly used up, so they decided to leg it.

The walk across town was an eye-opener for everyone. The seed-bombs were falling again from a bruised-purple sky turning red where the sun was washing its hands of the whole affair. Everyone had surgical masks on in the street, since close proximity to a seed impact at pavement level could seriously infect the lungs. The symptoms could be neutralised if medical treatment was sought quickly, but otherwise the body would become a living host for weeds within forty-eight hours. Occasionally one would pass a vagrant oblivious to the warnings, whose twitching body was bursting forth with flowers and leaves as his blood turned to green sap and chlorophyll, his toes and fingers taking root through tarmac.

The facemasks were fortuitous in the respect that they helped conceal Benson's handsome snout. Together with a long raincoat and hat underneath which he could pin back his long sensitive ears, his disguise was complete, especially after nightfall.

Wait! -Benson exclaimed as they turned into an empty street.

What? -Claudia asked. *The place is deserted, ...what's the problem?*

Benson took off his mask and let his nostrils twitch and inhale for a whole minute before he turned to them and explained: *it might be an empty street to you, but in the realm of scent I can see back in time, the street is alive to me with ghostly images of every animal, human or otherwise that has crossed it for the last four days, subject to rainfall of course.*

Look... -he said, and they ventured forward a little, -*in this doorway an old man was attacked and robbed yesterday, I can smell the sweat and blood, teenagers did it, they smell different, fresher: contrary to what you might think. And here I smell oil and tyre rubber, a police van an hour later, taking the old man away. He has cancer by the way, he just doesn't know it yet, I can smell that a mile off. The assailants jumped over that wall, it's plain as day, but the police didn't even look over there for fingerprints because, like you, they are blind, trapped within their own timeframe and their own bodies, entombed within their own smells.*

Wow... Vivienne marvelled, -*and we thought you just brought us our slippers.*

And I haven't even told you about the nice things yet. Flowers and children and ice cream, kisses and near-misses. Have you any idea, Benson said, tears appearing in around the red rims of his big sad eyes, *...how alive every street of your city is to me, to us? How brimming with life, with stories and possibilities? The realm of scent... you walk over it daily as if it doesn't exist. But I see through time and walls and clothes, I taste all of life's sweet and bitter flavours, and when I die, this dies with me. It's not that you won't miss it that kills me, it's that you've never wondered or thought to ask. What a noble tower of knowledge Man has built, but his ignorance throws a longer shadow...*

But Benson wasn't all ethereal philosophy, he had a decidedly earthy side. Claudia and Vivienne fretted nervously as he stopped at lampposts to sniff near their bases, then parted from them with a surreptitious raising of his leg and a deft blast of urine aimed out from beneath his raincoat.

But more alarming still was his encounter with a Golden Retriever bitch whom he circled, sniffed repeatedly showing a morbid interest in her anus, then knelt down behind in a darkened alleyway to penetrate from behind.

Oh, that's gross! -Vivienne hissed, burying her face in Claudia's shoulder. *Can't he refrain from that?*

He's just doing what comes naturally, Viv... -Claudia exclaimed, but they saw to their surprise that he was done already and the bitch was sauntering off as if nothing had happened.

Not even a look over her shoulder... -Vivienne gasped, *-don't you even want to take her phone number?*

Ahh... that's a very human joke, Benson growled, resuming his stroll casually, *...canines are more matter of fact about such things. A bitch goes on heat and everyone wants to fuck her, big deal. Think of Kylie Minogue or Keira Knightley. Difference is with dogs, anyone and everyone gets a shot. Looks like I'm the only male not locked up in his kennel tonight, that's all. No need to rip some rivals ear off with my teeth. She's not even interested in how witty my chit chat is or whether my clothes are fashionable. I suppose I should thank you guys for taking me walkies...*

No need, -Vivienne interjected, *...just thank us by telling the next one you've got a headache.*

But self-discipline wasn't his strong suit. By the time they had reached the City Zoo, Benson had fucked two Yorkshire Terriers, three Collies, a Pit-Bull Cross and a Labradoodle. Every dog has his day.

Aren't you worried about conceiving with those dogs, Benson, starting something unnatural? -Vivienne asked, half in disgust, half laughing.

Not at all, -he barked, *quite the reverse, -this could be the start of something big, don't you think? The animals of this earth need a spokesman, someone to stand up for them, and I won't be around forever...*

*

I've always wanted to do this... -Benson was saying, as the last of the zookeepers and night security staff went limp in his paws as Claudia withdrew the hypodermic needle.

Enough to knock out an adult gorilla for 2 hours, boy is he going to have a hangover, -Claudia whispered.

To set all my brother creatures free, what a gesture... Benson said exultantly, *-most of them will get run over of course, but the point will have been made.*

No one's going to run over the elephants, that's for sure... Claudia said.

And Benson... -Vivienne said as they took the keys towards the first of the cages, *-absolutely no fucking anything, got it? Not even the hyenas.*

*

Later that night as she dressed for bed, little Lucia could have sworn she saw the kindly and bewildered face of a giraffe peering into her second floor window, its big eyes blinking in the confusion of newfound freedom, looking for a road sign to the

Serengeti plains. She didn't bother to tell her mother about it in case she didn't believe her.

*

Claudia was careful to drop the children off at Franco's herself in the morning, and apart from the sight of a few penguins on a pedestrian crossing, some vultures perched outside a butcher's shop and a near-miss with a charging rhino on the dual-carriageway, the trip back over to Vivienne's place was plain sailing.

Claudia arrived to find Vivienne and Benson sitting watching television together, Benson in Leo's borrowed blue bathrobe with a glass of Dry Martini in one hand. They were laughing their heads off together at all the talking dog characters that seemed to crop up in children's television: suddenly it was the biggest joke in the world.

Feeling slightly excluded, Claudia offered to pop out to the corner shop for some more milk for their morning coffee, but half way down the stairs she realised she had left her purse and handbag behind and turned around.

Claudia walked back in the door to find that Benson had thrown off his bath robe like a prize-boxer and mounted an inexplicably naked Vivienne, right there on the couch, his long pink tongue hanging over her damp face. Apart from concern for the cotton weave cushion covers, there was the thought of injury, infection and possible cross-contamination between species. It was also a betrayal, somehow worse than her enjoying sex with a man again. Who was guilty, had Vivienne been cajoled? Raped? The red in her cheeks, the alarmed expression, and her heels wrapped around Benson's thrusting thighs between which his stumpy tail twitched like a metronome, all seemed to point to an unsavoury answer.

You bitch! -Claudia spat, and both accomplices' faces turned towards her and replied in curious unison, melody and growl:

You wish...

~

There will be a meteor but it will miss. But the gravitational force it exerts will weaken the earth's crust and trigger earthquakes and volcanoes whose ash will overcast the atmosphere and eventually produce global crop failure. This might have been survivable had it not been for the man-made build-up of carbon emissions and the centralising and industrialising of farming and trade which renders vast populations incapable of self-sufficiency. The infrastructure goes, everything goes. The gulf-stream shuts down and a mini ice-age is triggered. It's all survivable, but not by the kind of digital-idiot populace we have propagated. They can't tie their shoelaces, never mind skin a rabbit. Game over.

*

Sylvow

It was with a heavy heart that Anton stumbled at last upon the body of Leo Vestra. He had wandered, searching through the forest for three years now in search of his missing child, his beloved Lenni. How could he ever return to Vivienne without him, without even a body or a trace, even a tragic scrap of clothing? If the search was fruitless then he might as well stay in the woods until he died, his life was over, his relationship with Vivienne as dead and lost as the child itself.

Their little Lenni. He still longed to hear his laughing cries. They echoed in his head; he didn't want the memory to fade. But in the course of this despairing search he had descended gradually into something resembling a hobo, a tinker, a wild animal: more hunted than hunter. He had come to resemble Leo in fact, Vivienne's long lost husband, whose body he stood over now like an image of his own death.

The coincidence, the symmetry, the cruelly confusing irony of it made his head hurt. He sat down and wept by Leo's side, eventually lifting the cloth of his jacket to reveal the bones underneath. Emotion overtook any sense of revulsion and he turned the corpse over, bones rattling, the grinning skull looking up at the sky again, at the world it had lost. Anton wept for Leo, this man whom he had never met or known alive but whom he had heard so much about, too much about, in whose shadow he had lived throughout every fraught moment, every painful and fleeting instant of his time with the beautiful and unreasonable Vivienne.

As with every death, as with Anton's own father's death, Anton could see that he was weeping for himself now, as perhaps everyone does at such times, a wordless despair to see what a losing end of a bargain Fate has imposed upon each of us.

He noticed some paper folded inside a chest pocket in Leo's shirt and, after his tears had dried and his head cleared,

238

he reached out and carefully prised the parchment out into the daylight and began reading it, it was like some kind of poem in a mixture of English and Latin and invented words:

Orbis. Luna. Mooncold, forestfrond licked, frettframe sylva. Glimpsed from rhuba crimson heartspace spiritgreen of freshspace immerse. Nocturna. Orbis. Luna. Ocularis. Eternum. Salve suave Materna. Here in forestheart the arteries womblike of her enclosure occlusion mindcloud crowd my cerebrum. Nocturna. Ocularis. Mindthought I am river run of earthblood tonguewild sacra become. Verdum sacra Eterna Luna. Towards the lacuna, this driftwood dispersum particulate stardust sawdust nightfrost of child memory versum sacra cerebrum versa verde. Freasdal. The crinkled leaves of old come gold aura auriculum imperium luna mundi nocturna eternum dorma. My tongue unlicked of all language sings as angel trumpets tearing night. Nocturna violatum, blaze of goldnotes as fingertrace across the velvet dark. Oh stolen jewel of godword absence in the beautitude of loss. Thanata sacrum nocturna dorma vita Deus finitum. Content to wait. Cantata, Staccato. Endura. Multifoliate resplendence of a trillion eyelids closed. Dormus domus figura. The beauty of the sleeping face, trusting, pallid. Pallindromic. Pandora. Child of no one, how we await your kiss of absence. The pure frostcold lifeblood of the blue skyflow far below the world's heart. Shed language clothes and Venus rise Aurora. Resplenda Eterna Solaris. Make tongue of speechneed tasting from the waveday waking utter unknow. Salve. Suave. Fine. Begin.

After the poem, Anton found something apparently more intelligible folded up behind it, an unfinished letter to Claudia perhaps, and began reading it. To his surprise, he found as he read that it seemed to refer to the future, describing it as if it had already happened:

> *To find me, you have to become me. Well done then, welcome stranger to my wilderness, the tangled forest of my heart. It doesn't matter what brought you here, the roots and paths of your own particular journey, the intricacies of your story. In the end, all human longing is the same longing, all love the same love, all despair only cured by this same self-imposed exile. Here is the bridge across the pit of Hell, by which you can only pass blindfold and in love, that is to say a condition of complete hopelessness and trust in the unknowable. It doesn't matter whether you feel up to this challenge. If you don't choose it, it will choose you anyhow. Sit, stranger, and weep. You are a dead man now too.* **Quod per sortem sternit fortem, mecum omnes plangite...** *Let us mourn together for fate crushes the brave.*
>
> *Your world had blinded me. In the wilderness, the silence entered into me, slowly, over many years, and eventually I began to see again. The noise of modern urban life is like a wall of static, a force-field scrambling human neurotransmitters. Although you all move in close-proximity, you have each become incredibly alone, closed-off from each other and the world.*
>
> *Out here nobody is alone. The boundaries of the human soul and mind melt quickly away and we become part of something vast and benign. It is like a glimpse of the bliss of death, but granted to us while*

we remain alive. It fills you up, it joins itself to your essence, you become one. A man is never less alone than out here in this deepest most sacred wilderness.

I stayed still for so very long, I watched the tiniest movements of clouds and leaves, for days on end. Something gave way. Time altered. I watched tendrils and roots climbing over my feet and hands, flowers rotating, clouds racing across the sky, moons dip and rise like waterwheels. The cycle of life accelerated, the wheel broke free. I unanchored myself from time.

I climbed to a clearing on the highest hill in the forest and watched the city in the distance. Clouds and dayscapes, fugitive flickers of borrowed light, brief flashes of fires like streetlamps, sparkling diadems of flowing water. The rain of days washing the dreams of men away. Crinkle curl of autumn half-light, bonfires and ashes. The rain came again, cold and grey from a far-off place. Different rain, blended with ash, a volcano venting Nature's spleen at the world's underside. The poison, slow-sweeping in the sky makes its way to here. The rain and ash fell and all crops failed. The waters rose. Glitter of silver like a beautiful shoal of fish. From the far horizon I saw the ocean rise suddenly to all but envelop the city. Distant boats like upended beetles, humanity insect-like, scattered and confounded, a flooded ant-hill. The fingers of water even spread out to here, the forest split into wooded islands as the waters advanced for years and other cities drowned. Humanity perished like insects in numbers beyond counting.

Just as the waters began to withdraw, the sparkle of frost gleamed. Fate's treacherous knife poised to thrust again. I watched the waters freeze and rivers become glaciers. Now there were no more jets in the clouds, no laughter or babble from the distant town. Only crows filled the sky, laughing about fresh carrion. Men had no new gimmickry to save them this time. I saw a few black shapes, little flies among the frozen ruins, I saw their world was medieval again now, reduced to horse and cart, sledges and log fires.

After years this Winter ended. Long after hope had ended, fresh sunlight shone again like a revelation. Spring came as never before, a Spring of the whole planet and new birds brought news of it to me with their song, twittering in my ears, rousing me at last, realigning me with my own time stream, taking me back to the human and everyday.

I roused myself and stood up at last. The city beckoned on the horizon, thawing and new-born in the unexpected Spring. My limbs took weeks to move, they were trunks and roots of trees now, ancient and resilient, slow but strong. I had to cut the bark off them, long hard scabs fissured as dry river beds, my flesh white and sap-sweet underneath. I set out towards Sylvow, resolved to go home. I walked and walked without rest. The motion and rhythm became habitual. I still felt static in a way, tree-like, as if I had merely learned to make the Earth rotate under me, like a child's feet on a football.

I reached the outskirts and I saw that many streets were canals now. I saw that groves of strange new species of trees had colonised avenues and alleyways everywhere. Sub-tropical roots and branches of huge diameter were reaching up out of the mud and water and digging themselves into buildings, passing through windows and doors and cracks and fissures. Some of these swollen plants resembled human body parts. I saw trees that looked liked enormous human hands rising out of floodwater and grasping and penetrating tenement facades. Other trees and thickets resembles dissected hearts and lungs and bones, their tendrils and roots swollen to red and blue as if mimicking veins and arteries, conveying strange liquids in and out of buildings.

I increasingly failed to understand what I saw. These roots and veins seemed to be pulsing with water and fire when I drew close to them, translucent: were they carrying blood or chlorophyll or both? It was as if all of Nature had re-booted and re-evaluated itself, as if human and natural inventions had been merged and subsumed into some new order.

On the few spare pieces of muddy land or timber jetties I saw feral children in rags, their faces blackened, some of their ears pointed, their backs covered with red fox fur.

I moved closer. Through open doorways I saw women being made love to by dogs. I saw birds the size of men crouching on street corners like policemen as destitute humans filed by in chains, the weak and the old, picking at the fallen.

In a clearing in an oak grove I saw a curious new plant like a swollen phallus, pale green, blue and pink, spitting sticky spores from its head, this spray carrying on the wind like some perverse mixture of candyfloss and semen. Closer to, I could dimly see through its translucent skin the partially digested corpses of stray dogs, rabbits, newborn babies. A yellow tendril with a red-tipped barb shot out from its head while I stood there and began thrashing about blindly as if looking for me by detecting my heat or scent, before I moved away quickly.

I looked up and a fluttering butterfly was trying to land on my head. I crouched beneath it and saw that its body was that of a naked woman, blending out into fantastical patterns of black and red fur and feathers where her head and feet and arms should have been.

I tried to fight, but this strange chimera landed on my face and wrapped itself around me, wings folded and encasing my nose and mouth until I suffocated. Its musky smells, sexual scent, anaesthetised me.

I opened my eyes and it was as if I wore a visor now, a diver's helmet. I walked forward into the reeds and under the muddy water. On the far bank, some upright dog-guards, Bullmastiffs and Rottweilers, were pacing around and angrily gesticulating towards me, toting guns.

I walked beneath the waves and moved effortlessly into the buried ruins of the old city. I walked down drowned streets and saw the places I had known and played in and loved. Here what were city parks were now overgrown with sea urchins and anemones and coral and seaweed blowing in underwater breezes. I found the house of my parents just as sharks swam out of the shattered windows, tangling themselves in the washing line and the local swingpark.

I found my wife's house, my old house, and I walked inside. Everything was as we'd left it, but floating around, up and down, bouncing off walls: cushions, table lamps, magazines, books with pages like flapping wings. Something was keeping everything in motion, demented: as if I were inside a paperweight that had just been turned upside down, shaken by an unseen hand.

My visor became unstable, the butterfly separated from my head but I found that the camouflage pattern of eyes on its back were my eyes now as it flapped off into the gloomy water and made to leave by the living room window.

With the eyes of the butterfly I turned to see the lost figure of my human self, grey and forlorn, standing helpless and trapped inside the house he had once abandoned, as we flapped away. His silent scream became a trail of bubbles that issued slowly from the drowned chimney pot as we flapped higher and higher, further away, as we headed back to the surface.

The darkened waters were like a forgotten memory of some nostalgic summer night. I saw the street patterns, the many rows and avenues and groves and parks of drowned trees, now stripped skeletons of impotently grasping branches.

I thought I saw the moon above us in the night, then I saw it was the sun pulsing through the murky waters. We swam towards it and emerged into fresh air again, the bright daylight on the ramshackle shanty town, the colony of the survivors.

*

Trees are everywhere. The waters are receding daily. I see at last that the forest has come to Sylvow and embraced it. The people live among the trees again. I was a worm once, a thing of the earth, slow and blind. But now I am a butterfly. Within the enormous span of earthly time, I can live but a day, a second.

I perch on a church spire, emerging only twenty feet above the displaced earth: all that is left of a great cathedral whose bells still toll perhaps a hundred feet below, buried in slime and tendrils. I fancy I can hear or feel them, pulsing in my quivering body like a lonely heartbeat, the lost tick of time: in cold storage until the creaking lid of God's eye flicks open again, rusting and sore, and civilisation resumes.

When the waters recede, the ruined and disfigured land below will resemble the wrinkled skin on the face of an old man, each ruined building a broken tooth. When this face is finally revealed in entirety, will it show a smile or a frown I wonder? A grimace of age and endurance or just a scream of indescribable pain?

For now, I flutter down onto the street's end in the blazing light of late afternoon. Sunset is on the way, then the sky and I shall compete for colourfulness. Six feet tall, I unfold my beautiful wings to reveal my body like a revelation. Perfect fusion of fur and flesh, my feline scent perfumes the air like honeysuckle. Pink and black striped, woman and insect, half and half. I unfurl myself, strategically placed at my town's end, and wait for the dogs to come sniff me.

~

14.

Dear Vivienne,

Is beauty good? Genetic advertising, beauty is Nature's incitement to procreation, but is has no moral component, at least not one open to Human understanding. New life must be created by any means. If beauty incites two men to fight to the death over a woman, or one to murder the other in his sleep in cold blood, then Nature has been served and is content. Only in the human world is there regret and anguish at the outcome.

If one species threatens the planet's survival, then the elimination of that species by any means, to Nature is good. No matter if Humanity took a few million years to develop, Gaia has plenty of time on her hands.

Gaia is blind, patient, amoral, selfish, all-powerful, savage, beautiful, resourceful, resilient. If this is a God, it is no human God, not one that it is safe for human beings to worship. Make ourselves too closely in her image and we become monsters, tyrants. But humans have a strange need to worship. Finding we could not safely worship Gaia, we chose to construct some other idols we could worship in her place. Maybe we should have forgotten about all idols, forgotten the need to worship. Maybe we should have stuck with Gaia, but forgotten the worship, swapped the worship for study and a wary respect.

The scientific mind is bound to question the relevance of such theological musings, but isn't that a product of their compartmentalised thinking? As well as being the high-priests of our technological age, scientists should work on being sociologists and historians and politicians too, if they want to be any less useless in the end, in the face of change, than the Archbishop of Canterbury. The question of what Gods to worship, for Humanity, will always be the question of what roles to aspire to. What archetypes to promote in a society. Put like that, the question isn't irrelevant at all.

In the twenty first century, our Gods stand all but demolished for most people in the west, there is no consensus on Gods. Thus there is no consensus on how to live, what to live for, even ultimately how we should each live from one moment to the next. This meaning of God is merely a signifier of an arbitrary but necessary moral code. We can and should reconstruct this God if we like, so long as we recognise it as arbitrary, as our necessary code to prevent rape, murder and war. Has any world religion achieved this aim yet anyhow, or has each eventually been hijacked in the furtherance of precisely these sordid outcomes: rape, murder and war, under some spurious and despoiled moral banner?

It is as if Mankind's true nature, violent and vile of course as any other creature on earth, will always come out in the end, and no matter how we try to suppress it, or perhaps precisely because we do, it will come out even more forcefully and dangerously in the end. Our invented Gods have all been made by us to help us with this problem. But they are of no avail. And never will be until we admit they are made up and stop parading them as universal truth.

But there is another God. Just because we couldn't look her in the eye doesn't mean she stopped existing. And run away as we might, over countless millennia in the desperate garb of various civilisations, in the end we will always have to stand and face that God again, and see that she is red in tooth and claw and does not share our human morality.

So maybe we might finally start finding the answers if we for the first time start phrasing the right questions and here is the main one: how to embrace the cosmic disconnect, how to resolve the contradictory challenge of how Humanity can best contrive to be moral in an amoral universe.

-Love, Leo.

*

The first tinge of frost bit into the edges of the leaves, autumn was in the air. Vivienne Vestra's garden had grown so out of control, so unruly since she lost her husband, lover and child that now perhaps nothing could retrieve it: it was Nature's domain. How the tendrils and creepers leapt and grasped, clutched at windows, unsettling, blind: as if trying to turn door handles and lift window latches. What an artwork they made, she thought, staring out into their midst as darkness fell, the endless folds of their tangles like Celtic knotwork, embellishing, worshipping, enshrining, enclosing her battered but still beating heart.

She almost never left the confines of her house and garden now. Too much out there in the world just reminded her of Leo and Anton and Lenni, the men, boys and babies that she had lost, that she had made the mistake of loving, of allowing into her garden, as it were. So never again. Now she would be impregnable.

It wasn't as if she was truly alone. Often she would sit outside on the patio or stroll along her pathways between the bushes and trees and gaze at the myriad armies of beetles and ants and spiders. Their tiny wars, the innumerable casualties, the violence, *Nature red in tooth and claw* as Tennyson had put it, was astounding.

She was simply the mute observer, or perhaps the inscrutable goddess, who got to preside over all this carnage. Mata Hari, Helen of Troy, she would do nothing to save the magpie eaten by foxes, the mouse disembowelled by a neighbour's cat, the wounded badger torn apart by seagulls. No, she would carefully and quietly just watch it all, take some photographs at the crime scene, maybe turn it into a disturbing oil painting later for her dealer in London.

The first trap she set was an accident. A wire to train climbing pea plants over, which a careless nocturnal fox managed to slowly strangulate itself in, taking hours to die.

With the constantly rising crime rate and increased incidents of civil disorder, Vivienne had invested in serious perimeter fencing, CCTV, Passive Infra-Red Sensors, Motion Detectors and Burglar Alarms. Her world was closed and complete now, if not completely happy. Fate or Nature had wronged her entirely without provocation, a meaningless and nihilistic assault on her contentment, not once but at least three times, and now there seemed something therapeutic in any unexpected act of cruelty she could contrive to call her own. It was as if an atrocity in the present might cancel out those of the past, and bring about a divine balance. The worst part of everything done against her had been the helplessness and lack of control and so now, conversely, control was scintillating to her.

So she began rearing rabbits in the garden shed, only so as to have them dissected by cheese wire at sudden and unexpected moments, as her complicated traps exploded and sent firecrackers and streamers up into the air.

She trapped some ravens in birdcages once then released them later with twine around their feet leading to a bound and gagged squirrel, and sat back to marvel at the spectacle of them all learning how to rise into the air together and dismember their mute ballast by flying in opposing directions.

The many recent unexplained changes in plant life across the country had also given rise to new possibilities for cruelty. The exotic species like Venus Flytrap and Pitcher Plants, the razor-sharp grasses and cacti, she put to good use for impaling and slowly dissolving in plant acid the various rodents and birds she could ensnare with bait and twine.

Despite all this entertainment, Vivienne, like most lonely people pushing middle-age, was increasingly reliant on the television as the social centre of her life, the other partner in her marriage.

The outside world ironically, or at least as reported, seemed even more violent and freakish than Vivienne's garden.

The summer rains of seed-bombs had finally stopped, but now more than fifty percent of the city's streets were choked and overgrown with Japanese Knotweed and Giant Hogweed, bamboo groves, Rhododendrons and several other new unknown species evolving too rapidly to have even been named or catalogued.

Public infrastructure was at breaking point as tarmac gave way to undergrowth too quickly for the Local Authority Roads Division to carry out repairs: who, like most Council employees, reacted in their usual helpful way to a public crisis by going on strike and demanding more holidays and pensions.

When the seed-bombs stopped falling, the rain had started. And rarely stopped. Global sea-levels had been steadily rising for years, bringing about widespread failure of third-world crops. Hyperinflation and unemployment had gradually followed from this, in the developed economies as much as anywhere else, increasing inequality and urban deprivation. Civil disorder was certainly at hand.

Many residential areas all across the nation were now either underwater or so regularly flooded as to be uninsurable, peopled by a new kind of white-trash developed-world boat people who seemed to thrive on hard drugs, tattoos and new age religion.

On top of all this, a super-volcano in Indonesia had been steadily puffing away, filling the atmosphere with so much ash that the sun's rays would soon be cut by fifty percent and crops fail in the chill, but still adding to greenhouse gases. A sort of gloomy global-warming-holiday, of little use to anybody.

On top of on top of all this, quite literally, the increased rain and thunderstorms had unexpectedly given rise to heightened levels of electrical activity in the upper atmosphere resulting in massive lightning strikes of a novel variety: their ultra-violet and electromagnetic content was thought to be so intense that they were causing epileptic fits in animals and children. Warnings of these *Gamma Flashes* and *Critical Shifts* were now being regularly broadcast in the streets to encourage people to seek shelter indoors throughout their duration.

All this exciting and unpredictable news Vivienne gathered nightly from her television. She hated when society made up new words, obviously and specifically as a means to try to make older people feel confused and ashamed that they weren't keeping up with things, out of touch with the current parlance. Nonetheless, unlike most other people, she was excited about the prospect of the *Gammas Flashes*, since she hoped she might be able to make use of them to eviscerate sparrows and fry ant colonies.

This happiness of sorts continued for a while until the façade of her self-sufficiency was brought down one day by one inconvenient mishap; the plumbing to her hot water cylinder in the attic stopped working.

*

Vivienne didn't like the plumber's tone on the phone, and his eventual physical manifestation on her doorstep did little to revise her opinion. Something was subtly impolite and obtrusive about his body language, the way he followed her to the kitchen when she grudgingly offered to make him a cup of tea, then stood there eyeing her in her dressing gown as if she were a sad specimen who needed more than her plumbing sorted out. She could even have sworn she saw an erection rising in his jeans, and the thought of some greasy sausage lurking there with her name on it, like a remnant from his full fried English, made her want to go over to the sink and retch.

She reckoned she could see the seed of the thought in his mind, and part of her almost wished for a moment that he would try to rape her. While she was still seriously fit, she could see he was a pathetic physical specimen, more fat than muscle, and the thought of the shocked expression on his face as she broke his arm with a half-nelson or crushed his testicles in her fist made a twisted smile break across her face. Men were truly pitiful and she sometimes wondered how they could be the same species as her, indeed how they could ever have built cities and machines between having to tug themselves off twenty times a day to drain their feverish little snot sacks.

He tried to maintain a conversation as she herded him up the stairs and practically threw him into the cupboard to start his work, saying something about all the flood waters rising and how his job wasn't what it used to be, spending more of his time trying to get water out of buildings than back into it.

I really couldn't give a shit, Vivienne said at last, *I live on a hill.*

The plumber looked at her wide-eyed, wondering if this was a poetic metaphor. *Wasn't a hill that saved Noah...* he began to say as he turned to look at the cupboard then jumped out of his skin: *Jesus Christ. What the Hell is that?*

Japanese Knotweed or something I suppose. I lose track. One of those new exotic and invasive non-native species they keep blabbing about on the News.

He wasn't so shocked that he couldn't fit in a long peek down Vivienne's cleavage. She thought of his hideous tapeworm turning around in his jeans again, looking for somewhere novel to unburden itself of its white vomit.

What's it doing there? He asked, and she looked up again, returning relievedly from the world of trousers.

What?

The knotweed thing? How'd it get in there?

Dunno. Must have been a hole in the eaves or the cavity wall head. It's come in from the garden and made itself at home obviously.

Didn't you notice it? Do something to catch it before it got this far?

I hardly ever come up here... Vivienne sighed.

The plumber shook his head and got his saw and chisel out. *You rich people, I don't know... more rooms than sense.*

As if this wasn't enough, he hit her with his final leering insult as she made her way down the stairs: *Is there a Mister Vestra?*

Vivienne lit a cigarette, then shouted up to him: *He's in the fridge in bits... his balls are in the ice box.*

She heard a thump which she imagined was him raising his head too quickly and hitting the roof joists, and smiled to herself in satisfaction.

*

She watched the television that afternoon and it became uncharacteristically original, highly entertaining. The rising water levels had rendered entire neighbourhoods homeless, who were now rioting and fighting with the police, the army was being called in. It made for quite an enjoyable movie, when you allowed yourself to forget that this was your city and your world that were going down the Swannee. At least it wasn't boring. Better than that, for Vivienne at least, was the sight of so much confusion and suffering in the eyes of thousands of strangers. She wanted the cameras to zoom in, she wanted still photographs she could keep on her walls to enjoy later. There it was, that look. The pain and suffering that life had contrived to give her, dealt out to someone else for a change. That was the most striking thing about human suffering when you stopped and really analysed it:

that look of surprise and indignation on someone's face when a bullet went through their stomach or their wife had just been crushed under an armoured vehicle. The look, that look said: *What? Can this be me? Surely not? Isn't there justice and divine order in this world? Is it just chaos or worse? Does God actually hate me?* The answer was amazingly obvious when you looked at the world, even at the murder and mayhem in your own back garden, and yet it was always equally amazing how little this news had spread yet, at any given moment in human affairs.

When the Council Parliament got fire-bombed and some of the clerks fell blazing from the broken windows to the streets below, Vivienne thought she heard a shout from the plumber upstairs but decided to just let herself ignore it. The lazy slob probably just expected another cup of tea, or a spanner brought to him, or a hand job, and the wait would do him good.

When the army finally got things under control by teatime by shooting twenty protestors dead on sight, Vivienne was about to cook dinner when there was a gamma flash from the horizon followed by a few more.

She switched the television back on, curious to see what effect this might have had on the riots, which side might have benefited from the confusion and the need to take cover. Then she remembered that the flashes always took the transmitters down for half an hour. Another two flashes crossed the sky, and she turned her back as the safety warnings recommended, then pulled the curtains.

Upstairs she opened the cupboard to find the plumber's ill-fitting jeans and backside cocked up in the air and his head entangled and garrotted by tendrils and stems and branches. In detached fascination she knelt and leaned forward to catch a glimpse of his contorted face beneath the leaves, as if he were Caesar with his laurel wreath or Christ enduring his crown of thorns. His eyes were tightly closed, but she could make out a vague pulse in his neck and feel the lightest of breaths escaping his nostrils. There was another gamma flash and she jumped in fright: instantly the tendrils rotated and gripped and crunched, breaking his neck by the sound of it, his trapped hands and feet twitching in some sort of death-throes.

Feeling a leaf brush her own back, Vivienne recoiled in disgust and stepped out and backwards into the attic, surveying the weird scene in its entirety.

A final gamma flash split the sky and Vivienne watched in awe as the complex pattern of tendril and branch now twisted and convulsed and drew the plumber in yet further, digesting his head through some unseen lacuna at the centre of its root system, contorting the rest of his body into radial segments. His training shoes fell off with a comical but mournful little sound, leaving the silence in the room somehow bruised and guilty.

Vivienne sighed and went to call the police, but of course found all the lines busy. She gave up and went and got a yoghurt from the fridge and sat down to enjoy the resumed civil emergency coverage.

The entertainment had died down disappointingly quickly. State of Emergency, massive army presence on the streets, splitting of the municipality into several separate administrative zones. Bread queues, food-relief drops by helicopter, safe-drinking water points set up to prevent the spread of cholera and typhoid. Shoot-to-kill policy for looters.

With her binoculars from upstairs, Vivienne could just about catch sight of the edge of some of this in the distance, many blocks away, but the T.V. was best and allowed for digital quality playback.

She went up and opened the cupboard door again and was relieved to see the plumber was scarcely recognisable anymore. Even the really tell-tale bits like fingers and toes were browning fast and could soon be mistaken for nuts or tubers or some other root protuberances. Soon nobody would know she had a dead plumber in her cupboard. There wasn't even any smell. This new plant technology was fiendishly efficient and non-wasteful. All that banging-on about recycling... Vivienne thought to herself. She wondered if the Council knew there was such a green and clean method of recycling human beings: surely the biggest ecological hazards in history.

*

Vivienne slept soundly the next few nights, safe with her high-tech security system, her electrified perimeter fencing. She expected the plant upstairs to have just finished digesting the plumber and returned to normal. She forgot about it until she heard a strange thumping sound around midday. Her stomach lurched for a moment as the irrational thought assailed her that the plumber might somehow have come back to life and she would find him up there looking at her with half-dead green eyes, asking in a hoarse voice for a cup of hot *Baby-Bio*.

She went upstairs and was astounded by the sight that met her. All the vegetation in the cupboard had continued twisting and digesting and developing and now presented to her a large erect phallus, throbbing against the back of the cupboard door. It was criss-crossed by leaf-veins, but apparently, possibly: half-human, maybe even functional, but at three feet high: enough to rupture a she-elephant.

Tentatively, against her better judgement, Vivienne tip-toed forward and touched the angry red tip of the thing, gorged with sap. A small cloud of spores blew out and a sticky residue wept over her fingers, smelling of fish-paste.

She stood back and admired it and to her surprise, then alarm, found herself wet between the legs, increasingly aroused. She looked around. Were the spores narcotic? Could she make out more of them in the afternoon sunlight from the windows, almost invisible, demonic little pilots, invading her consciousness and her blood, trying to bend her to their will as if she were only an organic puppet, only DNA, only weak flesh and blood, a helpless pawn in some larger strategy?

She put her hand around the phallus in curiosity, and couldn't suppress her pleasure at the way its multiple skins easily encouraged her hand to slip and stroke the thing up and down.

She knew deep down it could be terribly dangerous, but her excitement was mounting, her heart racing, her blood pumping in her ears. She closed the curtains carefully lest the gamma flashes produce some unpredictable psychotic activity in her mysterious host, then undressed and turned around and presented the dilated opening to her moist interior towards the phallus, like a spring flower quivering before a bee.

*

Vivienne awoke gradually from a strange dream in which every vein and artery in her body had flowed not with red and blue blood but with white sap and green chlorophyll. Her ears had been drooping leafs and her two breasts some swelling fruit whose ripeness she was eagerly awaiting within a season.

She stumbled out of bed and walked to the toilet to wash her face then remembered why the hot tap wasn't working and how she'd have to get it fixed before autumn and winter set in. She looked at herself in the mirror and saw how much she was ageing, saw how her undeserved suffering had made her skin into a map of the world. The twisting lines and her tousled hair seemed to be fusing into some menacing undergrowth bit by bit, revealing her crueller nature, taking her back into the earth with all its armour and savagery.

A shot rang out from somewhere outside. She went to the front windows and saw a plumber's van outside with a policeman and a soldier poised around it, one taking notes, the other one talking into his lapel microphone to some hidden comrades.

Vivienne went to the back window as another loud bang went off. She laughed then went upstairs so she could admire the spectacle in greater detail.

Several soldiers and police had penetrated her outer defences and were making their way through her back garden. Unheeding of the initial warning blasts, she now watched their confusion as they set off the various traps and cheese-wires, slicing each of them into unexpected pieces, as little fireworks went off in odd celebration of each new and unwarranted atrocity. A gun was drawn, then the arm that held it separated from the body that commanded it. Some legs rushed forward then stopped dead as the body they carried plummeted forward into a duck pond filled with piranhas, and all the time party streamers, bird feathers and coloured smoke were billowing into the air.

It was automatic and blameless, senselessly savage and entirely without redress to an absentee creator. A microcosmic model of a universe too close to our own to bear comparison for long without that immortal look of shock: the steadfast human refusal to accept the patently obvious.

Behind her on the floor at the half-open cupboard door, a training shoe lay with its laces disarrayed in indolent and unrequited anguish, while the roots and leaves on the wall behind it folded themselves contentedly in preparation for another long harsh winter.

~

15.

THE RED QUEEN

Who needed psychiatrists anymore? Now everybody's dreams and nightmares had come out of the shadows, shuffled like shackled convicts from the dark folds of their brains and been granted their freedom. Now nightmares roamed the very streets, unopposed, a reign of terror. There was nothing hidden anymore, nothing to analyse, only facts to doubt and anecdotes to reel from.

In the flooded half of the city, an army, or perhaps it was better called a navy, of looters and scavengers now ruled largely unchallenged. The damned, the drowned, were occasionally filmed from passing helicopters, which they raucously endeavoured to shoot down like game birds. But bullets were scarce. The whole gamut of human ingenuity had now been unexpectedly unleashed at this last moment in makeshift spears, converted swords and improvised crossbows.

In the respectable enclaves, the gated neighbourhoods on higher ground, school classes struggled on, and in these, playground games were played by still well-dressed children who enacted, as if by proxy like little puppeteers, the terrors of their parents. In these they often spoke of "The Red Queen", a fabled leader of the scavengers. She was said to sail the flooded streets in a Viking long-ship made from welded hulks of crashed cars with lampposts for masts, half-torn billboards for sails – huge faded awnings still advertising the ill-fated promises of a dying world: girls in pastel underwear laughing knowingly about million-dollar apartments and low-cholesterol sandwich spread. We had wanted it all. But we weren't worth it.

Laughter, dark laughter, had found a new vogue in human affairs, in both halves of the divided city. From the ruined financial executive, his bank stock razed to zero, reaching for the revolver in his bureau drawer, to the half-mad drunk eating the raw carcass of a dog on the steps of a defunct cinema, looked down upon by posters of judgemental Disney characters, the "hot dog" sign given new irony. Where laughter had previously been at some clever comedian's description of our familiar cosy world, now laughter was a kind of belch, a drain gurgling, the sound of a human being having taken too much and crying out for air, for relief. Where laughter before had been in reaction to some alternative vision of reality, now it was a plea for that reality, any reality, to arrive and replace the horror before us. It also had something of the death-rattle about it, that unmistakable sound of when the human heart and lungs begin their shutdown sequence, a sound once familiar in the First World War trenches and now familiar again among the damned, the drowned, the abandoned.

As the waters rose, wild animals had become trapped in strange places and strangest of all were the deer who now stalked the city parks and boulevards, taken to moving by night to avoid the attention of the scavengers. With little need for his psychiatric services, Franco had turned himself in at the local accident and emergency and had been surprised to find himself treating among many other things: those grazed and gored by deer antlers.

Reverting to type, even as he dressed the wounds he found himself fascinated, asking questions about how and why the victim had tried to catch a deer, trying to picture the scene. Usually the ribs showing under the T-shirt, the teeth falling out, were all the answers he needed: malnutrition due to bad diet, lack of protein as rationing and food-shortages took their toll.

Franco lived alone now in a single room apartment provided by the hospital, a monk's cell in his self-image, in which he could atone for some sin he vaguely acknowledged blame for but could still not accept with his rational mind.

Veronika had thrown him out, and it had been senseless to pursue her to reconsider. The friends she had been associating with were increasingly menacing, tattooed, pierced and bejewelled to the point of irrefutable tribal supremacy: warlords in waiting, nursing baseball bats and swords on street corners.

Following a call-out, Franco found himself walking through one of Sylvow's strangest current anomalies. The Dry Districts, formerly the Civic Centre and Financial District, surrounded by thirty-foot concrete walls, some blocking entire streets to keep back the waters behind them in a vain short-lived attempt to preserve the nerve-centre of society from the chaos all around. Now these streets were abandoned and eerily calm, as the concrete cracked and the waters occasionally dribbled over the ramparts, intimating an imminent doom. Turning into a moonlit street of smashed shop displays, darkly reflecting a frost-like carpet of crushed glass underfoot, Franco was confronted by the spectre of three Red Deer: a stag and two hinds, frozen like statues, eyeing him, transfixed.

He remembered glimpsing these creatures in the distance as a child on summer holidays, and always being awed by their majestic rolling motion as they pranced along on spring-loaded legs, their unnerving habit, just as now, of looking at you, scrutinising, as if waiting for you to impart to them the meaning of life, as if you were God himself. But one was always left with the sense that they were the divine ones.

A sound behind them startled them, and they turned and fled, then Franco made his way towards the scene that required his assistance. Two paramedics bent over a teenage boy bleeding from his stomach, a machete on the ground pushed out of reach of his right hand, the leg of a deer still clutched in his left.

Franco felt a strange spasm of disgust as he approached. He remembered all the discussion, arguments even, that he and Claudia had had about animals and humans, how unjustified or otherwise our assumption of superiority over the animal kingdom might be. Something about the machete enraged him. He gave the boy morphine then bandaged him, staunching the wound, radioing for back-up. In the shop window behind him, against whose glass the youth's head rested, eyelids drooping in pain and slumber, he saw posters of pinewoods and mountains, a travel agents, an anodyne dream of primordial freedom. He had a momentary sense of Man and Deer hunting the same lost paradise, fighting for it, stabbing each other while sleepwalking in their restless dreams.

A noise at the street's end startled everyone, the paramedics stood up. A night breeze stirred the branches of some of the new invasive species growing from a shattered towerblock above them and they released an eerie rain of mutant cherry blossom that descended, weaving, showering the whole scene with confetti, three standing figures and one horizontal, like some ancient Greek carnival offering for the splendid dead.

The unidentified sound came again, and a hairline crack progressed a few feet down the tall rampart at the street's end, and to Franco's disbelief: some sort of galleon sailed slowly by there, its white sails billowing in the moonlight, dark figures moving on its decks and rigging, pointing down at them with bows and spears.

Where the pink blossoms fell they opened and closed their serrated petals like the mouths of piranha fish, emitting disturbing squeals, as the medics brushed them off the shivering boy.

*

Francis and Jenny let me go The Red Queen all day today, Vittorrio... it was superb, we made a boat out of a wheelbarrow and sailed up and down the grass slopes in the playground...

Bully for you, mumbled Vittorrio, having long-since entered that adolescent unfriendly stage and impatient with his sister's childishness. Then again, the prospect of her behaving flirtatiously any time soon also filled him with trepidation in a household of women, with no father to call order.

His mother was having one of her chaste afternoon tea and cakes sessions with the elderly and odious Professor Bartholomew, and more than once he had overheard them talking about him and recoiled at the thought of it. He had even thought of running away recently, but in a city like this it would not have been his greatest brainwave.

What are you doing? -His sister asked over his shoulder, with a certain trepidation.

Scrapbook...   collage,   he   mumbled,   taciturn, recalcitrant.

But what is that? Eughhhh... I'll tell mum on you!

Vittorrio sighed and put his hands over his collection. It was true. His assemblage of photographs, some from newspapers, others taken himself with the aid of a telephoto lens, were of scenes of disorder, vandalism, violence, looting, dead bodies, glimpses of hands and feet uncoiling from doorways and spoil heaps. Blackened skeletons amid burnt-out cars.

You wouldn't understand! He spat, red-faced with anger. *I'm recording everything, trying to make sense of it all, the bigger picture. I need all the pieces, even the sordid bits. Maybe especially the horrible bits. You wouldn't understand. You're too soft, being a girl.*

Lucia snorted, with her hands on her hips, and this made Vittorrio smile despite himself, as she looked a little comical. Unable to resist the effect, she slowly smiled in turn, against her better judgement. *You miss Dad, don't you?*

Why do keep saying that? -Vittorrio asked, on the back-foot, surprised by her sudden maturity.

Our English teacher said a boy without a father lacks a moral compass, today. She was talking about a book we were reading.

Well this isn't a book, Loo. No one's been at this moment in history before. A lot of families have been split up by all this mess, by The Inundations.

And you think you can make sense of it? Jenny says you're creepy, she says you might be a prevert.

The word is pervert, Vittorrio sighed, standing up and ushering his tiresome sister to the door, *...and Jenny Watts fancies me, any fool can see that, all my friends can.*

This was only half-true, but enough to make Lucia's face burn and her pigtails positively writhe in rage and confusion as the door was shut firmly in her face.

*

Professor Bartholomew took another piece of homemade walnut cake as Claudia Reinwald poured the mint tea. Outside, birds still twittered in the hedgerow, but the street was dying under attack from Knotweed and Rhododendron, the once pristine tarmac pavements outside now ruptured beyond repair, the street impassable to traffic, even if there had been any affordable petrol left.

You're worried about the boy? -Bartholomew ventured.

I'm worried about everything... Claudia sighed, *who isn't?*

There's a new academy you know, a kind of special academy, Claudia. I might be able to get him a place in it...

Oh yes...? -Claudia averted her eyes, trying not to look too interested.

Bartholomew paused, until he felt the warm humid air had acquired just the right consistency for his next verbal kite. *The government is failing, as you know, and some well, what used to be called captains-of-industry in happier times...*

When there was industry to captain, you mean? Claudia affirmed wryly.

Yes, well, such men... and women, are forming a kind of conglomerate now, a survival committee, if you will, of all the best people.

The best people... Claudia repeated, and couldn't seem to keep the revulsion from her voice.

Your son could be part of that, should be part of that.... although numbers are limited.

At this point, Vittorrio, not entirely innocently, sauntered into the room and decided to pretend he was about four years younger. Perhaps it was not too late to still enjoy the special dispensations of youth before he joined the brave new crusade of tomorrow. *Mum, how come you never see Aunty Vivienne anymore? Did you two have a fight or something?*

Caught off guard by this broadside, Claudia nearly spat tea down her front, and the professor could even be seen to briefly place protective hands over his still only half-eaten cake. *Vittorrio... darling, don't be so rude. Professor Bartholomew and I were just enjoying a private discussion when you butted in. You know perfectly well that Vivienne moved away to a different district, one cut off by the floods now.*

But Vittorrio showed no sign of interest in the response, which he disbelieved and had probably heard before, as he paced back from the kitchen with a spam sandwich and lemonade in hand. *What are you a professor of, actually?* -He blurted at the old man, who sputtered in return:

Why... Linguistics, dear boy.

Languages... Claudia added, and irritated by the unnecessary elaboration, Vittorrio left a final comment sailing on the air in the wake of his departure:

...Much in demand in Babel.

And Bartholomew and Claudia were left looking at each other, both with eyebrows raised, both with mouths twitching into smiles.

The future is an untamed horse I see... the professor mumbled, and Claudia wasn't sure that she liked the metaphor.

*

Lucia had never wandered this far from home before, but here she was, outside the boarded-up house in a condemned district, the place she could dimly remember having spent four years of her life in. She was running her hands over the faded name "Reinwald" on the peeling wooden post-box, when a deer strutted out of a neighbouring thicket of Rhododendron and stared at her. Frightened, entranced, noticing its prominent horns and twitching nostrils taking her scent, she backed away from it, still holding its gaze as she retreated down the street.

Suddenly she was winded, as dirty hands gloved in black lace reached around her and dragged her sideways, another hand covering her mouth as she tried to scream. She could still see the deer and wanted to warn it, but a figure concealed in a thicket fired a misshapen bolt from a handmade crossbow, straight through the animal's neck, and its delicate knees buckled and it fell to the earth.

Before Lucia could despair in turn over her own fate, several gunshots rang out and the hands holding her suddenly loosened. Two soldiers and a policeman, then two others, emerged onto the street. One of them pushed over the man who only a moment beforehand had held the crossbow, then dragged his body behind him like that of a slain animal.

Lucia looked down in horror as he and the man who had held her briefly captive were now thrown in a heap at her feet, one of them shot through the eye. She sobbed and shivered in confusion, as a soldier knelt and embraced her then lifted her roughly onto a passing truck.

Your mother still alive? -The nurse inside the vehicle asked her, and she nodded, shocked by the question. *You know your way home, your address?*

Lucia remembered her address but knew no way home. Her childhood was over.

*

The few days or nights Franco had off now, he would spend walking the streets, but why and in search of what, he couldn't precisely have explained, even to himself.

Some streets were safe and dry, others condemned by failing barriers, increasingly waterlogged, threatened and eroded by encroaching crime. Franco's frames of thought, his long internal dialogues, wouldn't permit him to choose or plan his route or take any special precautions. He carried a knife, a letter-opener, in his inside pocket, and other than that was resigned to lose his own life or save another, as each day and whim of the Gods saw fit. He no longer greatly valued his own survival.

He often saw the ghosts of his son and daughter, sometimes aged as he would imagine them to have done, other times frozen in some previous remembered idyll. He saw them on the arms of and in the hands of countless other parents – strangers, worried, distraught, moving through the Displacement Zones, anxiously seeking food and inoculation, as new epidemics spread daily.

Sometimes Franco's walks would take him to neighbourhoods he remembered – some still inhabited, some ghostly quiet, others drowned beneath the nightmarish waves. He puzzled over how architecture could so guard and embody the dreams of men and yet go so un-lauded for its stewardship. Memories lived in buildings and never more poignantly than in ruins where the sadness of those displaced seemed almost to have bled backwards through time and buckled them with the weight of love.

He walked until his legs and feet ached, until his whole body hurt so much that he could no longer feel his heart. He longed for his daughter, for his son, his wife. He longed for a lost life he could no longer recapture. But in such times as these, and in the patients he treated each day for malnutrition, dehydration, scurvy, he took comfort from knowing that such longing was now universal. Humanity longed to go home, but went on mechanically, in hope of easing the pain even if that easement might only be obliteration, because even that, who knows, might be enough.

*

It was hard to remember a time in history when a famous woman had been so scarred, still less when that scar had somehow suited her, or had at least added to rather than detracted from, the sense of awe about her. Veronika was one such. It was said that the man who had raped her she had later captured and tortured and killed by her own hands. Perhaps that was a myth, but there were so many around her and more now every day. "Boudica" they had joked at first, but those few who knew their history might have recalled that Boudica had sewn the severed breasts of noble women over their mouths while she slaughtered Roman collaborators in ancient Londinium, and they might have recoiled from the comparison lest it become prophecy.

Her ships were moored around the shattered crown of what had once been the Stock Exchange, an irony not lost on her followers who declared that Mammon had been displaced by their fearsome queen. Insane paraphernalia of looted wealth littered this ruined palace: antique thrones and jewels from museums, rusting sports cars, suits of armour, DIY tools adapted into murderous weapons.

Children were routinely kidnapped and ransomed from the surrounding Dry Zones and, in the ensuing pitch battles, bounties offered for every "uniform" brought back. Piles of their helmets and skulls adorned her palace entrance like pyramids, triumphal stelae to a living goddess.

Through the new canals, once streets, the Red Queen's galleon sailed, surveying her current kingdom, always seeking to expand its borders, sending out scouts and emissaries into the transitional zones to harass the survivors, convert them if possible, slaughter them if necessary. Fresh meat, from dogs, cats, sheep, cattle, foxes, deer, was their greatest bounty, the quick fix, the easiest way to stay alive. Inevitably now, cannibalism was also occasionally amongst the dark necklace of rumours the Red Queen wore.

Tonight, her consorts Arundel and Vernon returned with the carcass of a cow and two frightened merchants whom they had captured in the Pines District. They were made to kneel before Veronika who asked them what their faith was. *Faith?* -they stammered.

Christian? Muslim? -she asked haughtily, fingering the string of enormous pearls around her neck, turning up the collar on her fur coat emblazoned with gothic studs and chains, sewn with stolen emeralds and sapphires.

We follow Leo... one of them said at last, and everyone present was surprised and touched by their Queen's unexpected interest. One of them even had a little black book, a new bible he said, of Leo's sayings, and after some tender cooing words from their dominatrix, he was persuaded to part from it.

Sitting cross-legged on a parapet above the flood waters, with her beloved tame crows feeding from chunks of blooded flesh in a silver platter at her side, Veronika read aloud from the Book of Leo and felt something stir deep within her, some wistful residue of the time before, some fragment of longing for a time to come which no one could believe in any longer. But perhaps, she smiled, her green eyes flashing in the setting sun, red lips caressing these new words, perhaps it would be her place to show leadership. To take her flock to a promised land when the waters receded.

...Man who turned away from Nature, how you suffocate, luxuriate now, in her killing kiss. You must lose yourself completely within her oncoming wave, embrace your own destruction before you can understand again your correct place in the order of things. From corruption and decay comes the green shoots of new life. The phallic stink-horn, the sly toadstool

or mushroom growing from Mankind's mulch, will nonetheless, once each has been tried and tasted and judged, nourish the new children through the hallowed dark in strange dreams and nightmares. When the fever subsides, the sustenance will have been imparted, the mandrake-man will arise...

*

Franco turned a corner and stumbled upon a scene of two youths confronting a pair of stags, having chased and trapped them in a cul-de-sac. He looked around, half expecting to see an audience of teenage females of both species, so evenly matched did the two sides momentarily appear, so much like some ancient trial of manhood from Crete or Rome.

One youth lunged with an iron bar and the stag he aimed for ducked then plunged for freedom between its two assailants while its fellow turned its horns towards the other youth's face. Something made Franco cry out, in warning or horror, directed to the deer or the humans, he wasn't certain, but the momentary distraction was decisive. One deer escaped a swinging sword blade while the other struck and impaled the youth through the neck, even as his accomplice stabbed desperately into its flanks.

Both beast and human groaned in pain and anger, ugly sounds that seemed to shake the ground and stop time for a moment, until they both clattered to the ground, limbs writhing weakly in horrid disarray. Somehow fearless, Franco found himself moving forward in a waking dream, walking slowly towards the wretched scene as the other youth dropped his weapon, panicked and sped silently past him.

Franco knelt and gazed upon the dying deer and the dying youth, his heart overflowing with love and pity, half and half. Both of them looked up at him with the same hopeless and fading stare, an imploring valediction. Both of them showered him with their red blood, dark as wine from their necks, soaking his shirt as he lifted and cradled each of them in his arms, weeping, unable to do anything. He remembered how Claudia had loved the animals and at last he understood.

At the end of the doomed street, a tall ship crossed the moon.

~

16.

The rain hadn't stopped for two months now, and Lucia's already intermittent school classes, like so many routines of normality, had eventually been abandoned as whole neighbourhoods had been evacuated and resettled on higher ground and on floating resettlement barges.

She hadn't seen her father in eight years, since around the time of his rumoured split with Veronika. But something about the worsening situation in the city had provoked a new urgency in her: a longing to find and make peace with her father again before it was too late.

Phone calls were no longer permitted except for emergency services, and even electricity had become strictly rationed and switched off entirely during evening curfew.

Lucia knew her mother wouldn't approve if she guessed her true intention, so concocted some diversionary tale about a friend's house then set out by boat to reach the main island. There she could make enquiries at the *Central Office Of Evacuations* as to where her father might now be stationed.

Fortunately the moon was full and almost bright, good enough to steer by even through the continuing rain.

The new trees, *the giant mangroves* as they had become known, were tall enough that their canopies still floated above the high tide level, like leafy islands. Perhaps this was why they had sown themselves in the city streets, bursting through tarmac to everyone's astonishment.

Was this also why so many indigenous trees and plants had been killed off by the *Gamma Flashes*? It was hard to say. Now that the web and television were mostly down for all but a few unpredictable hours a day, firm facts and knowledgeable people were increasingly hard to come by and rumour ran rife instead.

Lucia moored her boat and sidled past the packs of stray dogs at the jetties and ran into the torch-lit crowds in what had once been the quiet and highly desirable Torr Avenue in the Elms District, now a makeshift town centre and marketplace frequented by street hawkers and refugees and off-duty soldiers: the three categories which seemed to make up the entire remaining urban population these days.

She was still shaken by the sight of the sentries with machine guns and live ammunition at the *Government Administration Compound*. All police had been replaced by soldiers, martial law was unopposed given the "transitional circumstances", as the government euphemistically referred to them. Justice, when it was dealt out, was now rumoured to be swift and rough. Looters shot and thrown in trenches above the high-tide mark or locked into steel crates and dropped off murky barges in the new lagoons.

Lucia queued for an hour before reaching the head of the line and felt self-consciously well-dressed among some of the pitiful flotsam of humanity she saw sitting around on benches, dressed in rags, shivering with pneumonia or despair.

Miss Reinwald, the computer database states that your father is now working in the Eastern Temporary Hospital Encampment, an hour away by helicopter... you could just about make it there before curfew.

Could I, could you... telephone in advance, can I get a message to him so he knows I'm coming?

The administrator shook her head and smiled, grimly. *Don't you get the broadcast announcements, sweetheart? Nobody's working shifts anymore. If he's there, he's on duty alright...*

*

Technically the helicopter shuttles were for *relocates* and relatives of hospital patients only, but Lucia was able to disarm an army lieutenant with her sweetest smile and a hundred dollar bill. As the chopper took off into the rain and she looked back down on the guards' faces, she realised the note was probably worth only half its value of a week beforehand and the look in his eyes had been more of pity than of love or lust.

She found the darkness underneath her almost comforting as the helicopter wheeled around. By day, she hated the sight of abandoned buildings lurking beneath the waves like grinning skulls, a looming prophecy of humanity's demise. The irrational thought of being trapped down there haunted her nightmares: an omni-present image of a watery hell in which the souls of the damned might wander interminably, their mouths stuffed with seaweed, their vain words become bubbles.

*

Franco was now treating a steady stream of cholera and dysentery patients. Incidence of water-borne disease and contamination from breached sewers had reached a critical level. He also expected typhoid and malaria cases to begin increasing within days.

Nevertheless he found the constant activity, the complete lack of time for cerebral reflection, strangely consoling. The exhaustion would only come when he stopped, and then he would sleep, standing upright if necessary. His greatest imperative until then therefore, was to keep on moving.

It was with great shock and confusion that he at first responded to the sight of his daughter walking towards him through the long chaotic ward: activity criss-crossing in front of her strangely beautiful and familiar face, like a coin falling through murky water.

Loo... Lucia, he stammered and one of his colleagues stopped, alarmed by the expression on his face, concerned one of their best doctors might be having an epileptic attack. *My daughter,* he said finally, by way of simultaneous explanation and salutation and they embraced instantly in a flood of tears.

In happier times the entire ward might have applauded, but as it was, the sea of people merely coalesced and continued to flow again all around them.

What are you doing here Dad? -you're a psychiatrist, not a doctor... Lucia asked as they made their way out onto the roof to sit under a dripping parapet.

I'm trained as both. My Hippocratic oath. I must save lives. It's the only thing that matters anymore... He sighed and placed his hands on her shoulders, *You've grown so much, you're so beautiful. You're a woman now, my little girl, how did it all happen so fast?*

Oh dad, I heard she left you...

Ahh, that business. Well, so news still travels in this town eh? Even by candlelight and rowing boats... maybe we can take some comfort from that.

Dad, you should come back. Mum will have forgiven you...

Will have? Future Conditional tense. Conditional on there being a future that is, I suppose.

Now of all times, it matters. Not for me, for her, though she never says it. Vittorrio and I are adults now, we will find our own way but Mum...

Franco looked away bleakly, -*Your mother made it very clear that I could never make her happy again... words matter Lucia, I found that out to my cost. Every word and every action matter every day, they all add up in the end to... a life... or death, to this* -he said and turned around with a gesture that took in all the horizon. *All of this tonight, all this water that makes its way towards us. It's not just falling tonight, it's been falling for thirty, forty, maybe a hundred years in our minds. This is the floodtide of a million tiny little mistakes, little ignorances, little white lies. It builds up and it comes back to haunt us. Two million, maybe nine billion people did this to themselves, to each other. And we're drowning now... drowning in a sea of consequences.*

Two by two... Lucia sighed quietly to herself, wiping her eyes.

What's that, sweetheart?

Two by two. Noah and the flood, you used to read me the story from a picture book when I was a child.

Did I really? I've totally forgotten... and how does that story end? –he asked morosely to his feet.

Noah and the animals survive, Dad, you know that... because they heed God's warning.

But what God, Lucia? Franco suddenly asked and his eyes brimmed with tears and they embraced again. *The God of the forest or the God of the sky?* -he murmured into her hair, *Leo's God, or the God of Science?*

They've made a book out of his letters, Dad, haven't you heard? They say it's destined to become an underground classic. That's a good one, eh? An underwater classic more like. Mum says they'll worship him like a messiah one day if we're not careful, start a new religion...

Religion eh? More blindness and stupidity. He would have hated that. Poor Leo, Franco sighed. *These messiahs can never save themselves can they? Where is he now I wonder. Is there a tree tall enough out there to save his neck?*

At that moment a huge flash of lightning split the sky and they both jumped. *A Gamma Flash,* Franco said, *we'd better get back inside before there's more.*

Leo said the trees would save us, Dad.

Mysticism... how's that going to happen?

Maybe it's happening already. This building is on timber stilts, the new boats are made of wood aren't they?

Ignorance might have derailed us, but superstition could finish us off, Lucia... Wait, did you hear that noise just there?

The thunder clap?

No, I don't think so... something deeper, like stone and water?

No, Lucia started to say but was drowned out by the sound of a new fleet of helicopters coming down to land on the roof.

You must go back now, Lucia, I can get you on one of these shuttles if I give you a patient number. We'll just tell them you've got something non-contagious like scurvy.

But will you promise to come and see Mum...

A cracking and rumbling sound rang out behind Franco again and he turned to listen to it. *I promise, I promise...* were the last words Lucia heard Franco say as he bundled her into the cockpit and mimed his love to her through the glass.

Rising up into the night air, the pilots paused and gestured to each other at a long white line on the horizon that was amassing and sweeping in towards them. She didn't know what it meant but saw that their eyes met then went dead and their lips stopped even trying to speak. She looked again and saw it was like a crescent moon on its side, a silver scythe swinging in unseen hands, the plaything of a demon.

Lucia beat helplessly on the glass as the black metallic birds beat their wings and hurried her away into the rain leaving her father and his patients down below to the mercy of the approaching sea.

~

Claudia's hair was entirely white now, her face lined, her gait somewhat of a shuffle, her posture stooped. She still slapped down everyone who dared to call her an old woman, but nonetheless she had finally become one. She seemed to remember that the society she had grown up in had often derided the old as out-of-touch and resistant to change, but now by merit of their rarity and their knowledge of a world that had gone before, the old seemed a little more respected.

Her new house was made entirely of dark-stained wood, with no glass in the windows, just thick shutters that could be pulled over at night or in winter. Its layout was open-plan, not in deference to some design caprice but for the simple logic of enabling its various levels to be safely heated by one log fire at its centre which was cradled in precious stone flags.

She shuffled through her house to answer the knock on the door and there stood Vittorrio with his young wife Marie and new baby Carlo. She embraced them both and doted over the baby. She was a grandmother now. Although she rarely spoke of it, she could see a resemblance in the baby's features to Franco: and hard as she still found it to forgive his leaving her, part of her wished he could have lived to see his grandchild born.

She didn't even have a grave to go and visit and whisper to and try to make peace with his spirit. His body had never been found, one of many thousands drowned during *The Second Inundation*. All she had was the mental image, the cameo conveyed to her by Lucia: of him fighting to save lives in a field hospital as the waters rose before the collapse of the *Southern Dam*. Although Claudia had no message from him in words, perhaps she had this statement in deeds: that he had dedicated the rest of his life to self-sacrifice in penance for what he had done, once *The Upheavals* had started and Veronika had left him. And perhaps in the end she wondered, might this language of deeds be all that any of us really have of substance, and all our words are just froth and bubbles?

But why had Franco never got in touch? -Claudia still wondered. Perhaps he had planned to and would have if only he could have survived the flooding. Now she would never know. She had always said that Veronika would leave him once he got too old and inconvenient for her. The young are so heartless, she found herself muttering until Vittorrio overheard her: *What's that, Mum?*

Oh nothing, I was just thinking about your father...

Oh...?

Never mind... it's just I still wish things could have turned out differently, then Carlo could have had a grandfather too.

Mum, not that again...

What do you mean, again? I never talk about this, do I?

Not in so many words, but we're always skirting around it, like stalking a deer.

If only he had got back in touch...

Well it wasn't easy was it, Mum? The tell-coms were all cut back then and they haven't been back on since.

Just at that moment as if on cue, a pigeon landed on the bird box and Vittorrio got up and went to retrieve its message.

Well, blow me down with a feather, he said as he returned, unrolling the parchment he had just slipped off from around the bird's leg. A flutter in the wooden grille behind him told them the bird was gone again already.

The note was handwritten, as most communication now was, on the back of a recycled bank statement; or at least that was what Claudia said they were, because to most young people now they resembled some kind of obscure number poem. *It's from Aunt Vivienne...* Vittorrio marvelled, *who'd have thought it?*

Hey, who says you can read my mail now? I'm not so old and dottery yet that I need you to read to me, keep your sticky mitts off!

Mum... Vittorrio tut-tutted, *don't be crotchety. Here I'll light a candle for you so you can read this better. The daylight is a tad dim in here today.*

Vivienne... Viv... you say... after decades, it can't be can it? After me talking about your father too and getting in touch and stuff. That would just be too much of a coincidence wouldn't it, don't you think?

Mum, you talk about him or her or Uncle Anton every time we're here, however briefly.

My God! Claudia put her hand to her throat and Vittorrio remembered this characteristic gesture of hers from an earlier world, an echo of the woman his mother had been when he was a child, before all the changes.

What is it, Mum? What's wrong?

He stood up, leaving Marie talking quietly to the restless baby, so he could take the letter from his mother and check what was affecting her. Tears were running down her cheeks and for a moment Vittorrio wondered if someone had died, increasingly the only kind of news his mother seemed to speak about.

But as she handed him the letter even he was amazed and had to run his fingers under the words to verify them, the kind of backward and childish gesture that his mother used to castigate him for when she tutored him at home after the school was flooded.

*

Claudia, Vittorrio, and Marie with little Carlo all stepped out onto the wooden porch and rang the call bells and pulled their furs around them, their breath clouding the air.

Snow was starting to fall from the sky again, like that of last week which had been the first in twenty years some people said, so much so that Vittorrio scarcely remembered it and had to put it onto his tongue and close his eyes as if tasting it for familiarity, searching for some comforting connection with a time he could not remember, an emissary, a calling card from the lost years.

Beating wings came down over their heads and they stepped one by one into the gull basket, whose aviator then whipped his flock back into the air with a practised gesture, his leather helmet stained with guano.

They moved off from the platform and swung across the rooftops and down avenues of stilted houses, beneath which the thick mangrove swamps were now flickering in a cold north wind under a covering of snow.

They say there'll be more of this snow, the pilot shouted over the bird cries.

Oh yes? Claudia rejoined, always keen to gain the best village gossip from these *Errand Men* with their keen ears and eyes.

Yeah. The Knowledge Men have even been saying, or so it's rumoured, that some current has shut down, a tide or some sort, a warm drift.

The Gulf Stream, you mean? Vittorrio shouted, and Claudia smiled to see the pilot's surprise, and felt pride at the education she had gleaned for her son with his cultured accent, even through the bad years.

Yeah, that's it right enough, now how you come to know that, son? Are you in training, one of The Initiates?

Marie took his hand and Vittorrio smiled and nodded, clearing his throat before he spoke on, checking his mother's eyes to see that such divulgence of knowledge was permitted. *I am apprenticed, yes. In three years I will be allowed into The Circle Of Esoterics. They say they will let me see The Golden Books of Electronica and Mathmagick...*

A great honour! -the bird man nodded his head as he brought the flock down slowly onto the forest clearing amid the low lands.

They stepped out of the basket and paid the pilot with bread and pork fat, bidding him a shivering farewell.

What will that mean? Marie asked Vittorrio as they walked, *if that 'stream' secret shuts down? Is that Esoteric knowledge?*

At best, Vittorrio sighed, *long hard winters for many years, at worst, well: what did you used to call it Mum. You knew a term for it?*

An Ice Age.

What does that mean? What would that mean? -Marie pressed her.

Claudia paused and looked over what had once been downtown Sylvow. She could still remember the towerblocks and lights, the constant traffic. She had thought at the time that she hated it, but now she felt a flash of yearning, of nostalgia for those happy careless years. It all seemed like a demented party now, when humanity had played and laughed and wrecked the world like drunken teenagers while their parents were away. But the homecoming, the morning after had been, and still was... terrible.

Thousands died... she found herself answering Marie as they moved on through the snow, across the frozen lake and into the woods. *Thousands died when you were a child, but if there is an Ice Age...* and here her voice failed her, and Vittorrio stopped and came back to take her arm, alarmed at the change in her breathing, *We will all die...*

Even the Initiates and the Esoterics, Mrs Reinwald? Wouldn't the Keepers of Knowledge save themselves with magic?

They would use their aeroplanes and helicopters to escape, yes, if they still have any left that work. They would fly to the equator or the tropics, yes, but we'd be left in the freezer compartment...

What's a freezer compartment? -Marie started to ask, but Vittorrio nudged her away from the subject, seeing his mother was becoming upset.

Claudia walked through the old streets but where once there had been the city of Sylvow, now there was a forest with streets and buildings in it, interspersed, some ruined, some ramshackle but inhabited, subdivided: a bedraggled family to each room. Vegetable plots could be seen in every forest clearing, even some pigs and goats and chickens in pens. People had no privacy and little of their former dignity but they had something else instead now: a communal street life, the need to rely on each other, to trust and defend and agree. Now the forest had come to Sylvow, now things were how they had probably been in the beginning, again, like the old medieval paintings.

Claudia smiled, her old worn face breaking into unfamiliar lines and fissures: a smile, tears. *Leo would have loved this,* she said, and Marie looked up at her again curiously.

My dear brother Leo, God bless him. This is all how he said it would be. Sometimes I feel as if he is on my shoulder or looking out of my eyes.

Just then, they reached Vivienne's street and had begun the walk uphill towards her side of the woods, when a commotion seemed to be breaking out over behind the market bonfire. Fresh dogs were being cooked on the spit and some orphans fighting over scraps were being chased by the butcher. But they all stopped and pointed at a distant figure and a small crowd that were emerging from the woods at the head of a long avenue. Something about the group seemed to be transfixing the onlookers, commanding everybody's attention.

Claudia! Claudia! A voice familiar and yet strangely aged and cracked was cutting through the wintery air and Claudia spun around to see the figure of Vivienne running to meet them. Her eyes instantly filled with tears again. Here was who she had always truly loved, in a flowing deerskin cloak with two tame doves fluttering at her shoulders, her flowing locks of blonde hair greying at last. She was still beautiful despite the harrowing years, like a glowing embodiment of Summer in her youth; now she was gaunt and white and austere as Winter.

They embraced and all they could both say to each other was *Forgive me...* over and over again as if after a while they weren't addressing each other but life itself.

I always loved you, Claudia whispered and Vivienne drew back and held her shoulders, bathing her in her sad blue eyes, nodding. Then something caught her attention over Claudia's shoulder and they took each other's hands and shuffled with the gathering crowd down to where the strange procession from the forest's edge was making its way through the town. *This is why I sent you a message,* Vivienne whispered.

Claudia suddenly felt Leo's spirit within her more than ever before, her feet moving strangely as if every moment was suddenly pre-ordained, already lived before, an immortal day to be written in history. The crowd parted and there sat Anton on horseback, his clothes stained and torn. He looked older and scarred and tired, but glowing from within with some mysterious new light. A smile was spreading across his face like the sun lifting over a frozen Spring meadow, waking the new buds. To the side of him, two fierce white wolves eyed the crowd and between them: pawing and stroking them as if they were his mother and father, stood an apparition of Leo Vestra as a fifteen year old boy.

Claudia fainted, thinking her dead brother had come back as a ghost. While Vittorrio and Marie revived her, Vivienne howled like a wild animal and ran forward and embraced the child, weeping and hugging him and staring disbelievingly into his eyes, while the two wolves looked on like stern but gentle guardians.

When Claudia was brought back to her feet, Anton turned and addressed the crowd, raising a caber of carved oakwood above his head like a sceptre or the bone of some fabulous animal he had slain.

The child is Leo Vestra's! It is a miracle. He is the son of Leo and Vivienne. He has been spared, reared by wolves, saved and suckled by a she-wolf. He speaks no human tongue. He has gone beyond all that is human. He is Leo returned from the forest, re-born. He is Man re-made in Nature's image!

The crowd cheered, old women wept, men thumped each other's backs while bemused children ran between their feet. As Anton spoke, his horse shuffled underneath him, its nostrils flaring, as if animated by his words or by the reflected force of the crowd's reaction.

Anton broke into tears at last, his voice choking with emotion, as the crowd moved to touch him and carry him forward. *The forest has been merciful!* -he exulted.

Claudia leant up to kiss Anton on the cheek as he bowed to her. Then she knelt before Lenni where he sat with Vivienne and ran her fingers through his golden hair. *He is so beautiful...* she whispered. His eyes were pure and raw, cleansed of all human guilt and shame. His mouth opened and he made incoherent syllables and diphthongs, like a child, like the first man on the earth, innocent and fearless, without the burden of knowledge of the future or the past.

~

"Then a few voices began to proclaim Romulus's divinity; the cry was taken up, and at last every man present hailed him as a god and son of a god, and prayed to him to be forever gracious and to protect his children..."

-Livy.

AFTERWORD

by David Rix

There's the thing about living in a city – the darkness beyond the firelight no longer exists. That great prickly fear of what is out there, central to true cosmic horror, is gone. You look up at the sky and all you see is a red haze. The stars are gone. The distance is gone. You look down at the ground and what do you see? Faintly embarrassed trees in lines along the streets. Mundane weeds growing in vacant or shadowy spaces. Opportunists snapping up our scraps . . . that's the city and that's the world. Hop on a train just about anywhere in the UK and that same city continues.

In the face of that total domination over the environment, we have lost a lot. Modern horror writing has turned inwards, away from laughable monsters and demons that don't exist. And why? Simply because the unknown is now known. The terror beyond the firelight is revealed in mundane detail by orange sodium lights and, these days, we basically know that the only thing in the world there is to fear is ourselves.

Or . . . ?

You know what? That's rubbish!

Here's a recent story:

When scientists sent an ROV inside the wrecked Chernobyl reactor, they found something truly amazing. A murky black mould growing right there in the poisoned depths. That alone was strange enough – nature the great survivalist who never ceases to amaze by seeming at home in places that would kill us – but soon the much more extraordinary realisation began to dawn that these fungi seemed to be actually deriving sustenance from the radiation in a similar way to plants deriving sustenance from light. The black came from the pigment melanin, which appears to be acting in a similar way to chlorophyll, making use of the ionizing radiation to create chemical energy.

Whether this can be called evolution or not is uncertain since melanin is not an unusual substance in fungi – or indeed elsewhere. But it can certainly be called change. A change of environment to take advantage of what is available. For any living thing to make the switch and occupy a habitat like a wrecked nuclear reactor is nothing short of amazing, right? It is hard to imagine a less-natural environment than that, but here is this form of life that has made it home.

Here's a second story:

Recently also, a surprise was unearthed in the Gowanus canal at Red Hook, which is supposed to be one of the most polluted places in the world (ironically, also the setting of Lovecraft's tale of watery horror). It's a place where any fish would die within minutes, or possibly come back as a ravening green mutant fish zombie bent on justifiable revenge. But there was a recent discovery of microbes that had developed the ability to live and thrive in this poisoned environment. That, in contrast, is most definitely evolution – adaptation – change.

The two points here are simple ones: Nature changes and nature surprises. And always and continually for both. Even in the small scale – even within our lifetime or in response to some specific event. Even in response to us ourselves. Creatures switch colour to blend in with the mess we have filled the world with. Life lives in new places – feeds on new food sources. Life develops the ability to resist and even turn to its advantage our transformations of and intrusions into the 'natural' world. It also appears that change begets change. In the past, massive change events have alternated with long periods of quiet – and it is those change events that have stimulated nature into a frenzy of activity and new development. And now, we are in the middle of another change event. Now as habitats vanish or are altered over literally the entire face of the planet. It is not my place here to start talking about ecology or saving the world, but the mess we have surrounded ourselves with is not a matter for speculation. It is not about politics or about blaming this, that or the other – it is about stepping outside and looking at the world around you. It really is that simple. So far, this current change event is young – which means we have yet to see just how nature will fully respond to it. But it can be observed – for example, in the disquieting dance of man and microbe or in the example of the Chernobyl mould.

Environmentalists talk of saving the world. Doomsayers point to the inevitable self-destruction at the end of our path through the world. Both are probably unrealistic. 'Saving the world' – i.e. preserving it as it now is or recently was – isn't going to happen while we still have little children squabbling behind artificial lines on the map (called 'borders') and while humanity as a whole is still so keen to reproduce itself into planetary overload. And total destruction also seems way too dramatic for a surviving opportunist like ourselves. What we have to look forward to is change – either our own changes or changes forced from without by nature adapting its implacable power to the new circumstances and environments of planet Earth. It is only a matter of time before that wondrous opportunist the black mould of Chernobyl metaphorically takes over our entire civilization . . .

And as to the surprise, what do we know about any of this at the end of the day? About the world that surrounds us = a little, yes. About the possible and the impossible = almost nothing. About the future and how things will change = less than that. Science publicises itself as a quest for some kind of truth and knowledge but at the end of the day, science seems more about stripping away everything we know and finally beginning to get a measure of our ignorance. Science has done an amazing job of cataloguing the species and observing nature but realises that we have little idea where they came from. Science can watch in great detail as the world changes, as species die or morph into something else, but can't predict how it will pan out. Throughout history, we have blithely taken the world for granted – we believed we *knew*. How things worked – how to behave – what to think. In the old days, we looked to imagined powerful beings to protect us. Then later on, we believed that science itself could find all the answers and save us. Now both have proved nothing more than wisps against the vast void that rings down through the stars or up from the ocean depths or out from under the nearest log. The path through the next few millennia – the next few centuries – even the next few decades – is filled with a mystery and unknown that humanity has never had to face before. That is a darkness we are as yet inexperienced at navigating.

And this is the point of Sylvow.

*

There's the thing about living in the city . . . the unknown is everywhere now – in every shadow. In the guilt we feel and the unknown consequences of everything we do . . . the fundamentally unpredictable natural world . . . in the death of any kind of certainty born of faith. Where is our firelight now? It seems to be flickering low – suffocating and flashing blue as the unknown threatens to engulf us . . .

- David Rix - August 2010

BACKGROUND NOTES

Sylvow is not a real place, but a city of the mind, a compound of *Sylvan* and *Vow*, thus referring to the childhood promise made by the characters of Leo and Claudia.

Geographically *Sylvow* is a perhaps unlikely fusion of three places: **Glasgow** (Scotland), **Osnabruck** in Germany, and **Novogrudek** in Belarus.

Glasgow, home of many great inventors of the Industrial Revolution such as James Watt and Lord Kelvin, is originally named from the Gaelic *Glaschu*, meaning *Dear Green Place*. At Glasgow's northerly outskirts lie the remnants of the Antonine Wall built in 142 AD and mysteriously abandoned only 20 years later.

Near *Osnabruck* in 9AD, 20, 0000 Roman legionaries were massacred in the Teutoburg Forest by the Germanic tribes led by Arminius. Despite subsequent war, the Roman world's boundary became fixed at the Rhine for the next four hundred years until the decline of the Western Roman Empire.

In *Novogrudek*, the Jewish population resisted their nazi exterminators in WWII under the leadership of the Bielski brothers partisan group by retreating to the vast surrounding *Naliboki* forest.

The leaves of the indigenous trees of Britain and Ireland used as chapter "seals" appear within this book in their traditional order conforming to the passage of one pagan year, as follows: Birch, Rowan, Ash, Alder, Willow, Hawthorn, Oak, Holly, Hazel, Apple, Aspen, Ivy, Blackthorn, Elder, Yew, Pine and Beech.

The medieval illustration used in the frontispiece is from the *Tacuinum Sanitatis*, circa 1474, artist unknown, depicting how to safely dig up a screaming mandrake root, while killing your dog.

Lightning Source UK Ltd.
Milton Keynes UK
178695UK00001B/30/P